a mirror made of rain

'By turns fizzy and funny, poignant and sad, *A Mirror Made of Rain* is an acute, intensely readable exploration of hurt and resilience.'
– Namita Gokhale, author of *Jaipur Journals*

'Naheed Phiroze Patel paints a delicate and ironic portrait of small-town India as seen through the rueful and self-ironizing eyes of a young Parsi who will not make a grab for the brass ring.'
– Jerry Pinto, author of *Em and the Big Hoom* and *The Loves of Yuri*

'Naheed Phiroze Patel's sharp, glittering prose powerfully reveals the raw underbelly of a damaged family in this terrific debut.'
– Mahesh Rao, author of *Polite Society*

'*A Mirror Made of Rain* is luminous – a blistering and unflinching commentary on family, love, pain, addiction and destruction. We are lucky to have Naheed Phiroze Patel writing.'
– Diksha Basu, author of *Destination Wedding*

'A piercing, glittering reflection on familial trauma and addiction, Patel's writing is sharp as the shards of a smashed mirror.'

– Doireann Ní Ghríofa, author of *A Ghost in the Throat*

'The writing is sharp, beautiful, very evocative. The characters pop off the page and are instantly recognizable. Noomi is so achingly human and alive. I love the subtlety of Patel's hand in the way she depicts Noomi and her world in *A Mirror Made of Rain*.'

– Brandon Taylor, author of *Real Life* and *Filthy Animals*

'A moving, multifaceted portrait of a modern young woman whose twenty-first-century mores can't quite protect her from the gravitational force of traditional expectations, which arrive like a sort of slow-motion car crash you can't stop watching. I fell in love with Noomi and rooted for her all the way through.'

– Susan Bernofsky, author of *Clairvoyant of the Small*

'Patel writes one of the first female Indian protagonists to reckon with alcoholism. She does not flip gender on its head so much as send it tumbling.'

– *Scroll*

'A dark, moody, brooding novel that explores the fissures of family with delicacy and conviction.' – *Los Angeles Review of Books*

'[Naheed Patel] explores themes surrounding self-destruction, relationships, love and mental illness, imbuing them with sharp detail.'

– *The Caravan*

'Patel goes into the heart of the ways in which trauma can often shape and surprise us.'

– *GQ India*

a mirror made of rain

Naheed Phiroze Patel

FOURTH ESTATE · *New Delhi*

First published in hardback by Fourth Estate 2021
An imprint of HarperCollins *Publishers*
4th Floor, Tower A, Building No. 10, Phase II, DLF Cyber City,
Gurugram, Haryana – 122002
www.harpercollins.co.in

2 4 6 8 10 9 7 5 3 1

This edition published in India by Fourth Estate 2022

P-ISBN: 978-93-5629-295-6
E-ISBN: 978-93-5422-390-7

Typeset in 11/16.3 Scala at
Manipal Technologies Limited, Manipal

Printed and bound at
Thomson Press (India) Ltd

To the memory of my father, Phiroze, who'd always find a kind word for anybody who needed one.

Once I went through a mirror –
from there too the world, so intact, resembled
only itself. When I returned I tore
the skin off the glass.

– Agha Shahid Ali

PART ONE

For March, it was unseasonably hot. Summer in Kamalpur usually began in late April, and by May, the earth became an anvil for the sun to pummel down on. Birds fell out of trees, stray dogs sheltered under parked cars. Rickshaw-wallahs tied damp cloths over their heads to protect themselves from the nau tapa – the nine days of fevered winds. The local paper published a weekly toll of the victims of heatstroke.

It was only March, and yet the night was warm enough for Sheila Sehgal to have pedestal fans placed around her garden, where their lazily moving blades provided for a paltry breeze. Rice lights were strewn over the trees; the champa's leaves were painted gold and silver. The glass gazebo at the end of the lawn had its air conditioners on and the dust covers removed from its sofas. Women in georgette saris and men in bush shirts jostled for room to sit. Light refracting from the gazebo's thick glass walls appeared to make their limbs move a fraction slower, as if floating in an aquarium.

For many years now, the parties Sheila Sehgal threw each season were the highlight of everyone's social calendar. Always, in the weeks leading up to Sheila's Holi eve do – more select than her Diwali open house and more opulent than her New Year's eve party – speculation would run wild about her guest list. Knowing who was *not* invited was as important, to some, as knowing who was. An invitation from Sheila was a golden stamp of approval; a snub meant that you'd been banished to the margins of Kamalpur high society. It was important to know who was out in order to properly know who one needed to look down on for the rest of that year. This time, the Seths were out: Sheila had caught her husband in flagrante delicto with Mr Seth's jiggly wife. The philandering wasn't really the problem – it was that they weren't discreet about it. The same went for the Tutejas, who'd neglected a few too many times to call and wish Sheila on her birthday. The Agarwals were *definitely* in; they'd recently purchased three new cocaine-white Audis and their son was going to marry a carpet-empire heiress. My father, Jeh, joked that if Sheila and her friends were shipwrecked on a desert island, they'd go all *Lord of the Flies*, certainly, but still maintain their social pecking order.

Jeh and I arrived at the Sehgals' at the fashionable time of 10 p.m. dressed in our finest: he in a white kurta, me in a blue sari. Heavy chandelier earrings stretched out my earlobes. The heat made sweat pool in my cleavage. I fought about with my ill-fitting blouse as Jeh nodded at acquaintances who walked past.

'Remember,' Jeh said, 'we are telling everyone that your mother is home sick.'

'I wish we didn't have to lie, Dad,' I sighed, adjusting the sari's pallu over my shoulder.

'Me too,' Jeh said. 'Stay out of trouble tonight, okay, Noomi? For my sake.'

'Okay,' I said. 'Oh, here comes Rhea.'

My mother's friend, Rhea Puri, lolloped over like a drunk rabbit. Rhea's husband, a politician–goonda, was both rich and controlling; she needed his permission for everything. Once, he'd caught Rhea smoking pot she bought off a waiter at the Gymkhana Club. He'd locked her in their bedroom as punishment. Rhea was forbidden from going anywhere by herself. A chauffeur bodyguard brought her, most afternoons, to our house, where she and my mother drank chai and bitched about Kamalpur. Jeh said that their friendship was based on a mutual love for self-destruction.

Rhea's high heel dug a divot out from the lawn. She stumbled towards us and only stopped from going splat because I pulled her upright by the arm just in time. The drink in her hand fell to the ground; the ice cubes gleamed like crystals in the dark grass. Rhea looked from me to Jeh to the glass and back to us again. Dismay etch-a-sketched itself across her forehead.

'Oh fuck. I had to work so hard to sneak in that drink!' Rhea said, looking like a child with a broken toy. 'Jeh, please. Get me a new one? My husband won't notice you in this crowd.'

'That's probably not a good idea,' I said, cutting off my father, who'd rather be struck by lightning than say no to anyone, let alone someone as glamorous and tragic as Rhea Puri. 'We don't want to get you into trouble.'

Rhea's hands grabbed the points of her elbows. One couldn't help but stare at her diamond solitaire ring, the size of an almond. She loved to tell the story of that ring, how her husband had slipped it on while she was asleep. 'He wanted it to be a surprise.' Later, we'd found out it was for surprising her with an STD – he made frequent 'business trips' to Thailand.

'Where's Asha?' Rhea asked, scanning the crowd, eyes hooded with boredom. 'I've been looking for her all over this stupid party.'

'Asha couldn't make it. She's ... not well,' Jeh said. He picked up the fallen glass and handed it to a passing waiter with a small smile. 'We're telling everyone that she's ill with ... with food poisoning.'

'Oh no, poor thing,' Rhea said with real sympathy in her voice. 'I hope she feels better.'

'She needs to sleep it off,' I said.

AT LEAST THAT WAS the hope – that Asha was sleeping off all the vodka she'd drank earlier that evening and hadn't dug back into her stash. An hour before we were supposed to leave for the party, I'd barged into Jeh's bedroom as he was putting on his kurta. His hands bloomed out of its sleeves; his head popped out from its pearl-buttoned collar.

'We can't take Mom with us. Not when she's like this,' I said.

'What are you talking about?' Jeh asked, sliding his feet into his shoes.

'Come out and see for yourself,' I said, throwing the door open.

We went out into the hall to find Asha at the dining table, her hands clamped on to a high-backed chair. She looked concussed, as if the alcohol had struck her like a mallet. A stain, like a dark shadow, staggered over the folds of her sari, a gara that had been passed down in the Wadia family for three generations. It was a wedding present from my grandparents. I was supposed to inherit it one day.

'Why are you staring at me like that? We're late. Let's ... let's go,' Asha said. A wilted rose drooped over her ear, pinned where she had made an attempt to sweep her hair back on one side.

Jeh and I didn't move. Asha said, louder this time, 'Chalo! I'm ready!' She wheeled her eyes from my face to Jeh's, then lifted the corner of her sari to wipe away the kohl smudges. A few shaky steps towards the front door, and her foot twisted in her heels. She cried out. Jeh grabbed her. Gently, he helped her back to the dining table.

Asha doubled over in a chair, rubbing her ankle. I watched her from a corner, rage filling me up like a balloon. The rose fell to the floor. Black kajal tears made tiger-streaks on her face.

'I'm not going to stay home, I'm fine,' she said. 'I'm fine, I'm coming with you.'

'You're not leaving this house,' I said. 'If you take one step towards that door, Mom, you'll regret it.' I pulled my cell phone out from my purse.

'You think you can threaten me, Noomi?' Asha said, all chinny and belligerent. 'I don't care. Call who you like.'

I decided to try another tactic. 'What's the point of fighting? Stay home and do whatever you want. No one will stop you. Let Dad and me attend this boring party.' I waved the cell phone in the air. 'But if I call Lily Mama or Zal Papa, they'll start talking about rehab again. You don't want anyone to see you when you're like this, trust me, Mom.'

Asha thrived on the toxic energy of a fight. But at the thought of my grandparents, who lived downstairs in the same bungalow, barging in, asking all sorts of questions, she shuffled off back into her bedroom. I waited a few minutes, then went inside to check on her. Jeh lingered at the doorway. Asha lay curled like a question mark in her blouse and petticoat. Her sari, my future sari, lay in a heap on the floor. Black tears dribbled on to the pillow.

'You hate me so much,' she said as I pulled the bedclothes over her.

'Ma, no one hates you more than you hate yourself,' I said. 'Go to sleep. We'll show our faces at the party and come back within the hour. It'll be really boring. You should sleep.' I sat with Asha until she blubbered into silence. Then, closing the door behind me softly, I left with Jeh.

BACK IN THE LATE nineties, Sheila's husband, Pali Sehgal, used to be a small-time government tout. For a certain amount of ghoos, he got you a contract for cement or small machinery or something like that. The details were, and are, fuzzy. Back then, Pali, Sheila and their son Siddharth used to ride triples on a Bajaj scooter. Hard to imagine now, when you saw the fleet of SUVs parked in their driveway, and attended their parties, where the alcohol was imported, and the DJ and the caterers flown in. There were rumours that Pali owned factories that produced the most low-grade, adulterated, your-building-will-collapse-in-a-year cement, and that he owed gangsters money. Every year, people predicted Pali's downfall, but the Sehgals' parties only got more lavish, their cars fancier and their holidays abroad longer.

Rich people in Kamalpur made their money in one of two ways: by mixing one thing in another – sand in cement, stones in rice, water in milk, kerosene in petrol; or by changing one thing into another – black money into white, agricultural land into commercial, employees' pensions into destination weddings – while the authorities mostly looked the other way. An income tax raid was considered a status symbol: if the IT people weren't snooping around your business, you weren't making a lot of black money, which meant you were paying your taxes, which meant that you were, as they say in Hindi, a chutiya, or in Yiddish, a putz.

In contrast to the Sehgals, my family, the Wadias, were the ultimate putzes. Not only did we pay income tax, but we also never cheated octroi, never hid assets from the company balance sheet, never ate into employees' salaries or bribed government officials. While everyone else's star was on the rise, ours was in slow but steady decline. Our bungalow and its sprawling garden were temple elephants: grand to display but gruelling to maintain.

It was universally anticipated that, this year, Sheila Sehgal's parties would be more extravagant than usual. Sid, her only son, was getting married in December. This Holi-eve soirée was to casually (yet ostentatiously) introduce Sheila's new daughter-in-law-to-be to the town, in an outfit that cost as much as a new car. At the start of the party, Sid and Anuskha had been led by their over-smiling families to a sofa under an arch of flowers and sat side by side like a pair of dolls. Sid held up Anushka's hand, and grinning sharkily, slipped a diamond on her finger. The crowd broke out into applause. Someone did a loud, two-finger whistle. I turned my head towards the sound and saw that it was Ammu, an old friend whom I hadn't seen since high school. A peculiar thing about Kamalpur was that the wealthy families had their roots all tangled up like banyan trees; it took some skill to figure out where one family ended and the other began. Ammu, who'd been my best friend, was Sid's cousin on his mom's side. Sid was one of the most popular rich boys in Kamalpur. Everyone knew Sid Sehgal. He went to expensive boarding schools and then college in America. His parents bought him a Mercedes at seventeen. He had a reputation for dating only the prettiest women.

When I saw Sheila Sehgal walking over to us, I grabbed Jeh's hand, and then, feeling a little stupid, let it go.

'Jeh, how are you?' Sheila said, tilting her head to one side. She had on a sari the colour of old ivory, trimmed with soft, white feathers that shivered gracefully with every movement. Around her neck were six strands of uncut diamonds. Her smoky eyes flitted from Jeh to me. 'And Noomi, long time no see.' A pause. A little frown. 'Where's Asha? Why hasn't she come?'

Jeh shifted his weight from one foot to the other. I saw his lips gather in a small, nervous moue.

'Asha's not feeling well. She's at home. She sends her best,' he smiled wanly.

Sheila Sehgal's eyebrows shot up into her luxurious hair. She raked and fluffed her layers with red, talon-like nails. 'Oh! I'm sad to hear that. I was looking forward to seeing her,' she said, sounding not at all sad. 'Achcha, you must go get yourself a drink. The bartenders are from Russia, or Ukraine, or someplace like that,' she waved a hand towards them. 'They make the most amazing cocktails.'

After Sheila sent Jeh off to the bar with a smile, she turned her attention to me. 'Noomi, where have you been hiding?' she enquired. 'Haven't seen you at any of the usual parties. Of course,' Sheila gestured at the crowd, 'I've been so busy with organizing Sid and Anushka's engagement.'

'I've been around, Aunty. Not up to much these days,' I said, not wanting to admit that I hadn't been invited to any of the usual parties. 'You look very pretty.'

'Bespoke Raaj Lulla,' Sheila said, preening. 'A gift from Anushka's parents. I hate his off-the-rack stuff, but this I adored. Did you know they've also got him to do the flowers?'

'The ... flowers?' I said stupidly. 'Raaj Lulla does flowers?'

'Not for everyone,' Sheila winked. 'Anushka's parents have a very close relationship with him. He's doing all her clothes.' She scanned my outfit. 'That's a pretty colour. Turn around so that I can see the whole thing.'

I turned. My sari was a blue chamois silk with a silver sequin border. I'd worn a shimmery blouse and high heels to match. My blouse chafed painfully at the armhole. I'd got it stitched weeks ago but forgot to try it on before the party. And then it was too late to get it altered. The hooks fought to stay buttoned across my chest; the front had gaps that I'd covered with my sari's pallu, praying it would stay in place for the rest of the night.

'Ah, lovely. I admire how you wear just anything, no need for designer brands,' Sheila said.

'Thank you,' I smiled, pulling at my pallu. One could detest Sheila yet crave her approval.

'Darling, you're twenty-three! I'll tell you the same thing I tell Anushka: at your age, you should look your best at all times,' Sheila said. 'Anushka works out for a couple of hours in the gym every day. I said to her: after marriage please take my son along with you!' She laughed.

'That's nice,' I said.

'Go congratulate them,' Sheila said, shooing me away with her hands. 'They're around here somewhere,' she added, searching the crowd on the lawn. 'Oh look, the chief minister and his wife have walked in. Excuse me, I have to go say hello.'

THE REASON WE'D BEEN invited to the Sehgals' in the first place was because Sheila always respected the tribal hierarchies. And my grandmother, Lily Mama, came from old, aristocratic money; she had enough power in her gaze to raise you up, or send you tumbling with a smile or a stare. When I was four, my nursery teacher used to pinch the inside of my thighs if I didn't 'sit like a lady'. Lily Mama discovered the marks one day while I was playing with a doll in her lap, shouting at it to sit like a lady. The next day, she marched into the principal's office, wearing battle pearls, purse under one arm, to roar at him. The teacher was fired. Apart from Jeh, she was my favourite person.

I wandered around the party looking for someone to talk to. I saw Lily Mama on a sofa placed under a twisty banyan tree. She was one of those large women whose girth enhanced their magnificence, like Aretha Franklin. I put a hand on Lily Mama's silken shoulder. Absent-mindedly, she covered my hand with hers. On her finger was a huge ruby mounted on a cage of pearls. I sat down next to her with a contented little sigh.

'Hello, pudding,' Lily Mama said.

'Hello,' I said and kissed Lily Mama's cheek. She smelled like flowers baked into a loaf of bread. 'Jeh went to get me a drink,' Lily Mama said. 'Your mother wasn't with him. Where is she?'

I blew out a puff of air. 'Mama was too drunk to come,' I said, flopping over a cushion.

Lily Mama's smile evaporated. 'She'd quit drinking if she really loved you,' she said. 'A mother has no business having such bad habits.'

'Dad drinks too,' I said. 'They should both quit, na?'

Lily Mama didn't answer. Her eyes had snagged on my badly fitting sari blouse. She grimaced. 'You didn't try this on beforehand, did you? I can see your bra through the gaps. Really, Noomi.'

'Forget it. No one will notice,' I said, covering the blouse with my sari.

'Give it to me tomorrow. I'll send it to Dashrath tailor.'

'Why don't you tell my dad to quit?'

'Jeh is a grown man, he can decide for himself.'

I let out a groan. 'Lily Mama, you are an MCP.'

'A what?

'Male chauvinist pig,' I smiled. 'Technically you're a female chauvinist pig.'

Lily Mama looked down her regal Parsi nose at me. 'Don't be rude!' she said, thumping my head.

'I didn't mean it like that!' I grinned, clinging to her. 'I'm sorry!'

'Come on, get away,' she said, prying me off. 'You're ruining my sari. Rude child.'

'Hug me back,' I said, clinging tighter. 'I'm sorry.'

'What a fancy party,' said my grandfather, arriving just then with a plate of food, sitting down next to us, shaking his leg. 'Bet they've spent a fortune. Why didn't your mother come? She's missing out on this lobster khao suey.'

'She's drunk again,' Lily Mama told him.

'I hope you'll turn out better than she has,' Zal Papa said, waggling a piece of lobster on his fork.

Zal Papa himself had been very fond of his daily two double-pegs until a stroke in his fifties had left one side of his face looking like Droopy Dog's. Now all he had to entertain himself was the annoying habit of minding everyone's business but his own. Even his friends looked a bit wary when he sidled up to them, his face stretched in a grin.

Soon after he moved to Kamalpur from Bombay to set up his business, Zal Papa bought an acre of land when my father, the younger of his two sons, was still a toddler. As his sons grew older, went to college, found love and got married, he built them each a home on the same plot of land as his own. So that they'd have a good income to support their wives and kids, he augmented his vast home appliances empire and gave each son a business. Zal Papa had given our family everything; for that we had to be continually grateful. And if we weren't, he'd be sure to remind us.

My mother told me that when I was five, my father had brought home a white-and-black kitten he'd found on the street outside his office. I have no memory of this, because before Jeh could even show me the warm animal curled up in his arms, Zal Papa had ordered him to take it away. No cats in this house, he'd said. Cats were bad luck, like living on a cul-de-sac or travelling on a moonless night. My father gave the kitten to a neighbour. He was his father's favourite – he craved his approval much more than his elder brother did. One of the rare times my father ever defied Zal Papa was when he chose to marry my mother. As in the case of the kitten, Zal Papa made it plain that he'd prefer it if Jeh would put Asha back wherever he had found her. Zal Papa prided himself on his good instincts when it came to character. 'Character is destiny,' he'd said. 'I never wanted your parents to marry. But at least we got you out of it.' I started to think of myself as some sort of consolation prize.

As it turned out, Zal Papa's instincts were correct. My parents never had a happy marriage to begin with. Then Asha lost a second baby in a late-term miscarriage, and along with that, her mental health, which was already precarious after a childhood filled with violence. There were moms who put notes in their children's lunch boxes, and there was Asha, who'd once picked me up from school five hours late, who sent me to birthday parties wearing torn underwear. Jeh's reaction to Asha's rapid deterioration was denial, and to retreat further and further into his books. I was raised by two women taking turns: my ayah, Shanta Bai, and my grandmother, Lily Mama, who would take me downstairs to her bed when I was sick, and put VapoRub on my neck and tie a handkerchief around it to ease my cough.

Sometimes, as kids, my cousin Adil and I would sleep in our grandparents' bed, between them. After they'd managed to get us to stop wiggling around and fighting about who was hogging the blanket, Zal Papa would put down his Jeffrey Archer, switch off his bed lamp, extend his hand to Lily Mama and say, 'Haath aapo.' Give me your hand. Their arms would form an arch over our sleepy bodies, as a slowly whirling fan dusted our heads with a soft breeze.

'ACTUALLY,' I SAID, LOOKING at my grandfather, 'I plan on getting nice and fucked up tonight.'

'Noomi! Your language!' Lily Mama said, crinkling up her nose. 'Apologize at once.'

'But Zal Papa is being mean!'

'At once, Noomi.'

'I'm sorry.'

Lily Mama put her hand over my forehead; her touch felt cool, soothing.

'Are you ill or something?' she asked.

'I'm fine,' I said, moving my head away.

'Why are you always so rude?' She lifted one of my earrings in her palm. 'Oh, these are pretty,' she said, frowning. 'They look expensive. Real or fake?'

'Fake,' I said.

'Not bad,' Lily Mama said. 'Could've fooled me.'

Jeh came up to us, holding a drink garnished with a flower. In a sweet, childlike manner, he kissed his mother's cheek. 'Mama, I had them make you a daiquiri,' he said. 'I hope that's okay?'

'Thank you, darling,' Lily Mama said.

For a moment, I admired their twin Mona Lisa smiles. Then more family members began to arrive. The Wadias were popular, and it wasn't unusual for all of us to be invited to the same party. Adil, my cousin, strolled across the Sehgals' lawn with his mother – all bright eyes and tall hair and broad shoulders. Aunties loved him. Adil responded to them politely, while his mother smiled like a pope. Five years ago, Adil was a pudgy teenager headed off to engineering college in America, his suitcase filled with hair gel and vast supplies of Haldiram snacks. Oftentimes when he got drunk, Adil would call at 2 a.m. and talk for hours about how much he missed home. He got a job in Bombay, but after several months of emotional phone calls by our grandfather, who wanted all his children and grandchildren to remain under his roof, Adil moved back into our bungalow.

'Ah, here he is,' Zal Papa said. 'My boy. Look at all these women eyeing you like a bar of chocolate.' He grabbed Adil's hand. 'How many shots have they forced you to have?'

'None so far,' Adil said, smiling. 'Mom and I just got here.'

'Come on,' Zal Papa said. 'At your age, I'd drink all my friends under the table.'

I snorted. 'It's like your double standards have double standards, Zal Papa.'

'Sarcasm is anger's ugly cousin, cousin,' Adil wagged his finger at me. 'I'm happy to see you, though. Didn't think you'd be invited.' He unclasped his mother's hand from his elbow and gave me a hug.

'Why wouldn't I be?' I snapped.

'They must've spent a fortune,' Adil said. 'And this is the engagement party. The wedding's going to be sick!' He rubbed his palms. My face must have given away my real feelings, as all of a sudden, Adil wanted to look everywhere but at it. 'Sorry,' he said.

'It's fine.'

'I mean, how long can it take to get over someone?'

'Well, I...'

'Never mind that,' Binny, Adil's mother, interrupted. 'I noticed Asha is not here. What's the story?'

'Well,' Jeh began, 'we planned to tell everyone that she's ill. Food poisoning, or something like that.'

'You mean, *you* planned,' I said.

'I ran into her at the supermarket this afternoon.' Binny shook her head. 'She tried to hide this big shopping bag that she was carrying with two hands, but I could hear the clink of bottles.' She gave a little sniff. 'Who buys alcohol in broad daylight like that?'

'You didn't actually see any bottles,' I said, frowning. 'The clinking could've been anything.'

'Oh, come on, Noomi,' Binny moaned. 'Let's not kid ourselves.'

When she was a teenager, Binny won a Princess Diana lookalike contest in high school, for which she'd chopped off her hair in Di's signature bob. 'Streamlined Working Princess' was the aesthetic she'd chased ever since. Back in the seventies when co-education was taboo, there used to be a prestigious girls' convent school that all the ambitious mothers in Kamalpur sent their daughters to, hoping that an education full of English poetry, choir, and crochet lessons would land them a good match. Asha and Binny had attended it a few years apart. So, when Jeh's mother expressed her desire to find a suitable wife for Jeh's awkward older brother, Asha, struggling to win favour with in-laws who didn't like her, introduced them to the pretty, polite junior who'd kept in touch with her: Binny. This backfired quite spectacularly a few years later, when there was a falling out about a ring or some other bit of Wadia jewellery that was supposed to be for Binny but ended up going to Asha. Binny's superpower was that if she had her knife in you, soon everyone else did too.

'Well, I'm off to the bar,' Adil said.

'Cool, I'll come with you,' I said, getting up.

'You'll do no such thing!' Zal Papa said.

'Why not?' I cried out. Fool that I was, I expected my family to treat me like an adult. At least a faint hope remained that they'd let me order a drink without basting me with lectures.

'This family doesn't need another scandal. And you're like your mother when it comes to alcohol, Noomi. You and your father need to come have another chat with me,' Zal Papa said. 'It takes years to build a reputation and only seconds to destroy it.' This sentence was punctuated by a smug little nod from Binny. 'I'm not about to see mine torn down because my son can't control his wife.'

'She's not his pet!' I yelled. 'You can't expect her to roll over, play dead and put out a paw to shake.'

'Noomi, that's enough,' Jeh muttered. Turning to Adil, he said, 'I'll need another whisky, or three, to survive this evening.'

'No problem, Uncle,' Adil smiled. 'I'll get you one.'

'Oh Adil, can you get me something to drink as well?' Binny trilled.

'Of course, Mama. What would you like?' Adil asked. I almost expected him to bow like the Air India Maharaja.

'I'm such a lightweight,' Binny simpered. 'Some Bristol cream, perhaps, or Baileys with ice?'

'I'll have a vodka tonic with lots of ice,' I said, grinning.

'I don't think that's a good idea, Noomi,' Jeh said.

'Why?'

'Because,' Binny hissed, 'as Zal Papa said, you handle alcohol like your mother.'

'This is none of your business, Binny Aunty.'

'Noomi,' Lily Mama said, 'I've warned you already. Don't talk to your elders like that.'

When I was little, on the nights my parents stayed up fighting with and screaming at each other, I'd creep into Lily Mama's bedroom to sleep. In the day, I'd follow her around like a puppy, holding the end of her sari. I loved her, but Lily Mama was acting like a total bitch. I looked over at Jeh, hoping he'd say something in my defence. But he didn't say a word.

'Apologize to Binny,' Lily Mama repeated. 'Come on, do it. Don't spoil everyone's mood.'

'Why do I need to apologize?' I said, wrapping the end of my pallu around my wrist.

'You'll do it because your grandmother said so,' Zal Papa said. His words hovered in the air like a bird of prey, ready to strike.

'I'm sorry,' I said to Binny.

The DJ began playing, and the bass travelled up through the soles of my feet, as I walked away.

An unspoken rule in Kamalpur was that well-bred women did not order their own drinks at the bar. They had to wait until a man was free to fetch them one. As I avoided my father's disapproving frowns and made my way into the press of shouting men surrounding the bartenders, I bumped into Ammu, also waiting for a drink. I immediately turned away, expecting to be ignored or shunned, but then I felt a hand on my shoulder and turned around to find Ammu smiling at me. Ammu Atale was one of those friends from childhood that you don't quite remember ever having met – they'd just always been in your life. It still hurt to recall how I ended up breaking her heart. In the decade since we'd last spoken, Ammu had moved abroad, and then recently returned to start an NGO. This Ammu was different from the quiet, intense teenager who'd left home with only one suitcase full of books. This older but even lovelier Ammu had a gold purse hanging by a strap from her bare shoulder. Her skin looked so soft; her long, black hair reached to the middle of her back. She'd always had huge eyes, which she liked to do up with lots of kohl. When she smiled, deep dimples appeared on her cheeks, like folds in light brown velvet.

To my surprise and delight, Ammu seemed to be suggesting that we sneak off for a smoke.

'*You've* got cigarettes? You?' I said.

'Argh, yes,' Ammu said, widening her eyes.

'When did you even start smoking?'

'There's a lot you don't know about me now,' Ammu smiled, raising her scimitar-shaped eyebrows. 'I mean, we haven't really been in touch for ... I don't know how long.'

'We were thirteen,' I said with a lopsided smile that I hoped was charming.

'Oh,' said Ammu. A shadow flitted across her face. 'But,' she said, brightening, 'that's why we need to get wasted and catch up. Come on, I know a place where no one will bother us.'

Holding our drinks away from our saris, we pressed up against the white stucco wall and skirted the dance floor, where paunchy uncles holding glasses on their heads and aunties eager to show off their Madhuri Dixit moves were gyrating to loud Bollywood music. No one noticed us leaving. We walked down the driveway, sneaking behind the multicoloured food shamianas, with their tempting odours of steaming pans of khao suey, Rajasthani dal, and the pasta station manned by a bored-looking boy in a crooked chef's hat.

Behind the shamianas was a badly lit courtyard that was as utilitarian and ugly as the front of the bungalow, with its sparkling garden, was lovely and impractical. I sat on the cement edge of a covered well, wondering how this evening would turn out, while Ammu took out a cigarette from her gold purse. The little wax match she lit burned so fast, she had to drop it, or risk singeing her fingers. She took a few puffs and offered it to me. I smiled. We could make each other out by light coming from the chauffeur's quarters. Through the open door, we saw a baby girl asleep on a charpoy, her mouth open, her hands curled into earthen cups. She must've been the child of one of the Sehgals' numerous live-in domestic staff. I assumed her parents were probably helping out in the party. The kid slept under a thin sheet. She didn't seem bothered by the mosquitoes alighting to feed on her little arms. Surely, I thought, Sheila could afford a mosquito net.

I WAS SIX YEARS old, the first time I ever held a baby. It was a rainy, noisy afternoon. I danced barefoot across the smooth tiles of my parents' living room. A radio played film songs. It was the eighties, so my hair was in a side ponytail that swayed rhythmically to the sound of Lata Mangeshkar's chaste yet sex-kitten-like voice. Over the song, I could hear my mother screaming. Apparently, our high-caste, vegetarian cook, the one we had before my beloved Shanta Bai arrived, had refused another delivery from our butcher.

'In this house, we eat meat!' I heard my mother scream from the kitchen.

The doorbell rang. Then it rang again. I turned off the radio, still sashaying to the music in my head. I pulled the heavy front door open with all my might to find ... no one. I shrugged and was about to let it swing shut, when a small noise made me look in the direction of my feet. An infant, naked except for a black thread tied around his swollen belly, lay on a dirty cloth, cycling his legs.

'Ma! There's another one today!' I yelled into the house.

'Bring it inside,' came the curt reply.

A children's home that my mother ran from the building opposite our bungalow had the depressing distinction of the lowest infant deaths of any orphanage in Kamalpur. As a result, people had started abandoning babies at our doorstep. At one point, it got so bad, Lily Mama stationed a chowkidar at each gate, with instructions not to let anyone holding a baby enter. As a result, a business associate of Jeh's, whom he'd invited over for dinner one night, became furious and started shouting where he stood outside on the street, because they would not let his wife, holding his infant son, enter.

I lifted the baby up the way I'd seen my mother do it, supporting his head, like a lotus on a thin stem. The rain had receded to a drizzle. I felt it on the back of my neck. The child's gaunt face was a skull painted the colour of flesh. He weighed as much as a bundle of twigs. He opened his lips and turned, hoping to find a breast. Disappointed, he let out a wail. I carried him back into the kitchen.

'Look, Mama,' I said. 'So tiny!' I waited for my mother to look at me. I wanted her to say that I was holding the baby the right way, that I was a clever, responsible girl. The orphan children called her 'Asha Mai'. They'd gather around her like chicks around a hen, chirping, 'Asha Mai! Look at this picture I made! Look how tall I am now!' My mother, in her cotton kurta and oversized sunglasses, would smile and say, 'Very good, Mira. Well done, Govind. I'm so proud of you,' as she ushered them all back inside. How jealous I felt of them with my mother, who'd never said she was proud of me.

'You crazy woman!' Apparently, my mother was too busy squabbling with our cook to pay attention to me. 'People who eat meat are not rakshasas. You're educated, goddamn it! Act like it!'

The cook threw down her frilly, turmeric-stained apron and said that Asha calling *her* crazy was the limit. She quit. I took the news with glee. I hated her watery dal and sickly bhindi fry. There'd be no dinner ready when Jeh came home tonight. He'd find my mother in a snit, and take us out for dinner to the

Gymkhana Club, where he'd order a whisky for himself, a vodka for my mom, and listen to me chatter while I sipped Thums Up through the gap between my front teeth.

'Here. Please, Mama,' I said and pushed the baby into her arms. 'I think he's wet himself.'

My mother took the infant to the window and held him up to the watery light. Turning him this way and that, she inspected his pointy little body. 'Hmm, malnourished. Probably dysentery,' she said. She pulled off his rough diaper cloth and gave him back to me. 'Hold him a little while longer. I still need to sort this stupid woman out.' She turned around to face the sulky, frowning cook.

'But Ma!' I protested as the naked baby was thrust back into my arms. My mother resumed fighting with the cook, barring her from leaving by standing in the doorway. As I watched them argue, I felt something warm and foul run over my hands. The baby, freed of his diaper, had pooped a watery mess. Vomit pushed up against the back of my throat. I fought an urge to toss the child out the window.

'THOSE ARE PRETTY EARRINGS,' Ammu said.

'Thanks,' I said. 'I swiped them from my mom's jewellery box.'

'How's your mom?' Ammu asked. 'I don't see her around tonight.'

'She's ... not feeling well,' I said, making quotation marks in the air.

'Oh,' Ammu said, 'I'm sorry.'

'Don't be,' I said.

'Nothing serious, I hope?' Ammu prodded further.

'The truth? She was too drunk to leave the house,' I said, shrugging. 'She drinks all day, these days. She's anxious, depressed, etc. Nothing new.'

'Poor Asha Aunty. She used to be such fun when I came over to your house as a kid,' Ammu said. 'Remember the time we carried all that mud through your living room,' she blew a plume of smoke and laughed, 'to make a garden on your balcony.'

'It was a disaster,' I said, recalling that day. 'Mud all over the floors and on the curtains.'

'Your mom wasn't even angry!' Ammu smiled. 'She yelled for the gardener to come upstairs, and he helped us make a little thing with bricks in which we could put the mud and some seeds. My mom would've had a meltdown.' She held her tongue between her teeth. 'I used to think of your house as Neverland. It was a place where we never got into trouble.'

'If you caught her on a good day, she could be amazing,' I conceded, grinning at the memory.

It was true. On the days when Asha's anger disappeared for a few hours, she transformed into the kind of mother one reads about in stories. She taught me how to play Scrabble, would read to me, we'd go to the fish market and she'd make the pomfrets move their mouths and pretend to sing. She had the most beautiful voice, like a crystal glass struck with a spoon. But her anger would always return. One mother sang me to sleep, while the other woke me up with her screams. After she'd hit me, her gold bangles clinking to keep time, I'd run crying to a mirror to see if I'd changed, if the beating had registered and I was more like the children Asha loved – the ones in her orphanage.

'Have you ever thought about taking her to a psychiatrist?' Ammu asked. 'Or rehab?'

'She won't get help.' I stared at my feet. My sandals glittered prettily in the dark. 'She doesn't trust anyone. Not even us. Perhaps Dad and I should see a psychiatrist. My mother certainly thinks so. She seems to blame us for everything.'

'Why does she blame you guys?' Ammu frowned. 'And what for, exactly?'

'I don't know,' I said, taking a big sip of my drink. 'Once, when I was really young, she and my dad had this massive fight. And it was because I … I pushed her. I mean, I was eight and lost my temper.'

'You're a good person, Noomi,' Ammu said, putting a hand, cool and dry, on my shoulder. 'I know how hard it's been for your family. Everyone knows. All anyone ever says about your dad is what a good heart he has. How patient he is.'

'Oh, and my mom can't stop talking about the fact that,' I paused, tilting my glass up to finish my drink, 'my dad hasn't touched her, you know, sexually, in fifteen years.'

Ammu took my hand. 'These aren't your problems. Have you ever thought of moving out?'

'Where would I go?' I said blearily. 'And what would I do?'

'What do you want to do?'

'It's not what I want to do, as much as who I want to be,' I muttered. 'Someone who isn't written off. Like you. Or even like Sheila Sehgal, Lily Mama, Binny. I want to … matter. I want to be,' I rolled my empty glass between my palms, thinking, 'the most important person in someone's life. Anyone's.'

'You could move somewhere new,' Ammu offered. 'A fresh start. No one about to tell you who you are or what you're worth.' She smiled, plucked the cigarette from my fingers and took a drag. She stood holding the cigarette up and away from her sari, which shimmered like ripples in dark water. There was a flash at her wrist. I realized she was wearing a bracelet I'd given her many years ago – a gold circlet with lion heads at its two ends. I took back the cigarette, then slipped a nail under the gold band.

'I can't believe you've kept this all these years,' I said. 'I thought you hated me.'

'I was an idiot,' Ammu said. 'I blamed you for things that weren't your fault.'

'Why didn't you reach out?' I slurred. *Reesh out*. 'All these years?'

'I was afraid,' Ammu said, letting go of my hand. 'I'm sorry.'

'Afraid? Of what?' I asked, studying the lines notched into her forehead.

'Afraid of looking you in the eye, once I understood what my brother had done to you.'

I'D GIVEN AMMU THE bracelet in her bedroom before going downstairs to attend a party for her older brother's law school graduation. In those days, I spent most of my evenings at Ammu's crumbling house. I loved that house. To my thirteen-year-old mind, it looked like an ancient wedding cake. The monsoon rains had battered its plaster-corniced façade. Repairs and whitewashing had little impact: the octogenarian house had stayed, stubbornly, in an aristocratic shambles, walls thrumming with the patter of small animals. Ants trudged into lightning-shaped cracks near the ground; through the walls a vine pushed out its green limbs; googly-eyed lizards and furry bats hid in the nooks; brown mice scurried along the floor, into doorways that swallowed the sunlight.

The inside was no better. Although the Atales had pots and pots of money, their furniture looked like the sort used in a government guesthouse: ugly, functional. The tables were topped with indestructible plywood. The curtains were synthetic and slippery. There was a large, ungainly hall on the ground floor, and the bedrooms on the first floor opened into each other like train carriages. Any notion of private space remained a theory. There was also a musty smell to the bed linen.

When I arrived, Ammu had been fighting with her mother over a top she wanted to wear that night. It was one of those sheer, confectionary pieces that Ammu preferred – chiffon with a collar bow. The argument was about whether the top was see-through: Ammu was firmly on the side of it wasn't, her mother insisted that it was.

'Aai please?' Ammu said, fidgeting with the collar, as she stood in front of a full-length mirror. 'Look how modest the neck is!'

'Amrita,' her mother said, pinching the bow like she wanted it to squeal. 'This blouse is *transparent*. We've invited all your father's colleagues to the party. Do you want the entire legal fraternity of Kamalpur to see your bra tonight? Think of Baba! How humiliated he would feel.'

'But Aai,' Ammu said. She was close enough to the mirror to almost kiss her own reflection. 'You can only see it if you look very carefully. Like they would literally have to be *this* close.'

'I think it looks really good,' I said.

Ammu's mother, who didn't like me much, threw me a look. 'That's exactly what men do, they look carefully,' she said to Ammu. She took a shimmery anarkali out from the closet. 'This is much better. Very nice and elegant. Wear this.'

'Why do I have to dress like a forty-year-old lawyer while Noomi gets to wear jeans and a cute top?'

'Aunty, Ammu looks so pretty in that blouse,' I said.

'Noomi, please stay out of it,' Ammu's mother warned.

Ammu snatched the anarkali from her mother's hand, marched into the bathroom and slammed the door behind her. She came out a few minutes later, a dark scowl stamped over her pretty features. I took her hand and slipped the bracelet on to it.

Ammu traced the lion heads with her finger and her scowl broke into a smile.

'That's cool,' she said. 'Where did you get it?'

'It's a secret,' I said with a little shrug.

'And why are you giving it to me?'

'Because it's pretty and I want you to have it,' I said and gave her a hug.

Standing outside the Atales' drawing room, we could hear talk and laughter, clinking glasses, plates, bangles, all muffled by the hum of an air cooler. I opened the door, and a damp breeze blew wisps of hair away from my face and encircled my bare wrists. Suddenly, in that room full of starched saris and pomaded comb-overs, I heard Simon & Garfunkel's 'Mrs Robinson'. My father loved that song. The music brought me to the other side of the hall. At the foot of an Akai music system sat the guest of honour, sifting through a bunch of LPs. He had on a simple white shirt with the sleeves rolled up, which I thought was the most stylish thing ever. There was something vulpine about the line of his cheekbones. The muscle that twitched in Ammu's jaw when she was thinking, twitched in his. When his mother ruffled Arjun's hair on the way to the kitchen, he bent his head sideways like a little boy.

'Pass me that one, please,' Arjun said, pointing to an album that lay by my feet.

I knelt and picked up *Led Zeppelin III*. 'My dad loves this one too,' I said.

Arjun took the vinyl from me without looking. 'Hmm?' he said. 'Who?'

'Dada?' Ammu seemed to materialize out of nowhere. I slid guiltily away from Arjun. 'Don't you remember Noomi? She's Jeh uncle's daughter.'

'Oh hey, nice to see you again, Noomi. I'm a big fan of Jeh's.' Arjun broke into a wide smile, as if it were a pleasant surprise to know there was a person attached to the hand that had given him the LP. 'Wow,' he smiled, his lips like an archer's bow. 'You've grown up! And you have your dad's eyes.'

'I do?' This was the best compliment anyone could give me: that I resembled my father. 'I don't have his moustache though, ha ha.'

'We have all this cool music, thanks to your dad,' Arjun said, waving an album cover around so hard that the record popped out of its sleeve. 'He used to get these albums for Baba on his trips abroad and then bullied him into listening to them, night and day. Eventually, Baba became a fan.'

At that moment, Ammu and Arjun's father walked past the stereo system with a colleague. Baba was a tall, imperious looking man, with hair like grey steel wool. In the high court, where less successful lawyers flapped about like crows, he stood out for his Buddha-like serenity. Rumours abounded that he'd been tapped to become a judge soon.

'Mr Kaptan, this is my son, Arjun,' Baba said to his partner. 'He has just graduated from the National Law School. And now he spends all his time telling me how I should run my firm.'

'Hello, young man.' Mr Kaptan, a gnomish gentleman well into his eighties, was the sort of person who looked like he called anyone under sixty 'young man'. 'I hear that you will be joining our chambers very soon. That's most wonderful.'

'No, Uncle, I'm starting a free legal aid clinic,' Arjun replied.

'A what?'

'See what I mean?' Baba rolled his eyes.

'Arjun, can't you put on Asha Bhonsle or something like that?' Ammu's mother said, walking past with a tray that she handed off to a maid. 'This music is giving Mrs Rai a terrible headache.'

'This will take care of all of Mrs Rai's aches and pains,' Arjun grinned, placing a record on the turntable. 'Immigrant Song' blasted from the speakers. There were loud gasps. Mrs Rai dropped her samosa. Another lady, quite frail and elderly, clutched her sari pallu and let out a frightened squeak. 'What is this unearthly sound? Is it a demon?'

'We're out of ... uh ... ice cream,' Ammu's mother punched the stereo's off button. 'Why don't you go to the store and get us some?' She pulled Arjun off the floor. 'Take Ammu and Noomi with you for company.'

THE NIGHT WAS QUIET but for the sound of crickets and the crunching of our shoes on the driveway gravel. Ammu's dad's car glowed silver in the moonlight, under a creeper of sweet-smelling night jasmine. Jauntily, Arjun held open the car door, first for Ammu, and then for me. The inside smelled like leather and Arjun's cologne, which was a bit too strong.

'All set?' Arjun rolled down the window and lit a cigarette.

'Dada!' Ammu gasped. 'What if Baba and Aai find out!'

'Shh, we won't tell them,' Arjun said. 'Wanna try?'

'No!'

'I'll try,' I said, stretching out my hand.

Arjun turned sideways and looked at me from the corner of his eye.

'I was only joking, Noomi,' he snorted. 'Good girls don't smoke. Your dad would kill me.'

'They'll be able to smell it,' Ammu frowned prudishly, waving a hand in front of her nose.

'Why do you think they invented cologne?' Arjun said, blowing a smoke ring. He took out a small travel-sized spray from his pocket and misted the air over his head. Then he pushed a tape into the deck. Some more Simon & Garfunkel. Parsley, sage, rosemary and thyme.

When we stopped at a red light, a young woman holding a baby in a cloth sling knocked on Arjun's window. Showing him the child's dirty, matted head, she begged for money, making a cup with her hands. Arjun rolled down the window and gave her a few rupees. She touched her forehead in thanks and moved off. The light changed and we drove on. Arjun's jaw muscle twitched. He made a sudden U-turn. Ammu braced herself by holding on to the dashboard, while I slid from one end of the back seat to the other.

'Dada, what are you doing?' Ammu said.

'We're going to make a quick detour,' he said. 'I want you guys to see what I've been working on.'

Something rolled out from under the front seat and bumped my foot. It was a cricket bat.

'Why is this in the car?' I asked, holding up the bat.

'Oh, that's for security,' Arjun said. 'In case anyone ever tries anything funny with you girls.' He parked the car in a narrow lane. 'Come on, it's over here,' he said, grabbing the bat.

'Wasn't this Baba's old office?' Ammu asked, squinting up at a building outlined by darkness. We looked at each other, clueless as to why we were standing outside a dilapidated office in the middle of the night. 'What are we doing here, Dada?'

'Come in and I'll show you,' Arjun said, fiddling with a rusty padlock. He used his shoulder to push open the door and was instantly swallowed by the dark. Soon, a tube light flickered on, and then another. The office, littered with leaves and broken light bulbs, smelled like mould and rodent droppings. In the middle of it stood a demented-looking, dusty old metal Godrej desk with a swivel chair that, miraculously, still swivelled. Arjun sat down and went round and round until I began to feel dizzy just looking at him.

'Umm, Dada, won't Aai be wondering where we are?' Ammu kicked at a box on the floor. Unwise. A lizard leapt out of it. Ammu and I clambered up on to the table, screaming. Arjun simply leaned back on the swivel chair and linked his hands behind his head.

'Relax, you're with me,' he said with a wink. I smiled and brought my knees to my chin. Arjun suddenly leaned forward, opened a drawer, and took out what looked like the blueprint of an open-floor office. 'See, this is what I have planned.'

I traced the white lines with my finger. 'That's cool,' I said and looked up. Arjun stared at me in a way that made me feel like I'd been running in a race. I hopped off the desk and dusted off the seat of my jeans.

'Dada, please let's go home.' Ammu slipped off too, and pulled Arjun up by his arm. We walked back to the car.

In the car, I kicked off my shoes and lay down on the back seat, my feet outside the window. I lifted my T-shirt a little, to feel the seat's cool, soft leather against my skin. I saw Ammu lean against her brother's shoulder and felt a pinch of jealousy.

No one talked on the ride home. I could tell that Ammu was dreaming by the way she stared out the car window, like the trees along the roadside were whispering to her. When we got back, the party was already over. Ammu's mother asked why we all looked like we'd been crawling around in a cave. Arjun told her about our little detour. His mother rolled her eyes and said we should go to bed. The office had been so filthy that Ammu said she needed to shower first. I sat on the cool, hard marble floor in the bedroom, thinking again about how Arjun had stared at me, and I began to feel nervous, like I'd done something wrong, only I wasn't sure what. Perhaps it was best to go home. I slipped my scrunchie off my wrist and tied up my hair. Then, I went to Ammu's closet (Ammu often borrowed my clothes because her mother only bought her frumpy kurtas and stuff) and balled up a T-shirt to toss on to the bed, along with a pair of boys' jeans that I'd been laboriously slashing with a pair of scissors.

'Hello, hello.' Arjun could also appear out of nowhere, like a cat. Evidently, the Atales had a talent for sneaking up on people. 'What have we here?'

'I'm leaving,' I said, pushing the clothes into a plastic bag.

'What's the rush? I thought you were going to spend the night.' Arjun yanked my scrunchie off from my ponytail, making my hair tumble all over my face. 'In fact, I was hoping you would.'

'I changed my mind,' I said, trying to grab the hair tie from him. 'Give that back, Arjun!'

'Try and take it, pocket rocket,' Arjun said, holding it up.

I dug my nails into his arm.

'Ouch,' Arjun said. He swung me around by the elbow and smacked my bottom. 'Bad kitty.'

'Ow, stop that,' I said.

Arjun still had the scrunchie. I stood on the bed to grab it from his outstretched hands and was taken by surprise when he scythed a foot under my legs, causing me to fall on my back. He began to tickle me. His fingers ran down the xylophone of my ribs. It hurt. Breathless, I told him to stop.

We heard Ammu turn off the shower. Arjun stood up abruptly and ran his fingers through his hair. He sat down at Ammu's desk. His eyes walked slowly over my body as his mask of playful irony slipped, showing something raw and greedy underneath. He looked away at the sound of the door bolt. When he turned back, his face was normal. Ammu stepped out of the bathroom wearing cotton pyjamas. She rubbed her head with a towel.

'Dada, please leave my room,' she said. Arjun gave a playful growl, flung his sister over his shoulder, shouted, 'Khamosh!' and galloped out the bedroom door. Ammu squealed and hit his back with her little fists, her long, black hair swinging wildly down Arjun's checked shirt.

IT BECAME THE SUMMER of Watching Arjun Do Stuff. At the Gymkhana Club, Ammu and I would look on as he and his friends jumped about in bulgy white shorts, playing badminton and swearing stylishly in English. We'd lurk in the shallow end of the pool while they took turns dunking each other and belly-flopping from the springy diving board. We'd watch Arjun drink beer and chain-smoke cigarettes on the club lawn, playing with his hair as he called to the waiters to bring more tandoori chicken, more beer, with his feet up on another chair. At home, we'd watch him argue nimbly, like a dancer, with his father, who wanted him to join his law practice instead of frittering away his time doing 'social service' at his new legal aid clinic.

'I don't care about money,' Arjun said, taking a book from the library shelf and flipping through it.

'Because you've always had money,' Baba said, puffing on his wooden pipe. I sat, unnoticed, on a leather chair, the seat of which stuck to my bare thighs. The library smelled of tobacco, books and well-oiled leather. It was Baba's pride: the only room in the house that got a fresh coat of paint every single year.

'My money,' Baba added, infuriatingly.

'I happen to think what I do is important, Baba,' Arjun said.

'Your mother wants you to get married, but will you be able to support a wife?'

'I hope for it to be the other way around,' Arjun said. Then he winked at me – me! – and my cheeks burned. A ballet dancer spun in my chest. Had Baba noticed? Did that really happen, or did I imagine it?

'I'll join your practice, Baba,' Ammu piped up from behind his chair, putting her arms around her father's neck. I rolled my eyes. 'I can't wait to appear in a case with you.'

'You?' Baba turned to look at her over his bifocals, wrinkles lining his forehead like a musical stave.

Arjun snorted – to show he'd heard enough. He slid the book back into its place on the shelf and loped out of the library through a side door that opened on to the driveway. Ammu's mother called her from somewhere inside the house. Obediently, Ammu went off to find out what she wanted.

After a few minutes of pretending to search for a book, I followed Arjun outside. He was in the driver's seat of his father's Mercedes, listening to music, one hand behind his head. Cigarette smoke floated like strands of hair around his face. He saw me looking in, threw the cigarette out the window, and opened the passenger door.

'Come on, let's go for a drive,' he said, starting the car.

I wiped my palms on my cotton skirt and sat in the passenger's seat. 'What about Ammu?'

'I don't want her. I don't want to be around anyone but you right now.'

'They don't understand you,' I said. I wanted to touch his hair, his face. The muscle in his jaw began to twitch violently. I managed to pat him, collegially, on the shoulder. Arjun leaned over and gave me a kiss on the forehead. It was a kiss that left sparks on my skin; it made me feel precious, delicate, like a porcelain doll. I noticed a gold 'om' on a thick chain under his unbuttoned shirt collar.

'Let's go,' he said, shifting the gear.

He took me back to his office, which was completely made over. It had a new desk and chairs, a new floor, a smart new coat of paint; the white tube lights had been replaced with expensive lamps. Arjun switched one on and unlocked his filing cabinet. He sat down at his desk. I attempted to drag over a chair.

'That chair won't fit on my side of the desk,' Arjun said. He patted the wooden tabletop. 'Sit here.'

I sat on his desk, bunching my skirt between my legs. Arjun pulled open a drawer and took out a brown file. From inside it, a picture of an old man fell out. He looked like his head had never known a soft pillow and his mind had never felt the peace of having enough food for his children.

'That's a senior abuse case I filed for Baba's old clerk,' Arjun pointed. 'His sons tried to throw him out. I got a magistrate to evict them from the house. I'm going to cite his case in my application.'

'Application?' I asked, putting the file aside. 'What are you applying for?'

'A master's degree in the UK,' Arjun said. Slowly, as if afraid, he slid his hand over my bare knee. I examined his face. It had that greedy expression again. I smiled and put my hand on top of his. Feeling shy and uncertain of how to proceed, I patted it. Pat, pat.

'Is it okay if I kiss you?' Arjun whispered.

'Yes.' My heart was a madman slamming against the walls of his cell. I closed my eyes and leaned forward. My eyes opened wide when Arjun thrust his tongue in my mouth. His hands crept under my skirt.

'Is this okay? Are you okay? Are you sure?' he asked, not really waiting for an answer.

A sharp pain made stars appear behind my eyes. That Arjun wanted me felt like I had a superpower. The idea that I, someone just out of middle school, could make beg, could make crazy with longing a boy who was ten years older – a man – was thrilling. Yes, yes. Every time he asked, I said yes. Because I didn't know I could say no. Because I was thirteen and he was my first love. And he seemed so excited. I was okay, either way. Because he'd winked at me when he said the word 'wife'. He kissed my forehead. I'd let him do anything in exchange for more of that.

I LEARNED HOW TO become invisible. A ghost. When, on the pretence of taking me home, Arjun drove me to his office for sex, I learned to duck down at the traffic lights. I hid in corners of the house while he put his hands down my shirt. I learned to stop myself from squealing when Arjun pulled me into empty rooms. He got bolder. We were nearly caught by a maid once, and once by his mother, wanting to know if Arjun needed the driver or if she could let him go. 'No, Aai,' Arjun said, as I, small and naked, hid under a cotton blanket, my lumpen shape obvious to anyone with a pair of eyes. But his mother had selective blindness: a common affliction amongst Indian women with sons.

One rainy afternoon, Arjun brought me over because the house was going to be empty. Ammu and her mother were heading out on errands. The staff, taking advantage of the lull in housework, had gathered in the kitchen for chai and gossip. Heavy clouds had turned the sun into a pearl, and it fooled you into thinking it was late evening. I walked down the upstairs corridor, listening to rain that sounded like deer running on the roof. As we passed by Ammu's door, Arjun yanked me inside by my arm. I managed to stifle my scream.

Arjun lifted me off the floor, hooking my legs around his waist. Then he tumbled me on to the bed. I giggled to hide my terror.

'What are we doing?' I whispered. 'What if someone comes in?'

'Shh,' Arjun said, locking the door. 'Ammu and Aai won't be home for another hour.'

'It's so gloomy today,' I said, hugging a pillow to my chest. 'Let's snuggle for a bit.'

'Shh now,' Arjun said, taking a leg in each hand. He flipped me on my belly and began to pull down my pants. That's when we heard the bathroom bolt slide open with a sickening shot, and Ammu stepped out. She dropped the hairbrush she'd been untangling her wet hair with when she saw that Arjun had me spreadeagled on her bedcover. Arjun leaped off me, and I scrambled up against the headboard, covering my body with Ammu's sheets. Ammu looked afraid, as if we were ghosts. She kicked the hairbrush away from her feet. It slid across the floor without a sound.

Arjun stood up and walked out of the room, head down, hands in his pockets.

I got up off the bed, my legs all wobbly and unsure, like a newborn calf.

'Get out,' Ammu said flatly. I stared at her, blinking. When I didn't move, she crossed her arms and walked past me out the door. At the window, a crack of lightning broke the world in half. Rain poured down from the ashen sky. Crying, I searched the house for Ammu, only to find her when I stepped out on the driveway, pacing up and down the gravel, her arms hugging her small body. I said her name. Then I shouted it. I caught up with her, grabbed her shoulder and turned her to face me.

Ammu looked at my hand on her shoulder as if it was a spatter of bird shit.

'I'm sorry you found out like this,' I said, wedging my hands in my armpits. The rain slipped inside my T-shirt and trickled down my back. 'We were going to tell you.'

'We?' Ammu said with a look that was both incredulous and mean. 'Who do you think you are? My sister-in-law?' She pushed me aside and began to walk back to the house.

I grabbed her hand. 'Maybe one day? He loves me. Look, he gave me this,' I showed her the 'om'.

Ammu shook her hand free so hard it made me flinch. 'That's fake,' she spat. 'He wouldn't waste real gold on you. You're cheap.'

For months afterwards, I'd call Ammu and she'd hang up. Everything that happened was my fault. I'd corrupted noble, kind, legal-aid-clinic-running Arjun – made him do things he never would've had I not tempted him. But my life was forever altered, while his didn't change a bit. His work thrived, and he was accepted to a prestigious master's program in the UK. Deprived of the validation of Ammu's friendship in school, I became even more of an outcast. Eventually, Ammu did stop hating me. We began talking again, but it was never the same.

MY HAPPY MEMORIES WITH Ammu had withered like a dying tree, leaf by leaf, until nothing but air remained between its branches. Luckily, at Sheila Sehgal's party, I was too drunk to wallow in the past.

'Men are terrible,' I said, squinting in the dim courtyard light at present-day Ammu's face. 'Sid once told me he'd only marry a virgin.' I threw my hands up. 'Is this Anushka a virgin? If you know, you have to tell me.'

'The men in my family,' Ammu said, avoiding my gaze, studying the dozing baby on the charpoy instead, 'they appraise a woman like they would a horse or a cow.'

'How's your brother these days?' I asked.

Ammu shifted from one foot to the other, clearly uncomfortable at the question. 'He's doing great. He's getting married next year. She's English. They met at Oxford.'

'That's nice,' I said, feeling lousy.

'Noomi,' Ammu said. She held my gaze for a second and then looked away. 'I know what he did to you was very wrong. I see now that it was ... You couldn't consent to anything. You were too young.'

I could see that it pained her to say the words out loud. 'It's okay,' I said. 'We were all very young.'

'I feel guilty about how I treated you after. I was brought up in a certain way.' She paused and gave me a soft, pleading look that melted me. 'And I didn't know any better. Can you forgive me?'

'It's okay,' I repeated with a smile. 'All is forgiven. Can we be friends again?'

Ammu looked at the ground. 'You see,' she began, 'that's the thing. I still love my brother a lot. It's hard for me to reconcile what he did to you with how loving and good he's been to me.' She took a puff of the cigarette. 'I think that's why I've been avoiding you for all these years. I'm a coward, I guess.'

'So ... we can't be friends again?'

'I want to,' Ammu said. 'I don't know how it would work. I was not just a witness to but one of the authors of your trauma. I don't know how you can want me in your life after that.' A strain of loud Punjabi music floated in from the party and Ammu looked in the direction of the garden. 'I mean, I'll always be here for you, and if you ever need any help...'

For a moment, I wished that the well I was sitting on wasn't covered so that I could jump into it. But then, I thought, wouldn't it be as good to get really, *really* wasted? I'd better get back to the bar.

'Okay, okay, I get it,' I said, standing up. 'Listen, my buzz is starting to wear off. Let's head back.' I was about to walk away when the baby on the charpoy stirred, sat up, and let out a wail. 'Isn't that baby too little to be left alone?' I asked blearily, walking towards the sound.

The room was smaller than it appeared from the outside. It was lit by a single, bare tube light. In a corner, on top of a rusty metal suitcase, was a little shrine with pictures of gods and goddesses. Durga, Rama, Sita, Lakshmana and Krishna, all resplendent in gold and jewels like the guests at Sheila Sehgal's party. The room had been recently cleaned, and a faint smell of phenyl lingered in the air. I sat down at the edge of the charpoy, which made a few complaining creaks under my weight. The child was blubbering softly, while sucking on the end of her bed sheet.

I looked around the room for something to distract her. Ammu stood quietly in the doorway, looking unsure about whether she should stay or leave. I nodded that it was okay if she wanted to return to the party. My heavy chandelier earrings swung back and forth. A tiny sound escaped from the little girl. I turned to see her staring in open-mouthed wonder.

'You like this?' I said with a smile. I took off an earring and twirled it in front of the child. The tube light caught it. Thousands of stars danced across the limewashed walls of the small room. The child smiled and held out her hand, and I dropped the earring into it.

'Perhaps it could be nice to have one of these, one day,' I said to Ammu, who smiled at the baby.

I heard the screen door of the kitchen across the courtyard fly open. A moment later, a woman ran into the room, glared at me in a confused way, and picked up the girl. When she saw what was in her child's hand, she became frightened and snatched it. Ignoring her daughter's screams of protest at losing such a sparkly toy, she gave the earring back to me, spouting apologies.

'That's okay,' I said. 'I was the one who gave it to her. She can keep it. It's fake.'

'No, no,' the woman said. 'Please, I don't want to be accused of stealing by someone tomorrow.'

'We should head back to the party,' Ammu sighed, crushing the cigarette pack in her fist.

'Thanks for talking to me,' I said as we walked away from the little room. On an impulse, I wrapped my arms around Ammu's shoulders. She'd always been so slight – all angles and points. It was like hugging a bird. She smelled like sandalwood and roses – the simple smell of the house temple. It gave me goosebumps, as if I'd heard a beautiful piece of music. I wondered what it would feel like to kiss her, to feel the shape of her small, neat breasts in my hands. I broke away and ran off towards the booming music.

THE DOOR OF THE gazebo flew open, and a young man ran past us to vomit into a hibiscus bush. 'Bitch!' Sid's booming laugh seemed to bounce around between the gazebo's glass walls. 'Lightweight pussy ass bitch.'

Inside, Sid and his friends were tossing back tequila shots. They stood about in groups, smoking, talking. The women sat demurely on the sofas, feet propped up on the coffee table, toes painted in shades of pink and pearl. In the centre of this shimmering group was Sid's fiancée, sitting on a jewelled pouffe, a champagne flute in one hand and a tiny, glittery purse in the other. Her outfit was identical to her mom-in-law's, but in pink. She looked like the sort who'd wear pink well into her fifties. Her brief blouse showed off a belly button studded with a diamond. She reminded me of Dinshaw's strawberry ice cream – pink, sweet and very cold. Or a heroine from a Yash Chopra film. But when she laughed, a vein on her forehead stood out like she was secretly plotting a murder.

A waiter came in with silver tumblers full of iced milk mixed with saffron and rose petals, and laced with bhang, that essential Holi narcotic: the slim finger that undoes our prudish corsets for a day. When it was officially Holi, at midnight, Sheila Sehgal would have a man with a dholak start playing. Tomorrow, her staff would clear away the remains of the party and put out vats of coloured powder. There would be plates piled with bhajiyas and mithai. There would be more bhang. Tonight's fine guests would return in their oldest, shabbiest clothes. They would smear each other's bodies with pink and orange colour and drink bhang. Laughing, men would touch women in ways that could get them arrested on any other day of the year. 'Bura na mano, Holi hai!'

I took a tumbler of bhang and drank it down. Nothing happened. Ammu had joined the circle around Anushka and had picked up the thread of their conversation. I didn't feel like introducing myself, knowing I'd get that look, once Anushka had placed me – that look, a mix of pity and contempt, which meant 'Ah, yes. You're *that* Noomi, aren't you?'

Standing outside the knot of women, I got tired of waiting for the bhang to kick in. A server passed by with tequila. I drank a shot and was then desperate for another cigarette. I glanced at Ammu getting all pally with Anushka. Couldn't blame her, she and Sid were first cousins after all. Ammu was out of cigarettes anyway. I'd have to ask someone else. I scanned the group and spotted Sid at its edge. He was in a kurta with loose salwar trousers, and I had to admit, he looked marvellous.

Sid was engrossed in his phone, as if his own engagement party was boring him to death. I sidled up to him and nudged his shoulder. He looked up at me but didn't smile or say hello. I grinned.

'Congrats, yaar!' I said, chock-full of fake heartiness. 'What an amazing party.'

'Thanks,' Sid said. 'Have you met Nushki yet?' he nodded in the direction of his fiancée.

'Oh. She's probably met so many people,' I said. 'I'll say hello later. At the wedding, maybe?'

'The wedding's in Goa,' Sid said. 'Mama's booked the entire Leela.'

'Wow.'

'It'll be a mad scene,' he said, while making it sound like a chore.

'Awesome. Cool. Achcha, listen, do you have a smoke?'

Sid patted his pockets. 'Looks like I'm out.'

'Oh, okay,' I said, a bit disappointed. 'Never mind.'

'I have a pack in my room,' he said, looking at me.

'Ooh, if you're going inside, can I come with you?' I asked, placing a hand on his arm.

'Why?' Sid shot a reassuring grin at Anushka, who'd begun to stare at us on and off. She smiled back, not looking reassured at all. The vein on her forehead throbbed like a hungry python. 'Why can't you smoke out here like the rest of us?'

'I'd prefer to smoke in your bedroom so there's no chance anyone in my annoying family might see.'

'For fuck's sake, who cares?' Sid said, looking appalled.

'Well, my dad would be pissed if he caught me. Good girls don't smoke, after all,' I stage-whispered.

'Why? No one in Kamalpur wants to, like, marry you,' Sid said. 'Okay, fine. Come on.'

OUR PROGRESS TOWARDS SID'S house was slowed by guests stopping Sid to congratulate him, their faces cracked open in ecstatic smiles. He had a way of receiving praise that I couldn't help but admire, like it was only natural. I lingered in his shadow. Waiters with trays full of canapés and drinks nudged past me. I took up a glass of wine. The dance floor blared Bollywood wedding hits.

Sheila Sehgal materialized out of the crowd like a figure pulled out of clay. She grabbed Sid's arm and whispered in his ear. Sid didn't resist as his mother steered him towards a prominent politician and his wife. 'This is my son, Siddharth,' she said. Sid dived to touch the couple's feet, his expression morphing smoothly from arrogance to subservience.

'Thank you, Uncle, Aunty, for coming tonight,' Sid said, straightening up.

'Of course, of course,' said the politician, slapping Sid on the back. 'Your father and I go back many years.' He nodded. 'And congratulations on your MBA. Harvard, was it?'

'Wharton, sir.'

'You know, we could use more smart young men like you in our party.'

'Maharashtra has never had a leader like you, sir.'

'And is that Anushka?' the wife asked, smiling, when she noticed me lurking between an outcropping of sofas. 'Hello!'

'Oh no,' Sheila said, whipping around to glare at me. 'That's ... a family friend.' She gave a pained smile. 'Noomi, what are you doing there – all by yourself?'

'Just ... taking a break,' I said, sipping my wine. 'Please, carry on. Forget you saw me.'

'I'm sorry, Sheila, but we must be going,' the politician said. 'I have an early flight.'

'We are so happy that you came tonight,' Sheila joined her hands in a namaste.

'Sir, you look so familiar,' I said. 'You were the one who once called South Indians Africans, right? Because of their skin colour? During one of your tevelized ... televished ... one of your speeches on TV?'

'Are you a journalist?' the politician asked. He looked around as if expecting an ambush.

'Don't mind her, ji. She's had too much to drink.'

'Oh,' the politician's wife said in an icy little voice, 'I see.'

'Siddharth,' Sheila said, 'go find Noomi some coffee.'

Grabbing my hand, Sid flicked his head towards the house. 'Come on.'

I MET SID FOR THE first time when he drove up in his big white car to pick Ammu up one day in ninth grade. Her friends, envious, whispered, 'Is that your boyfriend?' Ammu wrinkled her nose, 'Eww! That's my cousin, Sid. Our moms are sisters.' Sitting a foot away – flagrantly ignored by Ammu and her new friends – I swung my feet up on to the parapet. I was fourteen and my legs were the only part of my body I didn't hate. Sadly, even though I was careful to show as much leg as I could without coming off as vulgar, Sid hadn't noticed me. He and Ammu drove off in his white car with black-tinted windows. Then Sid began to cruise by school every afternoon at dismissal. And I realized that he had. He was seventeen, while I was fourteen and very stupid.

One night, my parents were out. The phone rang. Sid's voice was like sand warmed by sun.

'I love you,' he said.

'What?'

'I love you.'

I laughed. 'Okay. Thanks. I'm hanging up.'

'Meet me tomorrow after school,' Sid said. 'I'll take you for a drive in my car.'

I thought about how Ammu looked at me nowadays, with a mixture of pity and irritation.

'Okay,' I said. 'I'll wait for you by the bus stop. Don't be late.'

'I won't,' Sid said. 'Bye, baby.'

After some months of sneaking around after school and having furious make-out sessions in the back seat, Sid said he wanted me to meet his mother. It was at the end of a long fortnight of exams. That day, as usual, I pretended to wait for the school bus and then hid as it harrumphed away in the hot afternoon sun. A little way from the bus stop, a street vendor splashed a fistful of water over his bright mangoes. My stomach rumbled. To kill time while I waited for Sid to pick me up, I bought six slices sprinkled with salt and chilli powder, wrapped in a banana leaf. I gave the man a ten-rupee note and he dropped two shiny rupee coins into my palm. Out of habit, I went over and gave the coins to an old woman who begged by the bus stand. Nobody knew who she was. Her thin sari was a cobweb draped over her collarbones. Her grey hair had been tied into two long, dirty plaits. Madness had shaken all the words out of her head like coconuts from a tree – leaving one phrase, which she repeated over and over: 'Dey.' Give.

'Dey,' the old woman said, as the coins fell in her lap, and then spat on the ground. Her foamy gob raised a small puff of dust. The woman sat leaning against a wall decorated with tiles of gods and a sign that said: 'No spitting or urination'. At the other end, a man in a polyester shirt urinated noisily. He finished, gave himself a shake, a squeeze, and zipped up with a bob. Then he sauntered over.

'Nice mangoes,' he said, leering down my shirt with a paan-stained grin. Fear rose in me like a scream. It was the kind of fear that boils over from your mind when you realize that you've made a miscalculation that has put your body in harm's way. Women feel this fear more often than men. I glanced at the mango seller, hoping he'd say something before the man tried to put his hand down my shirt or worse.

The mango seller seemed hesitant to get involved, but reluctantly he murmured, 'Leave her alone.'

The man said, '*Teri biwi hai kya, behenchod?*' Is she your wife or something, sisterfucker?

The mango seller came from behind his cart with his fruit knife, holding his dhoti. He looked at me as if to say, you shouldn't be here. Fear, it seems, like a common cold, can be contagious. The two men and I stood in a triangle, and I looked at the knife the mango seller gripped in his hand. I felt guilty for making them fight. There was no way to go back to the school for help. I'd have to answer questions of why I wasn't on the bus in the first place. Not knowing what else to do, I was about to scream, when Sid's car drove up in a cloud of dust and both men dispersed like alley cats. When Sid opened the door to let me in, loud music blasted out, causing a flock of birds to take off. I got in hurriedly, and Sid made a fast U-turn that I think was illegal. As I mentioned before, he was seventeen, and didn't have a license.

'Had a good day?' Sid asked, trailing a finger down the length of my arm.

'You're late,' I said, feeling breathless. 'Where were you?'

'Why? What happened?' he frowned.

'N ... nothing,' I said. 'The bus stop gets a bit deserted.' Something in Sid's voice warned me not to say anything to him. Rule number one of being a girl: we were like medicine bottles. If our seals were broken, we were sent back to the store. It was important to appear untampered with at all times.

Sid pinched my chin. 'Let me know if someone's giving you trouble, and I'll kick his face in. Now forget about the bus stop. Tell me, how was school today?'

'Uneventful,' I shrugged. 'I suck at exams. A time clock turns me into an idiot.'

Sid pushed his Ray-Bans to the top of his head, where his gelled, spiky hair held them in place. 'My dad said...' he said and looked at me. His eyes, light brown with flecks of green, and his skin, marked him as high caste, with a drop of ancestral wrong-side-of-the-blanket Portuguese merchant blood running in his veins. 'He said,' and here Sid attempted to sound like his father, '"No point stressing yourself out with studies when you're going to inherit my huge business. I've worked hard all my life so that my son can enjoy."'

'How lucky,' I pouted and crossed my arms. 'Wish my dad was that rich.'

'You'll marry a rich guy,' Sid said.

I smiled: whatever could you mean, please elaborate.

'Are you excited to meet my mom?' Sid asked.

'I wonder how she convinced my parents to let me come over during mid-terms.'

'Oh please,' Sid scoffed. 'No one says no to Sheila Sehgal ever. Everyone is legit too terrified of her.'

'Should I be terrified of her?'

'She asked,' Sid said, and his voice took on a wary edge, 'if you were anything like your mother.' He looked at me. 'What do you think about her question?' He took my hand.

'It's fair, I guess,' I nodded. A pebble formed in my throat. To make it go away, I kept talking. 'I was wondering,' I said, nibbling on my lip, 'does she ... does your mom know about us?'

Sid smiled. His smile could pick open locks, it could make you feel like the centre of the universe. But add a raised eyebrow, and it could make you feel like the biggest fool in the universe.

Sid's house was the largest on their street. In the corner of the garden, with its sweet-smelling mango, frangipani and chikoo trees, was a fountain with a lotus pond. Every day, a maid picked out a single lotus to set at the feet of the gods in the house temple. The living room, which we entered through a short hallway, had a floor-to-ceiling mirror, gilded and clouded to look antique. There was more gold on the armchairs and the sofas, upholstered in muted shades of grey and white velvet. In the corner, by the gold bar, was a floor lamp made of white ostrich feathers.

Sid took my hand and led me up a flight of marble stairs to a family room, where we found his mother curled up on a white sofa, watching television. Her hair was perfectly coiffed, and her off-white trousers had sharp press-lines down the front. The thick-framed glasses perched on the tip of her nose were Burberry, as was the stole wrapped around her shoulders. Issey Miyake perfume hung in the air around her like an aria.

In contrast to her thoroughly modern appearance, the show Sheila was watching was a popular Hindi soap opera full of horrible, backward stereotypes – the dutiful wife, the vamp in red lipstick, the girlfriend in a miniskirt, the book-nerd in salwar kurta and glasses. The women spent all their time scheming for the attention of the men. The men seemed to be happily oblivious of the women's schemes.

Sid, crossing the room in two steps, practically dived into his mother's arms.

'My Sidoo,' Sheila said, squeezing his face. 'Where have you been all day?'

Sid looked up at me, smiled, and said, 'Mama, this is Noomi.'

'Ah,' Sheila said pleasantly enough. 'Noomi. Welcome.'

'Thank you, Aunty,' I smiled. 'It's so wonderful to meet you. Sid talks about you all the time.' Something in Sheila's gaze made me realize that I was hunching. But straightening up drew attention to my breasts, my least favourite part of my body. They all had a ranking. My legs were number one, breasts were number ten. My nose was a solid three and a half. I clutched my backpack to my chest.

'Sid hasn't told me much about you,' Sheila smiled. 'Now I can find out for myself.'

'Of course, Aunty,' I said, and giggled a little stupidly. 'Feel free to ask me anything.'

'Oh, I will, don't worry,' Sheila said, and pressed a bell on the table. Within minutes, a brown-uniformed man appeared at the door. 'Ramu, we're coming downstairs for lunch,' Sheila ordered, not looking at Ramu but at the television screen.

'Ji, Madamji,' Ramu said, and bowed out of the room.

'Come on, children,' Sheila said. The soap opera's credits began to roll as she pressed the off button. 'Oh, Noomi,' she pointed at my backpack, 'leave that bag here.'

The dining room had white and blue porcelain vases, and white silk screens painted with cranes. The napkin on my lap was white, as were the orchids tumbling out of a white marble urn. Sheila's love of white seemed very intentional. She could keep the white untouched by the besmirching sweat and dust that plagued the city's ubiquitous poor.

'So,' Sheila said, as Ramu laid out the dishes, 'tell me something interesting about yourself.'

'Well,' I said, making folds in the napkin on my lap, 'I like to read. And I write poetry sometimes.'

Sheila groaned. 'I said interesting. All this poetry-showetry flies above my head.'

'Noomi is a good singer, Mom,' Sid said and winked. 'Ask her to sing something.'

'What? No! He's joking. That's not true, Aunty,' I said. 'I'm a terrible singer.'

There was a glint in Sheila's eyes, like a knife catching the light. 'Let's hear you sing.'

'Come on, Noomi,' Sid grinned. I told myself that he didn't mean to be cruel.

'No, please,' I said. 'When I start singing, dogs start to howl.' My cheeks began to feel warm.

'Sing *now*.' Sheila's voice took on a flinty quality, even as her expression remained pleasant.

I sang an old Bollywood song, wincing as my voice cracked like an adolescent boy's. I glanced at Sheila and Sid. Their expressions of amusement made me want to cry. Still, I swallowed my anger and kept singing, screwing my eyes shut so that I wouldn't leak tears.

Then, in the middle of my song, I heard Sheila scream, 'Ramu, you bloody idiot!'

My eyes flapped open. Ramu's face loomed above me, blanched in terrified confusion. Down one of Sheila's white trouser legs ran a long brown smear. By her foot was the errant spoon that must have escaped when Ramu was clearing away the plates.

'Do you know how much these pants cost?' Sheila screamed again. 'They're worth more than what I pay you in the whole year.' She threw her napkin at his chest. 'I should cut it out of your salary.'

Ramu clasped his hands over his midriff. He bent at the waist, his head lowered and tilted to one side. 'Madamji, I'm so sorry,' he begged. 'Please, I will clean it up.' He dipped a napkin in a glass of water and approached her.

'Don't you dare!' Sheila yelled in accented Hindi. 'I'll fire you on the spot.'

Sid's eyes met mine. He gave a sideways glance at his mother and mouthed, 'Do something.'

'Sheila Aunty,' I said, rising from my chair. 'Mom had bought this powerful stain remover on her last trip abroad. Give me your pants. I'll send them back in perfect condition.'

Sheila seemed to mull this over. Then she shrugged. 'I want them back tomorrow.'

'Yes, of course,' I said, gesturing to Ramu to back off with the wet napkin. 'Tomorrow.'

'Say thank you,' Sheila said to Ramu. 'She's saved your job.'

'Thank you, Babyji,' Ramu said. Nodding at him, I followed Sheila out the door.

'YOU DID SO WELL,' Sid said a few minutes later when, on the pretext of retrieving my backpack from upstairs, we snuck into his bedroom. 'My mom likes you – I can tell.'

'She wasn't impressed by my singing,' I frowned. 'Or my poetry.' A lovely perfume emanated from his body. Every time he moved, I got a whiff. 'I didn't mean to sound snooty or superior or anything.'

'I love girls who read,' Sid said.

'Really?' I said.

'Sure,' he said. A look drifted across his face. 'Well-read girls have great imagination ... it makes them wild in bed.'

He pushed me up against a poster. I slipped away from him. 'All my work in impressing your mother will go to waste.'

'You're right,' Sid said. He took my backpack from the foot of his bed and swung it on his shoulder. 'I'll save it for the car.' He held my hand and we cantered happily down the stairs like a pair of dumb colts.

An hour later, Sid parked in his usual spot on the far edge of Rani Lake. 'Do you know,' I said as Sid began lazily unbuttoning my shirt, 'that my nani, my mother's mother, had a peculiar word for lake. She used to call it a "chashma". That means mirror, doesn't it?'

'Um,' Sid said, clearly not interesting in talking. 'It means spectacles.' He undid a few more buttons.

'No, that's in Hindi,' I persisted, brushing his hand away. 'I think in Urdu it means looking glass. Isn't that pretty? A lake is a mirror, one made of rain.' I stared out the window at the glittering water. My mother didn't talk much about her parents, who'd both died when I was a baby. She did, one time, let slip that she had trouble sleeping, because as a child, she had to sleep with her fingers in her ears to block out the sound of her father whipping her mother with the metal part of his suspenders. Even now, Asha was startled by any sudden, loud noise.

'No babe,' Sid said. 'Chashma means spectacles. Aina means mirror, okay? Now stop talking.'

A policeman strolled by, twirling his lathi. Sid, cool as a melon, gave him a nod. The policeman tapped a finger to his black topi and sauntered off.

'My dad has all the police in this town in his pocket,' Sid said, when I gave him a questioning look. 'They all know my car. But still, it doesn't hurt to hand out a little bribe once in a while.'

'Really? Who else do you come here with?'

'Just you, sweetheart,' Sid said, putting my hand to his crotch. 'Just you.'

The first time Sid asked me to blow him, I'd made sure to look as if I didn't understand. Sid put his hands behind my head and pushed me down. I opened my mouth and put my lips around his penis. Sid moaned like he was having a sex dream. Maybe we should do it, I suggested. Sid bolted upright, opened his glove compartment and pulled out a condom. He tore the wrapper with his teeth and rolled it on while holding the tip. 'That's so no air gets trapped,' he explained knowledgeably.

We shifted to the back seat. I remembered to cry out in surprise as he entered me. I could see from the look on his face that it made Sid feel very manly. After a while, we found a rhythm. I began, to my actual surprise this time, to enjoy myself. It dawned on me that the sex I'd had with Arjun was not very good, despite him being very beautiful. His face popped, uninvited, into my head. Before I realized what I was doing, I'd whispered his name – right in Sid's ear.

'What?' Sid said, realizing that the name I'd whispered wasn't his.

'Nothing,' I said, pulling him back on top of me. 'Keep going.'

'You said Arjun,' Sid raised his voice. 'Who the fuck is Arjun?'

'Ammu's brother?' I bit my tongue. Why hadn't I lied?

'My cousin Arjun?' Sid screeched. 'Arjun? You fucked him? My fucking cousin?'

'No,' I said, getting up, 'you don't understand.' With a blind hand, I fished out my underwear from between the gaps in the seat. My bra, it seemed, was lost forever. I did up my buttons. 'It was a stupid, one-way crush.'

'Why did you say his name like that?' Sid twisted my arm behind my back. 'Tell me.'

'Ow, Sid,' I cried. 'You're hurting me.'

'Tell me the fucking truth.'

'Okay, okay! We had sex, but he wasn't my boyfriend,' I burst out. 'Please, I'm sorry.'

A hand slammed down on the window. I yelped and threw myself, still half naked, to the car floor. Sid dived back into the driver's seat. He pulled his T-shirt over his head, zipped his fly, fixed his hair and got out. I heard him talk in rapid-fire Marathi with the policeman – whose hand stayed on the car window. After a few minutes, he got back in.

'Keep your head down,' he snarled. 'It's some new guy. I've given him a few hundred bucks, but he wants more.'

By the time we got to my house, I'd cried so much my eyes began to hurt. I'd ruined everything.

'I'm sorry, I'm sorry,' I kept blubbering, my body wedging the car door open.

'Shut the fuck up,' Sid said. With one hand, he pushed me away from the car. I stumbled backwards a few steps. 'You're a whore, like your mother.' He slammed the door shut.

SID SLAMMED HIS BEDROOM door, cutting off the faraway noise of the party. I turned with a little start. 'Shush!' I said. 'What will people think if they know we're in here together?'

Feelings, it turns out, are harder to get rid of than a turmeric stain on a white kurta. While Sid and I never did get back together, some part of me had always remained infatuated with him. We'd continued to – in Sid's case mainly because booty-calling most Kamalpur women could get you taken out by their menfolk, and in my case because sleeping with an ex-boyfriend was one way to keep my 'number' low – hook up every couple of months.

'They'll think that you,' Sid grinned, 'are a slut. I'm the golden boy, remember?'

Sid's bedroom was unrecognizable from the last time I'd been there. But it smelled the same. His bed still had white sheets and a snowy comforter. Above it hung framed photo collages: Sid with his parents somewhere in Europe, Sid making a toast at an American wedding, Sid in New York City with his arms around his Toosh-shawl-clad mother, etc. Happy memories, like cash in the bank. In the corner opposite the bed, was a flat-screen TV with videogame remotes scattered at its base. On the bedside table was an ashtray filled with cigarette butts – the only disorderly object in the room.

Sid rolled open a drawer, from which he took out a pack of cigarettes. The wrapping crackled as he crushed it in his hand and tossed it into a basket. He pulled out a slim, long cigarette, tapped the filter on the face of his watch, and handed it to me along with a lighter.

'Thanks,' I said. I lit the cigarette and took an extremely satisfying drag.

'You still can't keep your mouth shut,' Sid grinned, moving closer to me.

'It pissed you off? Wasn't that politician fellow like, your dad's low-level tout back in the nineties? I remember seeing him running around with a whisky bottle at Sheila Aunty's parties.'

'Yeah, well,' Sid said. 'Now he *is* the government. He can block our construction projects.'

'Sorry,' I said, ashing the cigarette and taking another long drag. 'I guess things change.'

'Life is like a see-saw,' Sid shrugged. He opened the drawer again and took out a baggie of coke, chopped out a line on the glass with his credit card and snorted it. Then he looked at me and smiled. I'd expected Sid to return to his fiancée. I'd hoped no one saw us go into the bedroom, even though I knew hoping was pointless. In the world I was from, there was always someone to see you when you least wanted to be seen.

'How's life?' Sid asked, brushing my cheek. 'I don't know anything about your life. So mysterious.'

If I were perfectly honest, tonight felt like a humiliation. Which was ridiculous. Sid and I broke up many years ago. But he was engaged, while I remained pathologically single.

'What's Anushka like?' I asked, hoping I didn't sound like I cared too much. Suddenly, I wanted to get out of this room, leave this party, get away from Kamalpur forever.

'She's lovely,' Sid said. 'Her parents and mine are good friends.' Someone laughed outside the door. We both looked up. I saw the shadow of feet walking away from the gap.

'Why haven't I ever seen you with her?' I asked. 'At parties or whatever.'

'She's been studying abroad,' Sid said with a smile. 'NYU. I like smart girls, remember? And also, her parents are super-conservative. You've probably seen her house. It's the big white one in Byramji Town with all the security guards.'

'Yeah,' I said miserably. 'I know the house. They must be very rich.'

'They are, they are,' Sid said and wiggled his fingers for my cigarette. He glanced down at my hard-working blouse like it was a present he'd like to unwrap. I felt a not unpleasant flutter in my chest.

'What?' I said.

'You know what,' Sid said, smiling.

'What? Here? Right now? Are you crazy?'

'Come on. You're excited. Don't deny it,' he said. With the flat of his hand, he pushed me downwards until I lay flat on the bed. He took the cigarette from between my fingers and stubbed it in the ashtray.

Halfway into being undressed by Sid, I felt my heart thumping nastily and had to sit back up for air.

Sid propped himself up on a pillow, looking bored. 'What's up?' he asked. 'You okay?'

'I feel dizzy,' I said, putting a hand to my head. 'I think that bhang's finally kicking in.' I turned to look at him. 'I think we should go back. I'm feeling all weird and floaty.'

'Float back down,' Sid said, pulling me by the wrist. 'Just let me finish.'

Sid got on top of me. Soon, my sari was bunched up at the waist and my bra lay across my neck. 'We should go back,' I said, trying to push him off with my legs.

'Listen,' Sid said, putting his weight on me. 'If Mama finds you in here, you're dead.'

'What! How would she find out?' I said.

'I'm saying,' Sid said slowly, as if explaining things to a child, 'if my mom finds out we were fucking at my engagement party, forget about being invited to the wedding, you will be on her blacklist forever. Okay? So, let's finish. Then you go out first, and no one will find out what you did.'

I let myself go limp. The floaty feeling got stronger. I felt myself waft up to the ceiling and stand there, upside down. I watched upside-down Sid's perfect buttocks bobbing over my body.

'My god, you're so dry,' Sid panted. He put his head between my legs, then thrust two fingers into me, pulled them out and pushed them into my mouth. 'Here, taste yourself,' he said.

I floated back down after what seemed like hours and he was still at it. Waiting for him to finish, I saw a sunset sitting on top of a cloud. It turned out to be a bedside lamp. The cloud was Sid's fluffy duvet. I turned my face towards the orange sun and pretended I'd slipped between it and the white cloud. I was flying away.

THE DHOLAK PLAYER WAS in the centre of a crowd in the Sehgals' marble driveway, his massive drum hanging from his shoulders by a broad leather strap. He wore an orange kurta and dhoti, and there was a long tilak on his forehead, like an exclamation point. He whacked the drum with his curved metal rods. Sheila had people standing on the rooftop, emptying sack after sack of white, red and orange petals on to the people dancing below.

Before I left Sid's bedroom, I'd made a half-hearted attempt to fix myself up. My sari was far more disastrous than before, but I was too wasted to care. I wanted to dance, to show them all that I was more alive, more full of beauty than Sid's fiancée could ever be. The dholak's music was enthralling, like an animal's wild heartbeat. I took off my sandals and ran across the wet lawn to the driveway. I ran into Sheila and Anushka. They stared at me, faces pinched with displeasure. Dressed identically in chiffon and feathers, they reminded me of a pair of angry flamingos. Sheila grabbed my wrist and pulled me aside.

'Who the hell do you think you are, huh?' she said, digging her red nails into my skin.

'What?' I said, trying to focus on her face. 'Sheila Aunty, let go. I want to dance.'

Sheila yanked me so close, I could smell her breath. 'I saw Sid take you into the house. When he didn't return to the party, I came inside to find out why. You were in the bedroom and the door was locked.' Her lips curled into a belittling snarl. 'You think you can do whatever the fuck you want? Look at that poor girl.' She gestured to Anushka, who was standing apart from us with tears leaking from her huge eyes. 'Don't you care about anyone but yourself, Noomi?'

I tried to yank my hand away. 'No,' I laughed, 'I don't. Now let me go. I want to dance.'

'You don't deserve to be standing here,' Sheila said. 'You are sick. Demented.'

'What?'

'I don't care what happens to you, I don't care if you get crushed under someone's heel like a fucking cockroach,' Sheila said. 'But if I see you try to interfere with Sid and Anushka again, I will make sure that your father knows what happened tonight. Do you understand? Do you want him to find out what a whore his daughter is? Poor man, he's already got so much on his plate with your mother. Do you want to add to that burden?'

'No,' I said, feeling burning insects start to crawl all over my brain. 'Please, let me go.'

Sheila didn't let go of my hand so much as throw it away in disgust. 'Then go.'

I nodded. Sheila hugged Anushka. They seemed to meld together into one strange and glamorous bird, all feathers and diamonds and chiffon. Anushka gave her mother-in-law a look full of love and gratitude. I turned away from the two women and ran off in the direction of the music. I found Ammu, and began to dance with her inside the storm of rose petals, not caring if the pleats of my sari unravelled, or if my pallu shifted to reveal the gaps in my ugly, ill-fitting blouse. I danced barefoot on the marble floor slick with petals. I bumped into Adil and almost toppled over, laughing.

'Noomi, your dad has been looking for you,' Adil said, pointing at Jeh, who stood staring at me from the side of the driveway. 'He was worried that something had happened. Are you okay?'

'Daddy! Come dance with me!' I said. I rushed up to Jeh and tried to bring him to the floor.

'I think it's time to go home,' Jeh said. He gripped my hand. 'You're not looking all right.'

'No!' I yelled. 'Dance with me na, please.' I began to yank him on to the floor. Jeh's face lit up with anger. He jerked his hand away. I lost my balance. The marble floor came rushing up to meet my face.

Darkness.

My whole childhood, I'd believed that if Asha disappeared, somehow all our troubles would disappear along with her. When she was late coming home, I hoped it was because her car had crashed into a truck. When she slept, I'd put a finger under her nose, hoping not to feel her breath. I wanted to be released from the prison of my shame. I wanted to not, when I looked in the mirror, see the image of my mother hanging like a veil upon my face.

Somewhere above my head, I heard Jeh shouting, 'Noomi! Get up right now!' I tried to open my eyes, but there was only darkness, the smell of flowers and the beating of the dholak.

They took me inside the gazebo and laid me out on the beige sofa. Faces loomed over me. My father, Sheila Sehgal, and a man I didn't recognize. He flashed a pen light into my eyes and asked me who the prime minister was and looked satisfied with my answer.

Jeh helped me to my feet and said we'd be leaving.

'Shouldn't you go to the hospital?' Sheila asked. 'My driver can take you.'

'Thank you,' Jeh said with a little nod. 'But I think she just needs to get home.'

'What's your opinion, Dr Kumar?' Sheila turned to the man holding the pen light.

'She looks okay to me,' he shrugged. 'Had too much to drink. She's taken after her mother, it seems.' He chuckled. 'Nothing to worry about except a bad hangover.'

Jeh managed a sad little smile. 'Thank you, Sheila. Sorry that we ruined the party.'

'Oh nonsense, Jeh,' Sheila said, patting his shoulder. 'I'm sorry you couldn't enjoy yourself.'

In her voice, there was no hint of the person who, a half hour ago, had been threatening me. Even in my state, I was impressed by how Sheila could tame her rage like a circus lion.

Jeh took me by my arm, trying to look like he was in control of things. I walked before him out the glass gazebo door. I stared at my wild-eyed reflection. I looked like a churail, a she-demon.

WHEN WE GOT HOME, I tore off my sari, and bundling it in my hands, threw it in a corner. I began to pull out clothes from my closet hangers to dump them into a suitcase. I'd almost finished packing when Jeh came in, wearing crumpled pyjamas. He looked surprised, as if he had expected to find me asleep. Yet here I was, at 3 a.m., full of energy, stuffing clothes into a suitcase.

'What the hell are you doing?' Jeh asked.

'I'm leaving,' I said, throwing a toothbrush into the bag.

'Leaving? To go where?'

'Bombay. I'll stay in a hotel until I can find a paying guest accommodation or a flat share or something.'

'So, this is your very mature reaction to tonight's behaviour, huh?' Jeh folded his arms across his chest. 'Running away?'

He made a shooing motion with his hands. 'Do you know how embarrassed I was tonight? No, Noomi, look at me. Like it or not, we live in a particular context, and we must live with decorum.'

'Do you hear yourself?' I screamed. 'You sound like some pearl-clutching housewife from the fifties. You talk about decorum. Where's your decorum, huh? Where's your dignity? You're spineless. You can't stand up to anyone, not even Mom.'

'What do you expect me to do? Throw her out on the street? Asha is my responsibility,' Jeh yelled. 'She has no one in the world but me. I can't abandon her.'

'What about me?' I yelled back. 'Don't you see what she's done to me? Or are you blind or just really stupid? By staying with her, you abandoned *me*. Now I'm abandoning you both.' I went to where Jeh was standing by the doorway, pushed him aside, and walked out of the bedroom.

'Where are you going now?' Jeh asked, scrambling after me.

'To get another suitcase from your room,' I said. 'And some whisky.'

'Noomi, if you dare drink right now,' Jeh warned, 'I will kick you out myself.'

'Perfect,' I said, running ahead of him.

In Jeh's bedroom – which was not Asha's bedroom – I pulled a dusty suitcase off from the top of his closet. Then, I felt about in his sock drawer until I found the bottle of expensive Scotch he hid there. Stupid Jeh, he lived in a house full of thieves and wouldn't lock up his treasures. I uncorked the bottle and took a deep swig. I could taste the drink's peat and moss. Something moved in the corner of my vision. For a second, I thought Asha had woken up and come into the room. I turned to look, but it was only me, reflected in the closet's long mirror.

'Give me that,' Jeh said, trying to grab the bottle from my hand. Topaz drops spilled on the floor as we tussled back and forth for it. I gripped its neck and it slipped out of Jeh's sweaty hand. Taking aim at the mirror, I flung the bottle at it. It crashed on the glass and a spiderweb of cracks appeared instantly. Hundreds of small Noomis stared back at me now. I swivelled, triumphant. Jeh's hands went up to his face and his body shook with sobs.

It was the first time in my life I'd seen Jeh cry. His grief held no artifice; he cried like a child whose toys had been smashed by someone big and mean. It was the saddest sound I'd ever heard. If I left tonight, I knew that sound would haunt me for the rest of my life.

'Daddy,' I said, rubbing the top of his shoulder. 'Don't cry. I'm sorry. I won't go anywhere. I was angry.'

Jeh mashed away his tears with the heel of his hand. 'Don't do this to me. My heart can't take it.'

'I'm sorry,' I said again. 'I love you. I don't know what else to say.' How had I turned out so cruel? This was Jeh – who'd read to me in funny voices, who'd get up in the middle of the night if I had a stomach ache and stay until I felt better, who'd lift me on to his shoulders whenever I felt tired.

'It's been a long night,' Jeh said, lying down and covering himself with a blanket. 'I'm exhausted.'

I lay next to him, watching his side rise and fall with each breath. His face became a mask of sleep. I picked up his hand and kissed his knuckles. 'I love you,' I whispered. 'I'm sorry.'

NEXT DAY, MID-AFTERNOON. ASHA was in her bedroom smoking cigarettes with Rhea Puri, lolling on her bed – surrounded by empty glasses, newspapers, ashtrays, handbags, and a stack of unopened letters and bills. Cigarette smoke drifted into the hallway like a lost guest at a wedding.

'Noomi bachche,' Rhea said when I walked in. 'Come sit with us. Did you just wake up, lazy girl?'

The walls of the bedroom were washed with sunlight. It made the bottles on Asha's drinks trolley sparkle like some sort of emerald city. Asha was propped up with pillows, holding an empty glass on which she tapped her ring, a signal to Rhea to make her a drink. Her face looked tender, like a peeled fruit. From experience, I knew she was at that point where the alcohol made her calm, before it began to make her angry, and long before it made her sad.

Rhea rose from the bed and strolled over to the trolley. She smiled at me and began to pour whisky into a peg measure. Her silk shirt had the first three buttons undone. A thin gold chain linked with tiny white diamonds lay against her pale skin. There was a beautiful mole on her collarbone. I cleared my throat. Rhea looked up at me. Alcohol overflowed from the measure.

Shaking her hand dry, she beckoned me over, holding up another glass. Taking the glass from Rhea's hand, I glanced over at Asha, who gave a non-committal shrug.

'What should I drink?' I said, and picked up the bottle of Lagavulin to look at its amber light.

'Nah, ah, ah,' Rhea said, taking the bottle from my hand. 'Too expensive for you.' She poured Old Monk into my glass, followed by Thums Up. 'Rum and Coke. Nice and sweet.'

It *was* sweet. I drank it down in big, thirsty gulps. The rum lit a candle inside me. I finished it quickly and made myself another, stronger one. Taking their drinks, Rhea joined Asha on the bed. It wasn't hard to figure out why Asha drank the amount she did, I thought, as my mind began to fill up with a delicious peace. Who'd want to feel like crap, when you could feel like *this*. Alcohol was a movie, a song, a conversation in a bottle. Like religion, music, art, it eased the symptoms of living as a woman.

I once saw a video of a man talking about an experiment called the 'Rat Park'. Scientists had offered rats two choices of water bowls: one regular, one laced with opiates. They noted that the lonely rats went for the drug water, while the ones with wheels and other rats for company chose the water without drugs. The scientists concluded that drugs and alcohol light up the same parts of the brain as love. Addiction came out of being unable to tolerate loneliness.

I dragged Asha's velvet dressing-table pouffe over. 'What's new, Rhea Aunty?' I asked.

'I was telling your mother about the party,' Rhea said, taking a sip of her drink.

I nodded. 'Yes?'

'Such a good-looking couple, no?' Rhea said. 'Can you imagine how gorgeous their babies will be? Oof.' She rolled her eyes. 'I heard their parents arranged the match. That always works out for the best, na? First the families should see if they get along.'

'I suppose,' I shrugged.

Rhea glanced sideways. 'Your mother doesn't think so.'

I regarded my mother, who blew smoke out of the side of her mouth and flicked ash into a Murano bowl. Smoke spiralled upwards from the cigarette between her fingers. 'You make them out to be a pair of pedigree poodles, Rhea,' she said. 'Being mated by their families to breed prize-winning puppies.'

When Jeh decided to marry Asha, Zal Papa had screamed, 'You're marrying a madhouse!' Jeh, who'd done everything (like going to a football-mad boarding school so that he'd 'toughen up' and taking up 'manly' hobbies like hunting and hiking) to please his father, decided in his own mild-mannered way to defy him. My parents were married. I was born. Six years later, their marriage began falling apart. My mother lost their second baby, suffered a breakdown, and had to be put on suicide watch. I remember visiting her. She was as scrawny as a sparrow. A nurse helped her use the bathroom. I didn't want her to hold me, because it was scary to feel her ribs through her hospital gown.

'Rhea Aunty,' I said, 'you've never told me the story of how you ended up marrying your husband. I heard that his family hates you. Didn't they,' I tipped my head to one side, 'try to disown him?'

Rhea took a sip of her drink and made a face as if it tasted bitter. When she looked up at me, I gulped, realizing that I'd overplayed my hand.

'I saw you,' Rhea said, 'at the party last night. You were with someone. I think it was...' Rhea put a finger to her chin and looked at the ceiling. 'Siddharth Sehgal?' She leaned forward. 'Why was he taking you inside the house?' She made a shoddy pretence of appearing shocked. 'Was it to sober you up? You looked pretty drunk. Is that why you fell flat on your back later, on the dance floor?'

Asha's eyes gleamed like a cat who's spotted a mouse's tail as it whisks around the corner. 'Were you drunk?' she asked. 'So drunk that you fell in front of everyone?' She smirked.

My mother and I were always circling each other like this. Some days she had the upper hand, some days I did. Today was not my turn. I decided to leave with what little dignity I had left. 'Excuse me,' I said, getting up from the pouffe. 'I think the rum and Cokes have given me a stomach ache.'

As I walked out the door, I heard Asha laughing.

I CHANGED FROM MY pyjamas into a plain cotton dress that smelled like it had been kept in the sun. I examined my skin in the bathroom mirror. I had a strange relationship with mirrors. I loved how they brightened up a room, echoing light from one wall to the other, but usually I preferred to avoid my own reflection, always afraid of what I might discover if I looked too closely. Blue veins ran below my skin like rivulets. My eyes were pink and small. An ache spread from my temples. I stuck a finger into my throat to vomit, curling over the sink. Black stuff ran into the drain like spiders. I rinsed my mouth; the water tasted sweet after the acid from my stomach.

Looking for comfort from my headache, I wandered into Shanta Bai's room with a bottle of hair oil. Shanta Bai was at her usual spot by the window, on a chair whose stuffing spilled out through the rips. The television flickered on mute in the background. Shanta Bai held a steaming tumbler of tea in one hand, while crumbling up stale bread with the other to feed a squirrel, her half-wild pet. Behind her, out the window, a white bougainvillea bloomed against the blue sky.

The bougainvillea had been planted when I was six. That was also the year that my mother hired Shanta Bai to be my ayah. Like most village women, Shanta Bai had never attended a school. She was married at the age of twelve to a man twenty years her senior. When she turned eighteen, she left him when he began drinking mahua liquor instead of working, and took up a room with her brother and his family. Shanta Bai learned English by working in the homes of families like mine. Her husband's name was tattooed on her arm in green ink. She never spoke it out loud.

Here is a great story about Shanta Bai from when I was around twelve: Standing on a tiny wooden stool, Shanta Bai liked to fret and mutter over whatever she was cooking. She swore at the dal like it was her nemesis, cursed the okra, and chastened the chicken curry as she stirred it with a long wooden spoon. Her pallu was tied away from the flame. Shanta Bai wore her sari the Maharashtrian way – without a petticoat, with the pleats gathered and looped between the legs and tucked in behind. Her buttocks, quite muscular for someone pushing sixty, looked like a pair of mushroom caps. I wanted to learn how to make chapatis, but I had to wait until Shanta Bai was free to teach me.

My aunt Binny sauntered in and picked up an apple from the fruit bowl. She leaned on the counter, but then seemed to think better of it. Dropping the apple back into the bowl, she inspected her white chiffon outfit for stains. To avoid her upbraiding gaze, I went over to chat with a maid who was lowering a batch of samosas into a pan of hot, spitting oil.

Binny folded her arms over her chest. She cleared her throat once, twice, like a terrible actor. Shanta Bai turned the stove to simmer and hopped off the stool. Wiping her hands on a towel tucked into her sari, she looked as if she was not thrilled to have visitors. Binny expected people to fall all over themselves to please her, especially the help. Her expression switched from benevolent to haughty.

'Shanta,' Binny said, 'I've heard you have a very clever niece?'

Her niece, a girl of nineteen or twenty, was Shanta Bai's favourite among her brother's three children. Her grumpy old face broke into a smile. 'Sumati,' she said. 'Just passed her exams.'

'Wonderful,' Binny said. 'Adil's ayah quit yesterday. I need an immediate replacement. Sumati can start working for us from next week.'

'No. That's not possible,' Shanta Bai shook her head vigorously. 'She's going to college. My brother is not going to let her work as an ayah. We've saved money for years to send her.'

The kitchen seemed to freeze. The maid frying samosas looked petrified; even the oil ceased to spit. Binny gathered herself up to her full, imposing height, almost a head taller than Shanta Bai.

'That money will be wasted,' Binny said. 'Who's going to give a girl from her background a job? The daughter of a chowkidar? Please. Send her to me. She'll be well paid.' Binny turned and started to walk away. 'Better than marrying her off. All the men of your class are useless drunkards, anyway,' she said as she opened the kitchen door to exit.

'No.'

Binny faltered, then turned slowly around. 'You better be careful how you speak to me.'

Shanta Bai drew up to her full height, all bristling four feet eleven inches. If she were a cat, she would've arched her back and hissed. Pointing her wooden spoon at Binny, she said, in English, 'Sumati will never work for you, awful woman!'

It was one of those very rare occasions that Binny got what was coming to her. The fact that Shanta Bai wasn't fired on the spot only spoke to how fantastic a cook she was. Her dhansak, which she made by first frying the mutton in ghee, garlic and onions, could bring tears to a grown man's eyes. That afternoon, Shanta Bai became my hero as well as my ayah.

I SAT DOWN AT Shanta Bai's feet. 'Give me a tel malish, please,' I said, handing her the bottle of oil. The floor was cool under my palms. Shanta Bai's fingers massaging my head were warm and strong.

'Always bothering me, Nooma, even now,' Shanta Bai complained lovingly. She poured oil into her hands. I heard the slick noise of her palms rubbing together. I closed my eyes and let my thoughts wander far from the room, into other possibilities, into the sort of life where I could have turned to my mother for comfort.

'I've never thanked you,' I said.

'For what?'

'For raising me.' I reached for her hand. 'I wouldn't have survived being a child without you.'

'You can thank me by going on your internet to find a nice young man to marry,' Shanta Bai gave my head a light tap. 'Should have his own business ... and look like Chunky Panday.'

'Shanta Bai,' I said, turning my head to meet eyes dark as two pieces of coal. 'Has Mom always been this way? Why don't I have any happy memories of her? Did she even want me?'

AS A CHILD, I used to get fevers so high that I felt like a tea kettle on a stove. My mother and Shanta Bai stayed up, swabbing my shivering little body with damp towels, listening to my tortured screams. By the morning, the fever had broken. Sitting up in bed, I pressed a palm to my forehead, which was specked with beads of sweat. Sunshine slid through gaps in the curtains, casting pale slats on my white sheets. Outside the bedroom window, loutish city crows cawed as they weaved through the white bougainvillea. Their racket cast me from my bed and out of my bedroom.

The door of my parents' room had a pneumatic closer, and it shut behind me with a moody hiss. A pashmina of cold air fell on my shoulders. It took a few seconds for my eyes to adjust to the room's hazy darkness. Thick blinds didn't let in a crumb of light. I slipped over to the bed and slid under the blankets between my parents' sleep-musky bodies. I put an arm over my father, pressing my nose against his back. His muslin kurta slipped about under my palm. He stirred, grunted affably. I flung one leg over his side, nudging his quaggy belly with my heel.

The AC turned on with a shudder and I sneezed. My right ear began to throb with a dull, regular pulse. My parents had my ears looked at by a number of specialists who'd scolded them both for smoking. It wasn't healthy for a child to get such frequent ear infections. And yet, overfull ashtrays still decorated rooms like potted plants. On my mother's bedside was a blue Murano one filled with cigarette butts. Smoke clung to the walls, curtains, sheets, and my mother's hair – which looked like black smoke shot across her white pillowcase.

The sneeze woke my mother. She lifted her head a bit off her pillow and frowned. I smiled and reached out a hand to touch her face. I thought she'd be happy to know that I was feeling better. She slapped my hand away and shouted, 'Get out! I was up all night with you. Let me sleep.'

'Better go, sweetheart,' my father urged, yawning. 'Maybe Shanta Bai is up. Go to her room.'

Quietly, I slunk out of their bedroom. Having finished with her bath, Shanta Bai was sitting cross-legged on her chatai, rubbing a small pat of butter into her leathery arms. I sat on the floor next to her and placed my head on her lap.

SHANTA BAI PAUSED TO consider my question, and then resumed her kneading. 'I think it's because of the child who came after you,' she said quietly. 'The boy.'

'Is that so?' I said, then paused. 'Wait, you said child. I thought that it ... it was a miscarriage?'

'He was a baby. When you were little, your mother lost a baby,' Shanta Bai said. 'He lived for a week. His heart was bad, or was it his lungs?' She shook her head slowly. 'I don't remember now. They brought me in to look after you because your mother refused to. Your father took him to be cremated, carried him in his arms. They covered him with a white handkerchief.

It looked like they were cremating a little kitten, he was so small and broken.'

'And my mother?'

'She was never right after that. They'd all told her – the doctors, your grandparents – that it was her fault. Even a village woman like me knew that it wasn't. But Lily Mama told her she'd lost the baby because her mind wasn't strong enough to keep him.' Shanta Bai braided my hair back into a shining plait. 'That's when the drinking got really bad.'

'Why hasn't anyone ever told me?' I asked, squeezing my head. 'Why would they hide this?'

'Ask your father,' Shanta Bai shrugged, stroking my head. 'What's this?' she asked, slipping an oily finger under Arjun's chain, lifting it from my skin. The gold leaf had come off, showing patches of brass. I'd kept the necklace as a reminder of what men were capable of when they thought no one cared. I didn't need that reminder any more.

I took the necklace off, dropped it in Shanta Bai's palm and closed her fingers around it.

CONFRONTING ASHA WAS ALWAYS tricky, and confronting her when she was drunk was a terrible idea, but my feet carried me back to her bedroom. How had Asha, and for that matter, Jeh, managed to keep such a thing secret? What else had they been hiding, I wondered, pushing open the bedroom door. The smell of booze was so thick, it was like running into a wall. Asha lay propped up with pillows, her long skirt bunched between her legs. As I watched, Rhea, who'd been lying next to her, got up and twisted her body towards my mother. She pulled out her clip from her head and her hair curtained her expression from my view. Asha was having a hard time keeping her eyes open. She smiled and thrashed a limp hand at Rhea's chest, snagging open the remaining few buttons of her shirt. Both women were very drunk, and seemed not much in control of their limbs, like newborn babies.

Rhea's necklace slipped out of her open shirt, diamonds glittering. The solitaire pendant, cut like a raindrop, tumbled towards Asha's face. The gold chain yanked it back. It hung in the air, suspended between them, flashing fire when it caught the yellow afternoon light.

The diamond resumed its downward journey when Rhea brought her face closer and closer to Asha's, and then pried open her mouth with her tongue. I wanted to shout something at them but found that I could only croak. My mother screwed her eyes shut and accepted the kiss. It seemed like she neither loved nor hated it when Rhea kissed her. As if this was the price she was willing to pay for intimacy of any kind.

I retreated from the room, turned on my heel and went to find Jeh. Perhaps I had no right to be angry; perhaps, like everyone else, I was a hypocrite. But my rage, as it rushed about to fill all the corners of my head, didn't care. I walked into Jeh's room to find him in an armchair, reading, a bowl of white mogras by his elbow. He loved the smell. Jeh picked up a white flower, shook off the water and put it to his nose, while turning the pages of a leather book embossed with gold print.

'Piglet,' Jeh said, smiling up at me. 'What's going on? Come here, sit with me for a minute.'

I sat on the arm of his chair, resting my cheek on the top of his head. Jeh read out loud:

'But that the dread of something after death –
The undiscover'd country, from whose bourn
No traveller returns – puzzles the will,
And makes us rather bear those ills we have
Than fly to others that we know not of?
Thus conscience does make cowards of us all...

'Isn't it lovely?' Jeh asked, sounding awed. 'Thus conscience makes cowards of us all.'

'It's not very comforting,' I said.

'So what?' Jeh said. 'It's true.'

'Dad,' I said, closing the book. 'Rhea is here. They are really, really drunk.'

Jeh considered this information for a moment. 'Let it be,' he said and put his nose back in his book. 'Peace at all costs,' he added, when I tried to object. 'Your mother will only scream and shout if I interrupt them. Why cause unpleasantness for no reason, hmm?'

'Don't you think they're bad for each other?' I asked. 'They're both so ... angry.'

'You know,' Jeh said, turning a page. 'As a child, Rhea would come along with her older brother to my birthday parties. Her mother always dressed her in these ugly frocks, the kind they made girls wear back then. On my tenth birthday, I got an air gun. Cyrus and I used my mother's crystal vase for target practice. When we hit it, the vase exploded, pieces of crystal flew out in every direction like birds. My father took out his belt and whipped us with it. Right there, in the middle of the party. I remember Rhea laughing. She was four, or maybe five? Such a small girl with such a big laugh. It embarrasses me even today, when I think of the sound of that laughter.'

'I'm going to call her husband,' I said, standing up from the arm of his chair.

'He won't be happy,' Jeh said, resting his cheek on his knuckles, turning the pages of his book.

I went into my bedroom, exhausted and sick, and fell backwards on my bed. The ceiling had leaf-shaped shadows cast by a tree outside my window. They shivered whenever the wind picked up. It reminded me of the puppets Asha used to make with her hands on the nights she was sober enough to tuck me into bed. Suddenly, I had this terrible, aching need. I wanted her to appear in my doorway. I wished Rhea would leave. I picked up my cell phone and left a message for Rhea's husband, then tossed the phone to the floor. To calm myself, I did what I used to as a child: I imagined that my room was floating in space, that outside my door was a vast nothingness.

I WOKE UP WITH my heart racing. How long had I been asleep? Minutes? Hours? There were screams pouring out of Asha's bedroom. I ran over and stopped at the doorway, shocked to see Rhea on her hands and knees. Small animal sounds escaped from her curled lips. Standing over her was her husband. He had Rhea's hair gathered in his fist and was trying to pull her off the ground with it, as if uprooting a carrot. In the opposite corner, next to the toppled drinks trolley, was Asha, also screaming, held back by Jeh. I crept to my parents' corner, giving Rhea's husband a wide berth. His face was twisted and cruel.

'Bitch,' he snarled, 'fucking lying bitch.' He slammed the heel of his hand into the top of Rhea's head and began to drag her out of the room. Asha broke free of Jeh and rushed after them, screaming that she would call the police. Jeh scrambled after, trying to grab her by the elbow, his face crumpling in shame. We all went downstairs to the driveway. Jeh split his efforts between handling Asha and trying to get Rhea's husband to stop hitting her. A pulsating red light of guilt swirled in my head. All I'd said on the phone was that Rhea didn't seem well, could her husband please come pick her up.

'Let her go or I will call the police!' Asha threatened. 'I will go to the station myself.'

Rhea's husband shoved Rhea headfirst into his car. 'Call the fucking cops, whore,' he said and spat on the ground. 'I don't care.'

'Jeh!' Asha shouted at my father. 'How can you let him speak to me like this? Do something!'

'You need to calm down, Asha,' Jeh said. 'All this screaming and shouting. What will my parents think if they hear it?'

When Rhea's husband got into the driver's seat, Jeh took Asha by the arm to steer her gently upstairs, but Asha refused to budge. The car screeched down the driveway and out the front gate. The night was silent again. Just when we thought it was over, I saw my grandfather, Zal Papa, coming towards us in brisk, long strides. Half of his stroke-blighted face was furious while the other side was calm. He moved with such menace for an old, feeble man. I was suddenly afraid.

'What the hell is going on?' Zal Papa demanded. 'What was that shouting?' He stared at Asha, who hung off Jeh's arms like a bouquet of dead flowers. I edged closer to them.

'Fucking bastard hurt my friend,' Asha sobbed, almost falling to her knees on the driveway.

'It's nothing, Dad, really,' Jeh said, pulling Asha up by the arm. 'I'll fill you in tomorrow.'

Zal Papa looked from one distraught face to the other and seemed to weigh whether to let it go or not. He decided on not. 'I want to see you both in my office,' he said, pointing at Jeh and me. Then looking at Asha, he shouted, 'I'm not putting up with this bullshit!' Thick cords in his neck stood up.

'Yes, Dad,' Jeh said, nodding. 'Of course.'

I grabbed Asha's other arm, and Jeh and I pulled her back up the stairs. Asha looked tired, her eyelids drooped as Jeh helped her out of her whisky-smelling clothes. Standing in the doorway, I watched as he put a nightdress over her head and pulled out her arms one sleeve at a time. Burying her face into his chest, Asha cried like her heart was broken. Jeh stroked her hair and muttered some soft words, staring up at the ceiling.

THE DOCTORS SUGGESTED ANTABUSE, because maybe if Asha got violently sick whenever she drank, perhaps she'd stop? Jeh begged me to give Asha the pill each night and stand watch until she swallowed it. Deprived of the sugar from the booze, Asha, who hated sweets, began to crave them: an encouraging sign. There were other encouraging signs as well. A month passed, then two, and we let out a slow exhale.

But events would show that we'd let our guard down too early. It didn't take long for Asha to find a way to hide the Antabuse in her cheek and spit it out once she was alone. I discovered this one night when I showed up in Asha's bedroom without warning. I never went to her room later than 10 p.m. – that's when she took her pills. The doctors prescribed more pills every time Asha complained of feeling sad. These pills were supposed to calm her down, which they did, but they also made her stupid, glassy-eyed and half-deaf. Asking her the simplest questions, like what do you want for dinner, or where is the TV remote, was like drawing water from a stone.

The first sign that something was off was that Asha had the TV volume so high I had to plug my ears. The second, the AC was on full blast and Asha was chattering her teeth under a blanket.

'Ma, you're shivering. Why is the AC so high?' I asked.

'What did you say?' Asha turned her head, but her eyes remained fixed on the TV screen. 'Stop mumbling.' Her bed was littered with cigarette packs, magazines, overflowing ashtrays, used tissues and a TV remote.

'Jeez, Ma, it's a cool night, you don't need the AC.' I shut it off. Then I picked up the remote and turned down the volume. As the room warmed up, it slowly began to fill with the reek of alcohol.

'Okay,' I said, folding my arms and glaring at her. 'Where is it?'

'Where's what?' Asha muttered, lighting a cigarette.

'Where's what?' I mimicked rudely, searching for the bottle in all the usual spots. I couldn't find it anywhere. No choice but to walk into my father's bedroom and get him out of bed.

'Dad, wake up, I need help with Mom.'

'What's wrong now?' Jeh asked.

'There's a bottle hidden in her room somewhere and I can't find it. Wake up.'

Like a soldier roused for his rounds, Jeh sat up, yawned, and swung his feet to the floor. Pulling at his pyjama strings, he ambled to the bathroom. Jeh's pants tended to slide down his hips, making his short legs seem even shorter. A bar of light moved across the bedroom walls as I heard a car drive past the window. It lit up Jeh's face for a moment. People often remarked that there was something kind about his eyes. In boarding school, a boy had once punched his face, and as a result, the tip of Jeh's nose bent slightly to the left.

I tapped my foot as Jeh took ages in the toilet, the sound of his urination echoing around the bathroom walls. His bedroom smelled like dirty socks and sweat. It was anyone's guess when the sheets had last been changed. A space cadet, Jeh was.

Finished with the bathroom, Jeh stepped out. I hadn't heard a tap running.

'Did you wash your hands?' I asked.

'Huh?'

I sighed. 'After you finished, did you wash your hands?'

'Uh, no,' Jeh shrugged, looking sheepish.

'Dad, please go wash your hands.' I pinched the bridge of my nose. How was he going to deal with Asha when he couldn't even remember to wash his fucking hands?

Jeh came out of the bathroom a second time, wiping his wet hands on his pyjamas. Together, we went to Asha's bedroom. The smell of alcohol was stronger now. I resumed searching, while Asha lit another cigarette. Jeh put on his best stern schoolmaster impression. Asha blew out a few puffs of smoke and placed her lighter next to a glass water jug. Drops of condensation slid down its sides. I snatched up the jug and took a sip straight from it. Asha had hidden her booze in plain sight.

'We can't trust you at all, huh, Ma,' I said, taking the jug to the bathroom to dump the alcohol. 'Zal Papa was right,' I turned to Jeh, 'this is not something we can fix by ourselves.'

'I'm sorry,' Asha said unconvincingly. 'This is the last time. I promise.'

'Sure,' I tucked the slippery jug under my arm and rubbed my wet hands on my nightdress. 'Sure it is. But just in case it isn't, I can't be your nurse any longer.'

'Oho! Listen to the big bully. This is my house too. Try and make me leave,' Asha said, her ears pulled back. 'What will you do? Throw me out? This is my fucking house!'

'Noomi's right,' Jeh said to Asha. 'We are in way over our heads.'

'Either she leaves, or I will,' I said to Jeh. I threw the jug on the floor, then turned and walked out.

'Suit yourself,' Asha said. I heard her lighter click, and then the smell of a fresh cigarette.

'Noomi,' Jeh called after me. But I didn't answer.

WHEN I WAS EIGHT years old, I pushed my mother so hard she broke a tooth. It all started with a fight I got into with my cousin Adil. I remember running down the stairs from my parents' apartment and out the back. It was Sunday evening, and I was going to have chai with my grandparents, as I did every Sunday. I walked along the curved driveway to the veranda overlooking my grandmother's garden. As I walked, I hatched a plan to beat up Adil for squealing about how last week after school, I'd thrown his bicycle in a puddle. Zal Papa would not stop yelling, so I picked up grapes from Lily Mama's dining table and plugged my ears, at which point he slapped me. Jeh never intervened with his father on my behalf. *Fight your own battles, Piglet.* Patiently, I waited for Adil the Snitch to trot over for evening tea with my grandparents.

The front lawn was foamy green, turned over by worms that scatter the grass with tiny mud laddus. Our dogs liked to suck up the worms from the ground like noodles. A mongoose slinked along the boundary wall to its nest, which was close to the patch of ground where the gardener buried the dogs when they died. Leaning against the wall was a hut that I had built using trellises stolen from the shed and covered with a blue tarpaulin. A bamboo thicket hid it from sight; it was my secret spot. Inside, there was a chatai to lie down on, a few books, a clock, a water bottle, a tube of Odomos, a packet of chips, and a skull that once belonged to a dachshund.

In the veranda, Lily Mama gave me a cup of tea with ginger biscuits. Zal Papa straightened his newspaper with a crackle and lifted it up. Noiselessly moving my mouth, I tried to read the thin, scratchy captions below the photographs when I was interrupted by the snick, snick, snick of a pair of scissors. Hidden between the wall and the back of the sofa, Adil had snuck in while I was distracted and was busy snipping off bits of my hair. I stared at the end of my pigtail in shock. It looked as if a rat had been nibbling on it. My cup clattered to the floor. I shrieked and dragged Adil out by the scruff of his neck. He unfurled on the floor like a rug. I sat astride him, pinning his arms, and snatched the scissors from his right hand.

'I'm going to cut off your pee-pee,' I said, pulling off his pyjama bottoms.

Adil's penis peeked out coyly from under his T-shirt.

I snipped the scissors and smiled a crazy smile.

Adil screamed in genuine horror.

Lily Mama dragged me off, yelling to her husband that I had gone insane. Adil stumbled, howling, into Zal Papa's lap, pyjamas halfway up his little apricot bum. Already exhausted from holding me back, Lily Mama shouted for help.

Ever so gently, Zal Papa slid Adil off his lap, as if releasing a hatchling into a pond, and stood up. Then, rolling his newspaper into a hard baton, he walked over to me wriggling in Lily Mama's arms and crouched so that we were face to face. His grip on my arms was like a pincer. I looked away.

'Look at me,' Zal Papa said, holding up the rolled newspaper as if I was a dog that needed to be housebroken. 'If you ever touch Adil again, I will thrash you.'

I nodded to show him I'd understood. When he was satisfied that I'd learned my lesson, he let go, and I immediately shrieked, 'Stupid goat!' before running away.

Angered by my humiliation at Zal Papa's hands, I decided to run away and hide in my secret spot. The tarpaulin had kept the hut's interior dry, even though it had rained last night. The rain-steeped earth underneath the chatai filled the hut with petrichor. I lay down and read the book I'd hidden there, *Five Go Down to the Sea*. I enjoyed Enid Blyton's tales of British children, foolhardy but always well dressed, with shiny shoes and not-torn underwear, with neat side partings and pink fingernails. Their mothers were good eggs, their fathers charmingly negligent. I was determined to live in England when I grew up, where I would eat buttered scones and crumpets every day.

My plan was to remain hidden in the hut until everyone frothed at the mouth with worry. I hoped that the loss of his only child would make Jeh stand up, finally, to his father. Zal Papa would have to beg my forgiveness, and in return for it, he would have to demote Adil to the position of least favourite grandchild.

I read until I was too sleepy, and then, placing the book under my head as a pillow, I put my arm over my eyes, listening to the chirps and whirs of the garden.

I woke up not knowing where I was for a moment. I poked my head out of the hut. The sky was pink with orange-gold feathery clouds; sparrows had begun their evening racket. I looked at the time. It had been two hours and no one had come looking for me. I sat at the hut's entrance, tossing the dachshund skull from one hand to the other. I could see everything from here: my grandmother's veranda, the sun-tinted windows of my parents' flat, a maid with fuzzy outlines hanging bed sheets on the terrace. Whining mosquitos kamikazed down on my bare skin.

The sun set behind the garden wall. Orange streetlights flickered on with a low buzz, and shadows ran across my arms and face. I heard the barking of street dogs. I heard a neighbour's baby crying, high and eerie. Or was it a cat? I hoped it was a cat.

My mind strayed to the stories Shanta Bai told me, about how men stole children who were wandering around outside alone. They cut off their legs before sending them to beg, pushing themselves along on carts. 'Ratri jhadam pasoon door raha!' Steer clear of dark places at night, she would say. Laughing at her, I would mime tightening a loose screw in my temple to Adil, who would laugh as well.

But alone in the dark now, I panicked. A thief could be in any one of these trees, ready to put his sticky hands around my neck. A blast from a car horn made me jump, my heart banging loudly. Too stubborn to leave, I decided to count to a thousand, hopeful that someone would come find me before I finished. I tapped on the dachshund skull to keep count: tick-tick one, tick-tick two, tick-tick three. I got to tick-tick one hundred when a shivering-shaking noise in the trees and a whoop-whoop-whoop sent icy ants marching down my spine. I jumped to my feet screaming, threw the skull in the direction of the noise, and didn't stop running until I was up the stairs and through my front door.

There was an invitation printed with a golden Ganesh on the telephone table. Jeh and Asha were in their bedroom, getting ready to go out. I went in to tell them where I'd been all this time. Jeh was on his side of the bed, facing the wall, polishing his shoes with a wood brush. He'd worn a white silk shirt that showed the outlines of his cotton undershirt. There was a small, coin-sized bald patch on the back of his head.

Asha was on the velvet pouffe at her make-up table, drawing her eyes with a black kajal. Her hair, which used to reach the middle of her back, was swept over one shoulder by a jewelled clip. Her sari was the rich jungle green of a monstera plant. Her oval face was plastered over with foundation. With her North Indian features and long, brown legs, she would've been a beauty, if not for all the acne scars that marred her cheeks from when she was a teenager.

'I ran away from home today,' I said, glaring at her in the mirror.

Asha threw a look that was like a middle finger and twisted her lipstick out of its gold tube to paint her half-open mouth. She smelled of cigarettes, perfume and minty toothpaste.

'And,' I said, turning to glower at Jeh's head, 'I was almost kidnapped ... by lunatics!'

'You can stop lying now, Noomi,' Jeh said, not looking at me. 'We know what you did. Why you've been hiding.' He gave an awkward little laugh, which usually meant that he was furious.

'I wasn't really going to do anything,' I said. 'You always tell me I need to fight my own battles.'

'So you threaten to cut off Adil's penis?' Jeh screamed, throwing the shoe brush at the wall. He looked down at his empty hands, surprised at his violence. 'You're ... disturbing. I am so ashamed. He's only five years old. We didn't teach you to behave like a ... like a...'

'A maniac,' Asha said from the pouffe, rubbing her forearms with Pond's cold cream. 'A slut.'

I am a bad person because whenever a little voice said, 'Wouldn't it be nice if Asha died?' I didn't tell it to shut up. Instead, I invited it further into my mind. Offered it a little sofa to sit on, and some tea and biscuits. Abandoning any chance at redemption, I charged at Asha like a small bear, and she tumbled from her pouffe with a terrified squawk. There was a flash of white underwear with black hair scribbled along the sides. The sight of it shocked me into realizing what I'd done. I felt like throwing up.

Jeh stood up and turned to find Asha dissolved in a green silk puddle. He rushed over to help, but her cream-greasy hands slipped out of his, and she landed again on the floor with a thump. She cried out in pain. Her mouth was full of blood. It looked like paan juice.

'Fuck off,' she said, slapping his hand away. 'I can get myself up. You can't do anything right, idiot!'

'I'm trying to help,' Jeh said.

Shaking, Asha pulled herself up to sit on the edge of the bed. 'Help?' she said, wiping her mouth on her sari, leaving a smear of blood. 'You both hate me. You want me to disappear, don't you?'

Sensing a chance to escape, I made a run for the door, but Asha caught my arm.

'Spoiled brat!' she yelled, hitting me across the cheek. The pain was a piece of hot metal lodged in my face. Perhaps unsatisfied because I didn't cry out, Asha grabbed my shoulders and began shaking me, the way people do to sad and hysterical women in the movies.

I decided to go limp like a rag doll, hoping it would appease, or at least frighten, my mother.

'Arey, arey, Asha, stop!' Jeh said. He pulled me away. I hid behind him.

Asha's jewelled clip fell to the floor. Her sari was ruined, and her bedraggled hair covered both sides of her face. She stood to unwrap the sari from her body, turning round and round until it fell to the floor, and stepped out of its green circle. Then she walked past us to the bathroom, where she locked herself in.

'Are you okay?' Jeh asked and brushed the back of his hand against my face. It tickled me in a way I didn't like. I stepped away from him, pushing my shoulder up to my chin.

'I hate Mama,' I said.

'Don't say that. Mama is sad at your behaviour. So am I. We expect more from you.'

It suddenly felt like there was a creature gnawing at the inside of my stomach. I hadn't eaten since biscuits and tea. Pity for myself bloomed like a mushroom in my throat. I gave in to my exhaustion and started crying. Jeh came over and picked me up in his arms.

'Daddy, I'm so hungry,' I said, sniffling. 'Can you get me something to eat?'

Jeh set me down on the bed and blotted my cheeks with his thumb. He stepped out of the room, and returned with a ketchup and butter sandwich, my favourite. In bed, we watched *The Jungle Book* on the VCR. I could hear faint sobbing coming from somewhere inside the bathroom.

THE YEAR HE TURNED seventy, Zal Papa had handed over the reins of his business empire to his two sons, loudly and repeatedly proclaiming that he wanted nothing more to do with it. But he kept his old office. Every day, Zal Papa sat inside his cubicle, devising new ways to drive everyone around him crazy. He was a restless man, prone to fits of dissatisfaction, which he alleviated by treating his sons, Jeh and Cyrus, to lectures on what they should be doing to make the business more profitable, calling friends on his telephone with a circular dial, or poring over architectural blueprints to add more follies to our bungalow on Banyan Street. One time, he'd built a bathroom extension with a plexiglass roof – to be 'closer to nature while answering nature's call' – those were his exact words. For a month, langurs peered down at Lily Mama when she was on the toilet, causing her to have panic attacks whenever she felt the urge to pee. There was also the disastrous vertical garden and the unsightly rotunda with a corrugated roof. Another time, he spent a fortune to encase half the front veranda in tempered glass, to create a sunroom. That was actually quite a nice room; I often spent my summer evenings in there, reading.

Jeh and I sat at Zal Papa's desk like students called into the principal's office. Opposite us, Zal Papa was signing papers, which he handed one by one to the peon, a young man with a large birthmark on the side of his nose, who stood at attention by his side. Zal Papa wrote with an ink pen that had to be refilled by the peon every single day – even on the days that he didn't come to office.

'Things with Asha are not going well,' Zal Papa said, handing papers to the peon, who hurried off. It was mid-morning; customers had started to trickle in. Jeh had a business associate waiting in his cubicle. He crossed his legs and clasped his hands uncomfortably over one knee.

'No, no,' I said, to piss my grandfather off. 'Things are going great.'

Zal Papa's solemn face dissolved into a petulant scowl.

'I'll spell it out,' he said. 'Asha's drinking is not acceptable to this family. Sober her up, or she's got to go.' He pointed to the cubicle door.

'It's no secret that you don't like her, Papa, but Asha is...' Jeh said, leaning forward in his chair, hands together on Zal Papa's desk, 'I can't abandon her. We're doing everything to get her better.'

Zal Papa took a letter opener out from his drawer and began slashing open a pile of envelopes, pulling papers out from between their jagged mouths. His elbows, resting on the desk, put small dimples in the brown leather top.

'Turning our home into a rehab isn't helping,' Zal Papa said. 'She needs professionals. Send her,' he said, more of a command than a suggestion, 'to a place where they know what to do.'

'You don't seem to care that she's sick, only that it hurts your precious name,' I snapped. 'She's been resisting all our attempts to get her real help. Do you propose we send her in a tied-up sack?'

'When you've raised a family and created a livelihood for them, you can flap that big mouth all you want,' Zal Papa said. 'Until then, you will play by my rules.' Pointing his letter opener at me but looking at Jeh, he said, 'I pity this one's future husband.'

Jeh put a hand on my arm, which I took to mean: Stop, you're not helping.

'I've been looking into places I can send her, Pa,' Jeh said. 'But you must give me time. I can't drag her out of the house to someone waiting with a straitjacket.'

Zal Papa looked at Jeh. His voice softened. 'Jeh, you're my son.' He put down the letter opener and steepled his hands. 'But you're a grown man, not a child. You need to take charge of your family. This whole thing with Asha is raising my blood pressure. She must go somewhere to get better.'

I was about to say something cutting when Jeh placed his hand on mine.

'Okay, Pa,' Jeh said. 'I'll have to make a few calls to find a place that will take her in immediately.'

'Fine,' Zal Papa said. 'But she must be gone in a week.'

'I promise,' Jeh said.

'You're a tinpot dictator,' I said, standing up. 'Let go of me, Dad.' I pushed Jeh's hand away. I didn't understand myself. Wasn't this what I'd wanted to happen? Why was I so angry, then? Maybe it was because of the way Zal Papa manipulated and bullied everyone and always got his way.

Zal Papa was an imposing six-foot-one when he stood up. 'This business, this house, it all belongs to *me*. While I'm the boss, I'll kick out whoever I choose.' He jabbed a finger at my face.

I wanted to sink my teeth into that finger. Before I could get into more trouble, Jeh hooked my arm and pulled me to the door, murmuring, 'No use arguing while he's like this. Let's go.'

'Thanks for coming by, son,' Zal called after us. 'This was a very good talk we had.'

EVENING. ASHA WAS ON her bed in a dressing gown, propped up with pillows, watching television and smoking. Her ashtray had about forty cigarette butts sticking out of it. She gave her cigarette a flick; a drift of ash fell on her bed sheet. I stood still for a moment, looking at her. If I crossed my eyes, Asha split into two women: what she'd become, and what she could've been. Shanta Bai had oiled her hair and put it in a braid. It made her forehead shiny enough to reflect the lamplight.

'Hi, Mama,' I said, approaching her bed.

'Hello,' Asha said, in a so-you're-back voice.

'Are you ready for your pill?'

'Fine,' she shrugged.

I popped a pill out of its blister. It looked like a pearl in the centre of my palm. I went to the kitchen, where I put it on a strip of newspaper and crushed it with a pestle. We had to crush the Antabuse into a powder now – it was the only way to make sure Asha wouldn't spit it out. Once the pill was a powder, I folded the paper in half and took it back to the bedroom.

Asha was watching politicians yell on TV. Her eyes glittered like a sunstruck river.

'Okay, open your mouth, please,' I said, folding the strip into a funnel.

Asha tilted her head and opened her mouth. Her molar had a shiny cap. I funnelled the white powder into her mouth, then gently tapped the paper to get the last bits. Sadness sat on my shoulder like a heavy bird. It was up to me to break the news about the rehab to Asha, because Jeh was scared of being swayed. Asha was better than any lawyer when she had to come up with reasons to keep drinking. Give her enough time, and she'd have you going to the liquor store and returning with two quarters of Romanov.

I broke the news to Asha a few days later, during lunch. 'You're going to rehab,' I said.

Asha raised her head from her plate piled with mutton curry and rice. She shovelled forkfuls of the food into her mouth, as if trying to fill a bottomless hole. 'Hope you're happy, knowing where you're sending me,' she said, sucking loudly on her marrow bones.

'It's a nice place,' Jeh said. 'Lots of, er, Bollywood types go there.' He slid a brochure down the table. 'And I've heard their food is pretty good. They even do Ayurvedic massages.' He looked at me and I gave him a little nod. *Keep talking*. 'It'll be like a vacation.'

In the days preceding her departure, judging by the empty bottles we discovered and the smell of vomit that permeated her clothes and hair, Asha began drinking like a camel preparing to go into the desert. The night she left, Jeh had to order a wheelchair to take her to the airport because Asha was too drunk to stand. He'd hired a nurse for the trip – a middle-aged woman with the air of someone practised in reserving judgement. They helped Asha down the stairs and slid her on to a wheelchair. The nurse stopped her from slumping forward. A small mercy that it was late at night and there would be no one around except a few sleepy porters. The nurse pushed Asha's wheelchair to the car and Jeh loaded their suitcases. He needed a backpack for Asha's papers. I gave him one of mine. The backpack had a bright tropical print; it made it seem like Jeh was going on holiday to Goa. Standing at the foot of the stairs, I watched them settle Asha into the car. Jeh turned and waved. The half-smile on his face nearly wrecked me.

THE STORY JEH GAVE out if someone asked about Asha's disappearance was that she was getting a treatment at an Ayurvedic spa. And to keep the lie afloat, we organized a huge welcome-home bash when Asha returned a month later. When he mentioned the idea of a party, a small smile bloomed on Asha's face like the first green bud after a drought. The shadows under her eyes had lightened. Once we got her settled at home, I went to check on her many nights in a row. No telltale smell. No hidden bottles. We planned for Asha's party with brio. Zal Papa and Lily Mama were so relieved at her improvement that they offered to foot the entire bill.

A few hours before the guests would start to arrive, Shanta Bai, irritated at me popping in to check on her progress in the kitchen, threatened to add a whole bird's eye chilli to the vindaloo, making it quite deadly. I ran off to Suzy's Parlour to get my hair done, and regretted this decision when I saw Sheila Sehgal coming out the parlour's tinkly door as I was about to step in. I smiled and twisted my body to let her pass by. She grabbed my arm and pulled me aside.

'Still gallivanting about, I see,' Sheila said, with a scorpion smile. 'Hope you remember my warning. The wedding is in a few weeks. I don't want any trouble from you.'

'Please let go,' I whispered, not wanting to cry. 'I have to get home soon.'

'I heard your mother was back,' Sheila scratched quote marks in the air, 'after her "spa" visit?'

'Yes,' I said, displaying a confidence that I didn't feel at all. 'She's feeling much better now.'

'Please, spare me,' Sheila rolled her eyes. 'Poor Jeh,' she shook her head slowly. 'He must've done something terrible in his past life to deserve the two of you.'

My heart pounded nastily in my ribcage. That was Kamalpur for you – disgrace lurked at every corner like a molester. I looked at the floor. 'Excuse me,' I said, and pushed past Sheila into the parlour.

'Imagine Jeh's face,' Sheila called after me, 'if he knew what you did at my party.'

THE GUESTS BEGAN TO arrive at around 9 p.m. The women in silk, tanchoi, crêpe de Chine, light chiffon, wearing 'casual' jewellery: pearls, solitaires, gold. They weaved, perfumed, into the living room and sat arranged in chatty rosettes on the sofas. The men went to pour themselves drinks and stand around in a circle, smoking. Everyone was in raptures about Shanta Bai's famous home-made mutton samosas and refreshing mint chutney.

I'd showered with a seashell-shaped foreign soap I kept for special occasions, which smelled like the inside of a rich woman's purse. I chose to wear the demurest outfit I owned: a blush-pink salwar kurta. I took a step back to audit my appearance. A glance was all I could stand before I began listing, in my mind, everything that was wrong with it. I picked and squeezed at a small zit on my forehead until it was red and unnecessarily unsightly. Shit, now what? Sticking out my tongue to one side, I tightened my dupatta around my neck.

Parties in Kamalpur reminded me of solar systems: there were usually one or two important persons around whose gravitational pull the rest seemed to orbit. I could tell that one old lady in a dove-grey sari was important, as everyone in the rosette sat pointing their bodies at her. I took a tray of samosas to show around. I heard a strange set of giggles from the side of the hall, and saw Asha and Rhea on a love seat, heads together, ignoring the rest of the party. Two flutes of champagne with strings of bubbles stood on the coffee table in front of them. They were drunk as parrots, under a gold-leaf painting of gods and goddesses dancing. I'd always hated that painting.

Sitting next to the lady in the grey sari, buttering her up like a piece of toast, was Binny. 'Noomi dear,' Binny said, giving me a bright smile, 'bring the mutton samosas to Mrs Rao.'

The corners of my mouth turned down. I walked up, knowing something unpleasant lay ahead.

'No thanks, I'm a pure vegetarian,' the grey woman said, putting up her hand with a small smile.

It amused me how vegetarians used 'pure' to describe their dietary habits. 'I'll find you some paneer ones,' I smiled.

Binny, with a vapid giggle, speared a samosa with a toothpick. 'Much too oily,' she said, rubbing her fingers together. 'This is Noomi.' She gave the woman a long look. 'She's Asha's daughter.'

'Hello, namaste,' I said. Unable to fold my hands because of the tray, I did an awkward little curtsy.

'Ah,' the old lady said. 'Is that your mother sitting on the sofa?' She pointed with her chin to where Asha and Rhea were cackling on the love seat, champagne flutes now in their hands.

'Yes,' I said, feeling my cheeks warm to the same pink as my outfit.

'She looks very happy,' remarked the old woman. 'Preposterously so.'

'She's returned from a relaxing holiday,' I shrugged.

'Is that champagne?' the lady raised her eyebrows. 'Lily Wadia allows her bahu to drink?' She lifted a hand to her chest. 'Very modern of her. My sons' wives are so old-fashioned. Of course, they're such dutiful girls, they would rather stay home with their children than attend parties.'

Unbidden, an image of two Pomeranians dressed in housewifely finery popped into my mind, raising their heads and whining when they heard their mother-in-law's car turn into the driveway. I let escape a weird giggle and the old woman gave me a frown. Then she stared at my mother. Asha was certainly not a dutiful girl.

Binny gave a martyr-like smile, which said: You have no idea what we have to put up with.

JEH WAS KNOCKING BACK a whisky with Ammu's father, whom he'd been close friends with since they were in college. I caught his attention, and he gave me a smile, which flipped downwards into a frown when I made a drinking motion with my hand and pointed my eyes in the direction of Asha and Rhea's sofa. Jeh excused himself. We huddled together in a corner, whispering like co-conspirators, shooting furtive glances.

'What do we do?' I said. 'She's drinking out in the open!'

'Let's not panic,' Jeh said, putting his glass down on a table. 'Let's find out what's going on first.'

'Okay,' I said, linking arms with my father. 'Let's find out.'

Our twin shadows crept up the arm of the sofa Asha and Rhea were on, and stuck to the wall behind them. Asha looked at us with a grin. 'Hello there, Tweedledee and Tweedledum.'

'Asha,' Jeh said, pointing to the champagne flute in her hand, 'is that ... what I think it is?'

In reply, Asha drained her glass and said, 'What're you talking about?'

Rhea treated us to a dismissive little smile. 'One teeny glass of champagne won't hurt her.'

'Do you promise this will be your only drink?' I asked Asha, my eyes rounded in warning.

'Of course,' Asha said, flicking a grin up at Rhea who'd wandered off in search of more champagne, probably. 'Mother promise,' she said, pinching the skin of her throat. 'No more booze for me.'

'Mum and Dad want this evening to go off well, you know,' Jeh said.

'It will, it will,' Asha said, nodding vigorously. 'I promise.'

'Noomi,' Jeh said, placing a hand on my back, 'get your mother some food.'

'Okay,' I said. On the way to the kitchen, I noticed my grandparents staring, first at Asha, then at me. I gave them a reassuring, we've-got-it-under-control smile, before disappearing into the empty foyer, where I leaned against the wall and pushed the heels of my hands into my temples. I wished *I* could get a flute of champagne – or five. I felt a hand on my other shoulder and straightened up.

'Relax, it's me,' Ammu said, taking a step back. 'Didn't mean to startle you. I followed you back here. You looked so upset as you walked past us.'

'Oh, hi,' I said, giving a little shiver. 'I'm a little stressed, that's all.' I gave her a hug. 'Why haven't I seen you until now? Didn't you come here with your dad?'

'No, Baba got here earlier. I brought someone else.' Ammu glanced to her left. She had a friend in tow – a tall, young man with the most beautiful art-film face, like he'd stepped out of a Satyajit Ray movie. 'This is Shiv,' Ammu said, smiling.

'Hi, Noomi.' Shiv seemed a bit embarrassed.

'Hi,' I said, shaking his warm, dry hand. 'Nice to meet you. Shiv is short for Shiva?'

'It's short for Shivraj, actually,' said Shiv, looking further embarrassed. 'I hate Shivraj, though.'

'Shiv's a friend from London,' Ammu said. 'He moved to Bombay to start a website. Hey,' she yipped, as if an idea had just struck her, 'aren't you looking for a feature writer, Shiv?' She smiled at me, 'Noomi always won the essay contests in school.'

'Not all the contests,' I said, brushing off the compliment. 'But most of them.'

'That's great,' Shiv said. He looked at Ammu, who beamed her approval, so he went on, 'I'd love to have someone like you on board. Here's my card.' He produced a small rectangle from his kurta pocket. 'If you're ever in Bombay, come see me. My office is by Churchgate station.'

'Thanks,' I said, holding on to it. I pointed to the kitchen door. 'I have to get my mother some food. But hang around, have a drink.' I smiled. 'I'd love to learn more about your website.'

HEADING BACK INTO THE party, I ran into a wall composed of Lily Mama and Zal Papa, all raised eyebrows and anxious expressions. 'Everything's fine,' I said, lifting the plate of food to show them. 'That was her last drink. She's promised not to make a scene.'

'Why is Rhea here?' Lily Mama said.

'Her husband must be on a business trip,' I shrugged. The three of us turned to look at Rhea and Asha clinging to each other on the sofa as if it were a raft afloat on a lonely sea.

'Well, if she's going to make a scene, we should make sure the party wraps up soon,' Zal Papa said. He looked for something to tell him the time. Lily Mama wore a gold watch with a mother-of-pearl face. He lifted her wrist to the non-stroke-afflicted side of his face. 'Have dinner served by 9 p.m.'

'Okay,' I nodded.

DINNER WAS READY TO be served, but none of the guests seemed interested in eating. All eyes were glued to the spectacle unfolding in the living room. When she was drunk, my mother believed she had superpowers. No one could be as charming as she, no one as compelling or intelligent. I couldn't cross the room fast enough to stop Asha from staggering over to the rich old woman in the grey sari, and Binny, who was still buttering her up. Asha settled into a high-backed armchair and threw one leg over the other, eyes glittering as if she were about to run a fever. The old lady gave her an ambivalent smile; Binny, an unambivalent scowl.

'Hello, Asha,' the old lady said. 'I don't believe we've ever met. I'm Reeti Rao.'

'Nice to meet you,' Asha said. 'I was admiring the colour of your sari. I thought I'd come over and ask where you bought it. Such beautiful material – it's as if you've wrapped a rain cloud around yourself.'

'Oh, thank you,' the old woman's eye crinkled up. 'It's a family heirloom. My mother's.'

'I'd like to buy it from you. How much do you want for it? Name any price.'

'Excuse me?' the old lady frowned. 'I told you, it was my mother's sari.'

'Mrs Rao's husband,' Binny sniffed, 'owns most of the farmland south of Butibori.'

'Oh, I'm sorry,' Asha bowed her head. 'Didn't realize I was in the presence of feudal royalty.'

'Here's your food, Mom,' I said, shoving the plate into Asha's hands. 'Why don't you come sit with me at a table? There's an empty one by the balcony. Let's get some fresh air.'

'Do you know, Mrs Rao,' Asha said, setting the plate on the floor, 'I've returned from a *spa*?'

'Yes?' the old lady said, looking like she wouldn't mind if someone yanked her away from this conversation.

'It wasn't actually a spa, stupid,' Asha cackled. Heads turned in our direction. Asha laughed like a hyena. 'It was,' she put one hand to the side of her mouth, 'a rehab! For alcoholics!' She made her mouth into an O and stared at the old lady. 'I was drying out there for a month.'

'Asha,' Binny shot up from her seat and grabbed my mother's hands to pull her up. 'I think I saw Jeh looking for you a moment ago. Let's go and find him, shall we?' She motioned for me to come too.

A FEW MOMENTS LATER, Jeh and I were huddled over Asha in her bedroom. With an extravagant sigh, Asha stretched herself out on her bed, crossed her ankles and put an arm behind her head. 'The bunk beds in that so-called spa were terrible,' she said. 'Hard, and so narrow. The room was always so hot. It was like sleeping in a baking tin.'

'Asha,' Jeh said, 'why are you doing this? We planned this party so that people could see that we're a normal family.' He placed his hands on his waist.

Asha, who'd been twisting about on the bed, sat up with a smirk and rubbed one foot against the other. 'You two honestly thought there would be no consequences to sending me away?'

'Ma, it wasn't his decision alone,' I said. 'Zal Papa basically gave us no choice.'

Asha's face seemed to fall apart for a moment and then it knit back together in a mask of spite. 'There's always a fucking choice!' she screamed. 'You could have chosen to grow a backbone.' She threw a pillow at us. 'Do you know how they treat women in those places? They put us, turn by turn, inside a circle, and hurled insults at us. Told us we were depraved, base.'

I peeked out the bedroom door to see if anyone had been listening in. It looked like Binny had everything under control. Everyone was heading to the dining room. I turned back to see Jeh sitting on the edge of Asha's bed, his face buried in his hands as Asha fumbled around for her pack of cigarettes, lit one and blew a smoke ring that wreathed Jeh's head.

The door opened and Binny popped in her head. 'Jeh,' she said, sounding supremely competent, 'your parents were tired, so they left. I told Shanta Bai to lay out dinner.'

'Thanks, Binny,' Jeh said. 'I'll be out very soon.'

'Don't worry,' Binny said, closing the door with a nod. 'Take all the time you need.'

Jeh turned back to Asha. 'We have to start all over again. The Antabuse, the doctors...'

'I realized,' Asha said. Then she laughed. A loud, bitter cackle. 'But your face when you saw me with a glass in my hand – priceless! Like someone had dumped a jug of cold water on your head. Your stupid, fucking face!'

Asha was still shrieking when I left her and Jeh in the bedroom. I had to find a way to leave this place, this city, my family. I loved Jeh more than anything, but I couldn't bear to go through that entire cycle again: vigilance, lies, shame.

I felt a need to gather all my miserable feelings in a bundle and lay it at the feet of someone kind. Ammu was talking to Shiv under the painting of gods and goddesses, the one I hated because it was too joyful. Joy made me uncomfortable, like a pair of ill-fitting, pinching shoes. As soon as she saw me coming towards them, Ammu broke off her conversation with Shiv and gathered me in a hug.

'What's up?' Ammu said. 'Where are your parents?'

'Dad's inside with Mom,' I snuffled.

'Oh, Noomi, I'm so sorry,' Ammu said. She turned to Shiv. 'What can we do to help?'

Shiv cleared his throat and tucked his hands into his armpits. 'Yes, tell us.'

'Let's make sure the party ends smoothly,' Ammu said. 'Shiv, can you manage the bar?'

'Of course,' Shiv nodded, and went off in the direction of the balcony. He turned back once and smiled at Ammu. I felt jealousy at the absent-minded way Ammu picked up love, the way a rabbit's pelt picks up burrs. I recalled a long-ago summer, when Ammu's brother plucked a flower and placed it behind her ear, while she, distracted, buried her nose in a book.

NEXT DAY, JUST AFTER dawn, I packed a bag and left the house while everyone was still sleeping. I'd kept Shiv's business card inside my purse. I'd apply to other journalist jobs as well: they didn't pay much but I wanted something with flexible hours. On the road in front of our gate, I managed to flag an autorickshaw to take me to the airport as a pink sun flipped over the horizon.

PART TWO

New Delhi's arid air shrouded me as soon as I walked out the sliding glass doors of its new snazzy airport. I clutched my handbag to my chest: a barrier between me and the eyes of the men standing behind the barricades, holding placards with travellers' names. It was half past midnight. I scanned the airport parking area, unsurprised to note that there were no women about at this hour. I hated this about Delhi. In Bombay, where I'd been working for a blissful three years as a journalist at Shiv's website, no matter the hour, women were everywhere – airports, restaurants, stations, tea stalls, even a booze or paan shop. They made themselves known in the flash of sandals getting out of a taxi, in the steady chopping of vegetables, in a wild, joyous shriek outside Grant Road station, in the clink and crash of glass bangles at an all-night bazaar.

Veer was standing with a bunch of flowers next to a fat white car with a red light on the roof. Before I could raise my hand to wave him over, a man in a white uniform had already come forward to take my bags, which he proceeded to efficiently Tetris-load into the car's trunk.

'Welcome,' Veer said, walking over with roses cradled in his arms like a child. We knew that we couldn't kiss, or even hug, as the men were watching us with much interest. Veer held the car door open for me and I slid in, dragging the roses after. In the back seat, once we were on our way, with the officer's and driver's eyes on the road and not on us, Veer took my hand, and rubbing his thumb over my knuckles (a habit of his that I loved), asked me in his taciturn way, 'Good flight?'

'Yes. I read a book,' I said, resting my head on his shoulder. He shifted uncomfortably and cleared his throat. With a small nod, he indicated the front seat. I sat up straight and moved away. 'What's with all this?' I whispered, gesturing to the men.

'Oh, Dad said I could have his official car to pick you up,' Veer beamed. 'I think he wants you to be ... suitably impressed.' He ran his thumb against the bristles on his chin.

Veer's father was a high-ranking bureaucrat in the Indian government. A mover of files, a purveyor of kickbacks. I found this fact amusing – and also quite terrifying. Veer had grown up in a stereotypically upper-middle-class New Delhi family: one filled with narrow minds and outsized ambitions. Veer once told me that when he was in school, his father would come at him with a belt if he ever scored less than 90 per cent in his exams. And his mother used her own make-up to cover the marks. Veer had hated them back then. But now he seemed eager to impress them. And so, I was too. What could go wrong? Everything. In the first year of our relationship, Veer's parents had refused to acknowledge me, protecting the family's brittle reputation from an unsuitable (meaning, non-Punjabi) match. Finally, Veer told them that they might as well get used to the idea, because I wasn't going anywhere. Now here I was, in New Delhi, on my way to meet my future in-laws for the first time.

'My aunt is so excited to meet you,' Veer said, corralling my thoughts back inside the car. 'She's waiting up for us, wants to make sure you'll be comfortable in the guest room.' Trucks rumbled past us on the Outer Ring Road – clumsy boxes that looked put together by a child with nails and a hammer. Swirls of dust slithered under their wheels like ghosts. They owned the road as shamelessly as bullies on a playground.

I stared at Veer in confusion. 'Hold on, why am I staying at your aunt's place?'

'I've told you about her,' Veer nodded. 'My dad's older sister?' He pushed his glasses up his nose. 'Listen, you know my parents are kind of traditional, right?' he said. 'They feel it would be ... I don't know,' he shrugged, 'inappropriate or something, if you stayed with us before the wedding.' He looked at the car's black window and fussed about with his hair. Veer loved mirrors, and mirrors loved him back. His good looks were an inside joke.

'But that's ridiculous,' I said. The attendant in the passenger's seat turned halfway around and gave me a look. I ignored him and rested my forehead on the window's cool glass.

'Of course, you're right,' Veer said, grabbing my hand. 'But folks of our parents' generation are too set in their ways. Why be antagonistic right from the start, na? They're so excited to meet you,' he said. 'It's only for a few days. Let's just make them happy.'

As the city flashed by outside my window, I thought back to when Veer and I had first met, two and a half years ago. I was still new to the city. Everything about it was fascinating. It was December and Bombay's streets were glittering with lights. Cool, dry, inland air had temporarily pushed away the standard tropical mugginess. One fine evening in Colaba, I decided to take a stroll down the Causeway after work, inspecting the street-sellers' wares – bags, scarves, cheap but pretty jewellery, and glass hookahs – to Café Mondegar – Mondy's – with its Mario Miranda walls, its uncurious, bow-tied waiters, and its extended happy hours. I walked under an old gulmohar blazing with orange flowers. Little boys, barefoot and dirty faced, pulled on my kurta. 'Didi! We haven't eaten all day. We're starving. Buy us some food.' My purse had one fifty-rupee note. I gave it to the smallest boy, who snatched it and shot off, the others running after him, shouting.

I was out of cash for beer and had to stop at an ATM. The machine was broken, but I didn't realize that until it swallowed my card. I turned to discover a small huddle of people. Maintenance was on the way, a woman said to me. Irritated, I went outside to smoke. A man crossed the street and walked to the ATM. As he got closer, I noticed that he was good looking in a Neanderthal sort of way: sloped forehead and full lips. He was dressed in a grey suit with a striped tie. He loosened his tie as he went around me with an apologetic smile. I considered warning him, but he would have walked away and I'd have lost him to the city night. I watched with interest as the ATM swallowed his card and he let out a barrage of curse words.

'Someone's on the way to fix it,' I said, walking back inside as the man stabbed at the buttons, muttering under his breath. I gave what I hoped was a dazzling smile, and perhaps it dawned on him that a not-bad-looking person was flirting with him. Crow's feet appeared around his brown eyes. 'I'm Veer,' he said, offering me his hand. I took it.

After we got our cards back, we walked over to Café Mondegar's and drank beer until the waiters started to put the chairs upside down on the tables. Sometime around 1 a.m., Veer snuck me into his paying-guest room at Sassoon Docks, which had green walls and rickety furniture. The toilet tank had a chain flush. The whole place smelled like balchao, Bombay's signature odour. Veer's thin, shabby bed made his body look even more gorgeous, like a fancy car parked in a dingy alley. The sex we had that night was exceptionally good.

The next morning, Veer kissed me and stepped out to buy cigarettes. He returned with a parcel. I tore open the soft newspaper to find two red glass bangles. They clinked prettily.

'A woman was selling these on the side of the road. Thought that colour might look good against your skin,' Veer said. This was the longest sentence he'd spoken thus far. 'I thought just two – instead of the usual dozen.'

I slipped the bangles on my wrist and smiled. 'Parsi women wear a red bangle once they're married.'

Veer ignored that information. 'I'm starving. Let's get coffee and some dosas.'

'Okay,' I said, rubbing my eyes, trying to remember the last time I'd felt this happy.

We spent the winter going to bars, having lots of sex and staying in bed on weekends. We explored the city together. With ships and ocean liners cruising in and out of its deepwater harbour, the busy wet docks and dry docks, the floating casinos and noisy little ferries that start at the Gateway of India, Bombay is a nautical city whose spirit is reflected in the details of its buildings – with portholes, ship deck railings and observatory towers a common feature.

Bandra was sparkly at Christmas time, with its Portuguese homes and palm-fronded lanes lit up with stars. At Mount Mary Basilica, you could buy a candle in the shape of a body part to light, with the hope that whatever ails it will be cured. I lit a candle in the shape of a heart. I spoke about my mother to Veer in dribs and drabs, always bracing for the moment that he might turn away. He didn't. Finally, I let out a long, slow exhale. Veer was a mirror that made me seem beautiful. One night, we kissed in a taxi hurtling down Marine Drive. The driver kept turning around to stare and almost drove us into the sea.

It was getting harder and harder to put up with the silence inside the white government car, as it beetled over flyovers and past dusty construction sites, glistening glass buildings and rundown tin shanties. Wobbly scooterists, cyclists and pedestrians were forced to leap out of our path. Around 2 a.m., the car arrived at Veer's aunt's address. The driver honked twice for the gate to be opened. I studied my exhausted features in a compact: wiping smudged kohl from under my eyes, fixing my hair, swiping on lip gloss. My anxiousness worked better than caffeine to drive away my exhaustion. A watchman, his face wrapped in a scarf, pulled open the iron gate.

A young man told us that madam was waiting for us in the living room. Veer handed my bags to him and let me walk before him down a short corridor. Dim lamps glowed in orange corners, throwing just enough light for us to see where we were going. In the living room, there was a white rug on the floor looking like spilled milk, and maroon curtains with tasselled edges, mahogany coffee tables with clawed feet that seemed to groan under the weight of crystal vases full of fake flowers, silver photo frames. It was an overcrowded room – as if the occupants of this house were terrified of empty spaces, of negative capability.

Veer's aunt, Kitty, was scrolling through her cell phone on a sofa in a velvet tracksuit and flip-flops. The Chanel glasses perched on top of her head were attached to a rope of small pearls. Her hair, with streaks of ash blonde, was twisted up in a French knot. Almond-sized solitaires dripped from her earlobes; her wrists seemed weighed down with gold and diamond bangles; her index finger had a ruby surrounded by diamond baguettes. Her lips were the same shade of maroon as her curtains.

'Hello, Aunty. Thank you so much for letting me stay with you,' I said, going up to her.

'Welcome, my dear. You can call me Kitty Aunty, or Auntyji if you'd like to be more formal,' Kitty smiled warmly but kept her arms folded over her chest. She looked as if she was waiting for me to do or say something. I scanned my sleepy brain to see if I'd missed some important bit of North Indian etiquette. I was about to thank Kitty again, more profusely this time, when Veer dived as if fielding an invisible cricket ball. I realized he was touching Kitty's feet. My eyebrows rose. I had no idea Veer did stuff like that. I didn't even know where to start. Veer had thrown me into the deep end of the pool.

Wanting for her to like me, I stared at Kitty's manicured feet, unsure of what to do next. Do I touch the toes or the foot? With my fingers or my whole hand? I grabbed hold of her toe for an awkward moment, and then shot back up, cheeks flushed.

'Oh, that's so unnecessary,' Kitty said with a chuckle. She pulled me up off the floor for a hug. Our cheeks grazed. Her skin felt like soft, expensive kid leather. She smelled like a bowl of mangoes.

'Auntyji, wouldn't Monty Uncle like to meet Noomi?' Veer asked. 'Or is he already in bed?'

'Oh, I sent him off at midnight. He has a 6 a.m. tee-off tomorrow at the Delhi Golf Club.' Kitty rolled her eyes. 'You know how he loves his golf.'

'I'll see him tomorrow, then,' Veer said, looking at his watch. 'I should get going, Auntyji.'

'Noomi, are you hungry? Do you want them to heat up some dinner?' Kitty said, turning to me.

'I think I'll go right to bed,' I said, picking up my handbag, which suddenly looked quite shabby and old-fashioned amongst all this Dubai-level opulence.

'Of course,' Kitty said. She led us down the hallway to a bedroom with peach and pink furniture. 'This is my daughter's old room. Make yourself comfortable,' she said in a tone that conveyed the opposite.

Standing behind her, Veer shaped his hand into a phone. 'I'll call you,' he mouthed, and left.

ALONE IN THE ROOM, I tossed my bag in a corner, sat down on a pink armchair and shucked off my shoes. Rubbing my aching feet, I looked around me. The bedroom, like the living room, was stuffed with furniture, pictures and gewgaws. The ornately carved bed in its centre had a fat duvet, a mountain of frilly pillows and a gauzy canopy. Kitty's daughter's photo stood on a bedside table. Her hair had ash-blonde streaks too. Her eyes, in blue lenses, shot sexy death rays. I willed myself to stand up and tossed all the frilly pillows to the floor. I read a few pages of my book, then put it on the bedside table and burrowed under the duvet. I was about to turn off the lamp when my cell phone began vibrating.

'Hey, what's up?' I whispered, and wondered why I was whispering.

'I'll pick your parents up from the airport tomorrow,' Veer said. 'You sleep in.'

'Sleeping in sounds great,' I said, pulling the comforter to my chin. 'But I'm sure *Auntyji* would not be pleased. Veer, listen, I'm not comfortable here. Your aunt – she has a weird vibe. Would it be okay if I moved into a hotel tomorrow?'

'You're tired,' Veer sighed. 'Auntyji's a lot to take in, I'll admit. But underneath it all, she's a very loving person. Can't you just play along for a few days?' Veer said. 'You were the one who wanted all of this marriage stuff. I was very happy with us living together.'

'You were happy not committing to anything at all,' I frowned.

Another sigh. When did Veer become such a sigher? 'And you wanted a commitment,' Veer said. 'Why? Our relationship was doing fine, no? Why did you want the families to get involved?'

'I'm going to read you a line from my book,' I said, switching on the bedside lamp.

'Which book?' Veer groaned. He wasn't much of a reader. 'How long will this take? I'm tired.'

'Which book?' I mimicked. 'The one I was reading on the plane.'

'Uh-huh, okay. Read it to me,' Veer said. 'But make it quick.'

'It's poetry,' I said, taking the book from my bedside and turning to a favourite page. 'There's this line that keeps echoing around in my head. It says...' I began reading, leaning towards the lamp on one elbow. 'Listen, it says, *I just want a humble, murderously simple thing: that a person be glad when I walk into the room.*' I lay back. 'That's it. That's what I want.'

'You lost me,' Veer said after a pause. 'Am I not always glad when you walk into the room?'

'Look, I don't know the exact reason why I want us to be married. Except, I really do. My parents' marriage is destroying them slowly, like termites eating a house. But ours will be different. Because I'm a nicer person with you around. Kinder, with softer edges, less angry.'

'Less angry?' Veer teased.

'Shut up,' I smiled. 'I need...' I paused, thinking of the right way to say what I meant, and failing. 'I have to prove to the world somehow that I'm not my mother.'

'Get some sleep?' Veer sighed again. 'I want you to look happy when you meet my parents.'

'You mean *be* happy.'

'What did I say?'

'You said *look*. There's a difference between looking and being.'

'Noomi' – I imagined Veer rubbing the bridge of his sharp nose – 'you'll probably meet my parents once or twice a year, max. Didn't we agree to play by their rules in Delhi? If you do the sanskaari bahu bit when they're around, it'll make them more comfortable.'

'All this sanskaari bahu and playing by the rules stuff,' I frowned, 'are tactics used to pressure women into having no boundaries. I hope you are aware of that, Veer.'

'Noomi' – I heard an edge creep into Veer's voice – 'please stop.'

'Okay, all right, whatever,' I said, too tired to keep this going.

'You really think having a traditional Punjabi wedding will make you less angry?' Veer said. 'Have you ever been to one?'

'Oh just shut up,' I said.

'Good night,' Veer said. 'I love you.'

'Bye.'

Too fidgety to fall asleep, I slid out of bed and went over to my suitcase, bare feet dabbing the marble floor. From under my clothes, I took out a small bottle of vodka. Pleasing Kitty had made me feel like a court jester trying to entertain a bored king. As I drank, I felt my confidence surge. Tomorrow would be better. I'd charm Veer's parents. I'd charm the hell out of them. Yawning, I hid away the bottle, crept back under the comforter and drifted off.

THE ALARM RANG AND I didn't know where I was. Oh right, New Delhi, in Veer's aunt's house. The realization dropped like a pebble on my chest. I lay in bed, gathering the courage to get up, watching the fluffy duvet rise and fall with my breath. I looked around for the remote to turn off the AC. Today I'd finally meet Veer's parents. I tried to imagine what they'd be like. Veer had said his mother was very religious. How did she feel about the fact that I wasn't? Or had Veer not told her? What had he told his parents about me? Nothing? Everything? I headed to the shower, questions multiplying like rabbits inside my mind.

I laid a few outfits on the bed. Indian or Western? The sanskaari thing, of course, was to wear Indian clothes when meeting one's future in-laws for the first time. I chose a pair of silk trousers with a loose cotton top, hooked silver earrings through my ears, and slid a pearl bracelet on to my wrist.

Once I was dressed, I wandered out into the living room, where Kitty was seated in the same spot as the night before, almost as if she'd never been to bed. The colour of her kurta and the carafe of gold bangles at her wrist made her blend perfectly with the room. A smell of jasmine incense haunted the cool morning air.

'Good morning,' Kitty said brightly. 'Slept well? Everything was comfy?'

'Yes, thank you, Auntyji.' I said, picking an apple out of a crystal bowl.

'There's cereal,' Kitty said, texting on her phone.

'Actually,' I said, looking towards the kitchen, 'could the cook make me an egg?'

Kitty, who'd been tapping out a message on her phone, looked up. 'Today is Tuesday.'

'T ... Tuesday?' I was confused. What happens on Tuesday?

Kitty looked at me sideways. 'Punjabis don't eat non-veg on Tuesday. You should know all this.'

'Oh,' I said, feeling stupid. 'In that case, cereal is fine.' I shrugged.

'Hello pretty girl!'

Here was Kitty's husband, presumably, from the way he ambled into the room, like everything inside it, including the two women, belonged to him. He took my hand. He was shorter than Kitty, but taller than me. He carried a golf club in his other hand. Tufts of grey-white hair poked out from his ears.

'Noomi, this is Monty, my husband,' Kitty said.

'Hello, Uncle,' I said, eager to get my hand back.

'Welcome to Delhi!' Monty said, trapping my hand in both of his. His goatee made his lips look oddly fleshy. His eyes were an overcast grey, framed with thick black eyelashes. He had a bulbous nose. His smile made me think of a lecherous koala.

'Did you rest well ji?' he asked. 'Has Chubby given you any breakfast?' He called his wife 'Chubby', even though she was as slim as a stork.

'Yes, thank you,' I said, smiling, still struggling to remove my hand from his grasp.

'Monty, please get ready fast, we're getting late, and *she* just woke up.' Kitty nodded in my direction.

I turned, surprised at the anger in Kitty's voice. 'Oh, are we late? Veer said I could sleep in.' I cringed inwardly at the words 'Veer said'. Not yet engaged, and Veer had become the one whose permission I required for things like staying in bed.

Kitty threw Monty a glance. 'You've come to meet Veer's parents. Don't you want to make a good impression?'

'I ... I guess it was a miscommunication,' I said, embarrassed.

'Okay, ladies, I'll be out of the shower in a jiffy,' Monty said. He gave us a twinkly wink and left.

'Oh, and Noomi,' Kitty looked me up and down, 'is that what you're wearing? Don't you have a nice salwar kurta or something? My parents, Veer's grandparents, will be there. I don't think they'll be very impressed by those tight trousers and that translucent shirt.'

I returned to my room, my hands shaking. This promised to be a very long day, and I was already failing. Could Veer's idea of me change based on his family's first impression? I didn't know. As I changed from my nice trousers into a salwar kurta that I wore for work sometimes, the thought of cancelling the wedding made me clench my jaw. I wasn't going to ruin this chance at a different kind of life. I took out my secret vodka and brought it into the bathroom, took two generous swigs, and brushed my teeth and my tongue. I could be charming if I wanted to – I just needed a little help.

THE SUN WAS IN the centre of a cloudless sky when Kitty Ahuja's car turned down a modest lane and stopped outside a two-storey home that looked lost amongst the mansions in that posh South Delhi neighbourhood. Veer's grandfather had built his house in the sixties, when that part of New Delhi was forest land. But the city had grown like moss, and the famous market, full of expensive restaurants and kirana stores selling foreign goods, was only a five-minute walk from the house. Veer's granddad's name, C.M. Malhotra, was spelled out on a mailbox. Two cars were parked bumper to bumper in the driveway, next to a shabby little garden, the kind Lily Mama would turn up her nose at. Its balding grass was bordered with red bricks embedded into the ground.

A woman in a pink chiffon salwar kurta stood framed in the front doorway. Her fluffy hair fell to below her chin. When she smiled, little crow's feet appeared around her eyes, like they did around Veer's. A big red bindi marked her forehead and a mangalsutra hung around her neck. How many signs marked a married woman, while a man didn't even need to wear a wedding ring. As we approached, the woman, who I guessed was Veer's mother, dropped her gaze and folded her hands in a namaste. Her gold bangles were not as heavy or numerous as Kitty's, and her fingers were adorned with only two rings: one was a single ruby set in gold, the other a pearl flanked with small brownish diamonds.

I went up to her with a smile. She held me lightly by the shoulders, cocked her head and regarded my outfit, beaming with honeyed impersonality. 'Noomi, welcome, welcome! I'm Veer's mummy,' she said. I smiled again mutely. It felt like I'd stepped into a play but had forgotten all my lines. 'We expected you a bit sooner. Didi, Jeejaji! How are you?' Parul Malhotra – that was her name, I remembered now – greeted the Ahujas with a namaste.

'Hallo, Parul Rani,' Monty said. 'How are you my beauty? Always lovely to see you.'

'Sorry, Parul,' Kitty said. 'Noomi took her sweet time.' She gave a mean little chuckle.

'I'm so sorry,' I said, suppressing the irritation rising in me. 'Veer said I could sleep in.'

'Oh-ho. Anyway, never mind,' Parul said with a slight bow of her head. 'Come in, the family's eager to meet you,' she smiled. With her hand at the small of my back, she waltzed me into the house.

AN ASSORTMENT OF RELATIVES, like chocolates in a box, were seated in the Malhotras' living room, which looked like a budget-conscious version of Kitty's living room: maroon curtains, white rug, knick-knacks and artificial flowers. In one corner, a Godrej refrigerator hummed next to a dining table covered in a plastic, eyelet-pattern tablecloth. Parul led me towards Veer's grandparents, seated side by side on a sofa like aging deities. C.M. Malhotra wore a blue cravat arranged around his sagging throat; his bottom lip stuck out, as if he was displeased about having to sit next to his wife of fifty years. Veer's grandmother reminded me of a brown hen, with a beaked nose protruding out of a round, soft face. Her pink satin kurta was taut and shiny over the mound of her belly.

Next to the old couple, with his hands resting on the back of their sofa, was a compact-looking man who appeared to be in his fifties, with a military posture. His short salt-and-pepper hair had been aggressively combed over, and he bounced on the balls of his feet while speaking.

'Hello, Noomi,' the gentleman said. 'Welcome. We are so pleased to have you in our home.'

'This is Veer's daddy, Mr Ajay Malhotra.' Parul said his name like an awards show host. 'And here,' she said, turning to the old people, 'are most respected Mummyji and Daddyji.'

'Has my sister been spoiling you a lot, mmm?' Mr Malhotra asked. 'She loves to spoil us, I tell you.'

'Oh yes, I'm being spoiled rotten,' I grimaced. 'Kitty Auntyji has such a beautiful home.'

'You should see how she dotes on my parents. Let me introduce you to them,' he said. 'Veer calls his grandpa Bade Papa.' General Malhotra beamed. 'And my mother is Badi Mummy.'

'Namaste, Bade Papa, Badi Mummy,' I said. There it was again, the expectant pause, like a single musical note suspended in the air. I added an enchanted smile to my face and bent to touch the grandparents' feet.

'God bless. May you have a long and happy life,' Bade Papa said gruffly.

'Your daughter-in-law is so quaint,' Kitty chirruped. 'Always touching everyone's feet.'

'Congrats on finding such a traditional girl ji,' Monty roared. 'A rare commodity these days.'

I imagined my father holding his sides, laughing that someone thought I was a traditional girl.

'God bless,' Badi Mummy wheezed and patted the snug space next to her. 'Come, sit next to me.'

'Please,' Mr Malhotra said. 'What can I offer you? Something to drink? Tea coffee juice?'

'No, thank you,' I said, squeezing in between Badi Mummy and Bade Papa. My answer displeased them. I was in a play, and I'd veered off script again. 'I mean,' I cleared my throat, 'if you have juice of any kind, that would be lovely, thank you.' I turned up the wattage of my smile.

'Bring madam some fresh lychee juice,' Mr Malhotra, emphasizing the 'fresh' very hard for some reason, ordered a young man hovering at the edge of our little tableau. He dashed off and returned with a tiny glass in the centre of a large silver tray.

'Thank you,' I said. 'Do you know when Veer will arrive?' I asked with another polite smile. In response, Badi Mummy picked my hand up and plopped it into her lap. Her fingers felt like chicken bones covered with soft, loose skin, on which her cold rings moved about.

'You are sweet,' Bade Papa said, looking me over. 'Small and cute. How tall are you?'

'Five two,' I said.

'And how old are you?' he continued.

'Umm. Twenty-six.'

'Slightly old for marriage. And less than average in height,' he said. 'But you'll make an attractive couple. Our Veer is six two. You two will look like Amitabh and Jaya Bachchan.'

'Thank you, Bade Papa,' I said. Jaya Bachchan indeed. I sat up straighter and made it a point to speak more clearly. Like a beauty pageant contestant.

'Veer is handsome, smart, earning well, you'll be able to enjoy.' Badi Mummy squeezed my hand tighter. 'Lucky girl,' she continued. 'You've found a real diamond!'

I TOOK MY HAND away, pretending I needed to scratch a mosquito bite on my leg. I closed my eyes. Bade Papa and Badi Mummy seemed to think I'd been waiting around for Veer to crash a champagne bottle on the ship of my life. In reality, I'd taken a taxi to the airport straight from the criminal courts. Because people were more likely to talk freely with a woman, Shiv had given me a tough beat. That day, I'd covered a trial where three men were found guilty of rape. The men – the boys, rather – yelled out threats at the lady magistrate as she read out their sentence. When the trial ended, the boys' families blocked my way in the corridor. They took out hospital bills, exam papers – anything to prove their sons had been elsewhere. I realized that a parent's love could stretch so far, even beyond the borders of morality.

Jeh and I would speak on the phone almost every night; sometimes I'd read out my latest article. It's surprising, what you find out about yourself when there's no one around to tell you who you are. In the anonymity that came with living in a big city, I bloomed. I made friends. We lived three women to a flat in the less expensive area of Bandra East. Much to our landlady's horror, the flat was littered with cigarettes, bottles of alcohol, and we behaved like banshees. The building across the road had its windows facing ours. On the second floor lived a woman who had a lover visit every Tuesday night. We'd make our drinks and gather to watch the show. The lover would enter and throw his briefcase, and if it was raining, his umbrella, to the floor, and they would begin kissing in the hall of her long, railroad-style flat. As they made their way from hall to bedroom, so would the three of us, carrying our bottles and ashtrays, running from one window to the next in our flat until the couple finally made it to the bedroom and began making love on the covers, flopping about like dying fish.

There were evenings when Veer and I would get off work early and go smoke hookahs at the rooftop bar of a seedy hotel, or share a joint in his room and go watch a really terrible, cheesy Bollywood movie at the Regal Cinema. We were always broke; drinking at posh bars was unsustainable. No matter. Unlike in Kamalpur, you didn't need to be rich to have fun in Bombay, just young. We weren't a lovey-dovey, date-night, exchange-looks-from-across-the-room kind of couple – we were more like two kids who'd found each other on a playground. The city suited us.

I found out that I was good at my job as a reporter. Shivraj turned out to be an excellent boss. He gave me the freedom to cover trials from any angle I chose, without the fear of being hauled up by a judge for contempt. I became known on my beat; sources trusted me and fed me leads. My cell phone contained the contacts of powerful people: commissioners, politicians, bankers, a Bollywood actor or two. My job was the thing, Veer said, that he found most interesting about me. In hindsight, this was perhaps a red flag.

As I PLOTTED MY escape from Badi Mummy's chicken-bone grasp, Veer the Diamond finally walked into the living room. He'd picked my parents up from the airport. Jeh walked in after, in office khakis, jacket draped over his arm. My brain flooded with relief. I was even glad to see Asha who, in her silk shirt and pressed trousers, made a smart, refreshing contrast to Parul's overabundance of flowy chiffon. I'd been in regular touch with Jeh, but I'd kept a self-preserving distance from my mother.

We spoke on the phone once in a while, but never about anything important. She'd try to ask me questions about my life in Bombay, but I always slipped out from them like hands from a loose knot. The details of my life were my wealth, to share with those whom I trusted. I didn't ask if she was sober or not; for the most part, I didn't care.

I gave them both a hug. No discernible smell of alcohol or cigarettes on Asha. Veer and I had decided his family could be given information on a need-to-know basis. I'd given up caring if Asha was sober, but I knew that the Malhotras' ears would prick up if they heard a single word of Kamalpur gossip. Before I could whisper a warning, Mr Malhotra had bounded up to my parents, hands outstretched.

'Welcome, sir!' he said, shaking Jeh's hand. 'And Madamji, welcome! I'm Ajay Malhotra, and this is my lovely wife, Parul.' Head bowed, Parul folded her hands. 'Welcome ji,' she said. 'I'm so glad to finally meet you in person. Please come meet the rest of our lovely family: this is Kitty Didi and Monty Jeejaji.' A round of compliments and counter-compliments began afresh and ended when Bade Papa ordered lunch be served.

AT THE TABLE, PARUL flipped a steaming, puffed roti on to my plate. I sat, smiling like a buffoon, with the women on one side of the dining table, the men on the opposite side, and Bade Papa at the head. Only Parul remained standing to pile rotis on to everyone's plates. I had to cover mine with both my hands. But Parul, it seemed, was not one to give up so easily.

'Noomi? Wouldn't you like some curry?'

'No thank you, er, Aunty,' I said.

'Some dal then?'

'I already have some, thank you.'

'Paneer?'

'Maybe a little later?'

'Yoghurt?'

'There's still some on my plate,' I begged.

'Then have some fruit?'

'I'll help myself, thank you!' I hadn't wanted to sound so irritated. Chatter pulled to a record-scratch stop. Veer shot me a look from across the table, and I shot a guilty one back at him. 'I mean,' I amended, 'I wouldn't want to waste.'

'Parul, what is this? You're only serving,' Kitty said. 'Come, come, come, chalo, please sit down, relax, eat. I'll make sure everyone gets enough rotis.' She grabbed Parul's plate.

'Please, Didi! Don't get up!' Parul sounded panicked. 'I'll eat once everyone's been served.'

'Arey, come on.' Kitty snatched up a large bowl and began to ladle yellow dal on Bade Papa's plate until he grunted for her to stop. Parul quickly offered him a roti, which he took and didn't say thank you. Then she offered a roti to her husband, who also took it and didn't say thank you.

'It's the bloody sanskaari Olympics out here,' Jeh whispered, making me stifle a snorty guffaw. I took the napkin from my lap and threw it at him. Bade Papa looked at us with a frown.

'Very badly brought up, this one,' Jeh smiled, pointing a thumb at me. 'Attacks her own dad.'

'Don't worry,' Bade Papa said looking serious. 'Soon she'll be a Malhotra. And we will fix her.'

AFTER LUNCH, EVERYONE RETURNED to the living room. Veer threw me a look over his shoulder, as if to say I should be helping Parul out in the kitchen, not lolling about on the sofas with my father. So I went inside and brought back a tray laden with bowls of fruit custard.

'So how big is … what's the name of your town again … Kamalabad or something?' Kitty asked.

'Kamalpur. It's not big at all, everyone knows everyone,' Asha said, blowing on the face of her coffee.

'Are there any decent hotels?' Kitty grimaced, looking from Asha to Jeh. 'Where will you put up our guests?'

Our guests? From behind his aunt, Veer gestured with his hands for me to calm down.

'Could Dad arrange a place,' Veer offered, 'at a government guest house perhaps?'

'Nonsense,' Monty said. 'Girl's family pays for everything.' He gave Veer's head a playful smack. 'It's the tradition. Don't try to be all modern-shodern, son. Let us do the planning.'

'We're happy to arrange hotel rooms for all your guests, Malhotra sahib,' Jeh said, 'once you tell us how many.' He put on his bifocals and took out a notepad. I glared at Veer.

Veer's father clasped his hands between his knees. 'Dekho, Jeh, we Malhotras are not old-fashioned. I mean, we don't ask for a dowry.' He nodded encouragingly, as if to say: That's pretty modern of us, right? To not sell our son to you? A breeze from the window upset his comb-over. He quickly patted it down. 'But,' he smiled, 'our relatives … they must get gifts. Only to keep face, you understand. And for Veer, we'd like a few new suits, maybe a watch?'

'Okay, okay,' Jeh said, jotting everything down. 'Relatives: gifts. Veer: suits, watch.'

'Dad,' I said, putting a hand on Jeh's shoulder. 'Can we discuss this?'

'What's there to discuss?' Kitty Malhotra said. 'This is absolutely nothing – compared to what we'd have received if Veer was marrying a Punjabi girl.' She put her custard bowl on the table. 'But then, we wouldn't have such an embarrassingly frank discussion. It would've all been understood. Bhaiya darling, I noticed that you didn't include our parents' gifts in your list. You don't have to include me, but they should be given a lot of respect, as they are the elders of our family.' She nodded at Jeh, who scribbled another note.

Mr Malhotra turned to his sister, 'Oh come on, Didi. As if we would do such a thing.' Then he turned to Jeh, 'It goes without saying that my sister is very important in the family.'

'Of course, of course,' Jeh said.

'Dad.'

'Your son is so good to our daughter,' Asha said. 'We worried that Noomi would never get married.'

'Mom!'

'Oh-ho, that's so sweet, Asha,' Parul smiled beatifically. 'It's been wonderful to have you and Jeh over. We really wish you weren't leaving tomorrow.' She turned to me. 'Noomi, do you know what tomorrow is?'

'Wednesday?' I offered.

'Silly girl, it's one of the most important days of the year! Tomorrow, we wives must fast all day for our husbands' health and long life!' Giggles escaped her lips like bubbles from a machine. 'And I have an unconventional request: we want you to keep your first fast for Veer with me.' Parul beamed like this was a special treat. 'Asha, if you can change your ticket, Kitty Didi offered to host a kirtan in the evening, before the moon rises.'

'Oh, thank you so much, Parul,' Asha smirked. 'But I think I'll let you and Noomi bond.'

Alarmed, I glanced over at Veer, who made an encouraging kissy face at me.

'I'd love to,' I said with a big fake smile.

BADE PAPA AND BADI Mummy retired to their room for a siesta. Veer's father, followed by his gaggle of attendants, said his goodbyes, got into the white car with the red light, and drove off to his office somewhere in the labyrinth of Lutyens' Delhi. Asha made Jeh take her shopping. Not in any hurry to head back to Kitty's, I asked Veer if he'd like to show me around Defence Colony Market. The sun was now lower in a dusty sky. We held hands, walking down a road that curved through the neighbourhood. Tramping on brittle leaves, we passed under the curious gaze of drivers and chowkidars, who appeared to have escaped their houses in the afternoon lull to chew tobacco and play cards.

The market looked best all lit up at night. Gleaming cars stood in the parking lot, and well-dressed South Delhiites went in and out of the restaurants and shops. Journalists and college students in colourful kurtas and silver jewellery stood around outside dive bars, smoking and arguing politics. The evening shadows were forgiving, not so the afternoon sun. The daylight exposed cracked, unpainted sidewalks, electrical wires that looped and sagged criss-cross over trees, cigarette butts and shopping bags that collected in corners and clogged the gutters. We stepped into a tiny bakery and found a table. Veer ordered us coffee. I looked out the window, feeling more than a little depressed.

'So, what's up?' Veer said, raising his eyebrows with a little smile.

'What do you mean what's up?' I said. 'What kind of guy-I-met-in-an-elevator question is that?'

'Why are you so pissed off?' Veer frowned. 'I thought everything went off really well.'

'I'm not,' I said, looking into my coffee. 'I'm just ... it's just ... all of this has been too much.'

'What has?'

'All of it,' I said, waving my hands in front of my face. 'Coming to Delhi, your aunt, your parents. I don't know. I don't think I could ever fit in with the Malhotras.' I drummed the scarred wood table with my fingernails. 'They are so ... different. Now this fast thing. You're, like, suddenly okay with me fasting all day for your long life?'

'You know I don't believe in all that stuff,' Veer said. 'But if it makes my mom happy...' He shrugged, showing me his hands. 'I mean, it's harmless, isn't it? It's a way for women to bond with each other.'

'Why can't we bond like normal people – over shared traumas and suchlike?'

'Nooms,' Veer fixed me in place with a stare. 'If you do this fast, it'll make my mother very happy.'

'Okay, why don't you go on a fast too?' I said, crossing my arms. 'For *my* long life.'

'No chance.' Veer let out a bark of laughter. 'You women are used to starving with your dieting and what not. I would pass out.'

'Okay, I'll do it,' I nodded, squeezing the sides of my head. 'Only because I want them to like me.'

'They like you a lot! You were amazing today.' Veer smiled, pulling my hands away. He opened my palms and kissed them.

'Yeah, that's because I wasn't me,' I said. 'They don't like *me,* they like some ideal of a daughter-in-law. They like a lie.' I took my hands back from Veer and covered my face. 'I had to worry and think about everything I said or did. I felt like some kind of cat burglar, twisting this way and that to avoid those laser beams that set off alarms.'

'Well, then, fucking relax!' Veer said. 'You don't need to be perfect. In fact, it made you come across as a bit snotty at times. Like, at the dining table, you didn't have to be so impatient with my mom.'

'What are you talking about?' I balked. 'Snotty? Really?'

'Mom was trying to make you feel welcome and you gave her a look like: *Oh god, stop it!* You've got to control your face, Noomi. You didn't have to put my mother down. She's a simple woman. Food is how she shows affection.' He stood up and left money on the table.

'Veer, I didn't give any look,' I said, feeling hurt. 'She wouldn't stop tossing food into my plate.'

'Be yourself,' Veer said. 'They will love you as much as I do.'

'I don't think you've put enough thought into this,' I shrugged.

A brown puppy and its mother had settled under the shop's steps. The pup was fat; his brown fur seemed free of ticks. He rolled around in the dirt by his mother who lay on her side, then flipped over to tug at her ear. The mother's flank rose and fell as she snoozed in the late afternoon sun. She let her pup nibble and pull at her ears for a while, then lifted one delicate paw to roll him away, a little ball of fur and dust. I sat down on the steps, not wanting to leave yet, and watched them play. Veer turned around and called out. I had to follow him back to the house.

*O*NCE UPON A TIME, *there was a queen whose seven older brothers doted on her more than on their own wives. When her husband, the king, was at war, the queen went to her maternal home to fast for his long life. On the day of the fast, the seven brothers returned home to find their sister collapsed on the floor, weak with hunger and thirst. 'Why do you starve yourself?' they asked her. 'Come, eat and drink with us.'*

'I am fasting for my husband's victory in battle,' the queen said. 'Only once the moon has risen and I make offerings to it, will I eat.' Unable to see her suffer, the youngest brother went out into the garden and placed a diya in front of a mirror on the branch of a peepul tree.

Running back inside, he told his sister, 'I see the moon, it's risen!'

The queen went to the terrace, and after praying to the false moon, came downstairs and broke her fast. With her first morsel, she sneezed; in her second, she found a hair; on her third morsel, a maidservant came running in – soldiers had arrived to say that the king, her husband, had died in a skirmish with his enemy.

'This has happened because you've angered the gods,' sneered her brothers' wives, who had not yet broken their own fasts and were waiting for the true moon to rise. 'Your brothers lied to you. The moon has not yet risen.'

The queen left her mother's home and rode with her guards until she reached the battlefield. She searched all over, and finally found her husband's body stuck with hundreds of arrows. Crying over him, she made a vow to not let a priest perform his last rites. She would bring him back to life with her devotion. For one whole year, the queen guarded the king's body, and each day, she pulled out an arrow from it. When the day of the fast came around again, only a single arrow remained.

This time, not wanting to leave anything to chance, the queen kept a fast so strict that she did not even swallow her own spit. When the moon rose, she looked at it through a veil, and then, satisfied that she hadn't cut any corners, she left her husband's body to the care of her maidservant and went to find water to break her fast. The gods would surely take pity and give back the king's life. While the queen was away, the maidservant, wishing to end her good mistress's misery, pulled the last arrow out of the king's body. He opened his eyes, and upon seeing the beautiful maidservant, took her for his wife. When the queen returned to the king, she was sent into the kitchen, and the maidservant became the queen.

AN OLD WOMAN SAT upon a bunch of pillows on the floor in Kitty Ahuja's living room, reciting this katha into a microphone, surrounded by a perfumed crowd – young and old – all dressed in red and pink like brides. The marble bar was emptied of alcohol bottles and had turned into a shrine covered with brocades, upon which sat gods and goddesses in silk and jewels. The smell of flowers, sandalwood incense and – maddeningly – food, floated above the floral scents of the ladies. The katha woman had henna-red hair and paan-stained lips. She closed her eyes and slowly shook her head from side to side at the queen's sad folly.

According to the Indian meteorological department, whose website I refreshed every few minutes, the moon was supposed to rise in another half hour or so. I'd had no water or food since Kitty woke me up at 5 a.m. that morning. Rubbing my half-open eyes, I'd followed her into the living room, where I found Parul, fully dressed in bridal wear and made up, waiting with a plate of sargi which she wished to feed me by hand. There is something very disconcerting about seeing your future mother-in-law dressed to the nines before dawn. I touched her feet, and then Kitty's feet. By the day's end, it felt like I'd touched everyone's feet but Veer's.

'What gift are you giving your new mummy today?' Badi Mummy asked. She was dressed in a red salwar kurta with gold flowers down the front. Her wrists were weighed down with bracelets that made a lot of noise whenever she moved.

'A sari?' I mumbled dizzily. After more than twelve hours of no food or water, my head was throbbing. My stomach felt like it was being gnawed at. Laughter wafted in from the terrace. Veer, his father and the other husbands were 'keeping watch' for the moon, fortified by whisky and chicken tikkas, the smell of which made me want to claw off my nostrils. A thread of saliva dribbled from the side of my mouth.

'Bas?' Badi Mummy clucked her disapproval. 'Arey, you're supposed to give your mother-in-law many things. Money, clothes, jewellery. After all, she has given you your life's happiness.'

'She has?'

'Yes, you're marrying her son. Veer is a diamond!'

If Veer were really a diamond, I thought, I would've gladly traded him for some chicken tikka. I managed to keep this thought private. Instead, I mustered up a smile for Veer's grandmother.

'Excuse me, Badi Mummyji,' I said. 'I need to reapply my lipstick.'

THE PEACHY CANOPY OVER the bed glowed with light coming from a window facing the street. I leaned against the bedroom door. Bursts of chatter and laughter buffeted it from the other side. I went over to my suitcase and scrambled through the mess of clothes for the hidden vodka bottle. I took a swig, realizing that by doing so, I'd technically broken my fast. Veer might be shot full of arrows. I didn't care. I took another swig and vodka dribbled down on my kurta. I needed to be polite and pretty for Veer's family, and for that I needed some liquid charm. There was a knock at the door. Hurriedly, I tucked the vodka bottle back into the suitcase, tossing a pile of clothes on top of it.

'Who is it?'

'It's me, sweetie,' Parul said, jiggling the doorknob. 'We were wondering where you'd run off to?'

'I spilled water on my kurta. I'll be right out,' I said.

'The moon is out,' Parul said, sounding inspired. 'Come quick. We'll break our fast together!'

'Oh wonderful, give me two minutes,' I said, glumly. I peeled off my kurta, which was not stained, but smelled like vodka. As did my breath. In the bathroom, I brushed my teeth until my gums bled. 'Come on,' I told myself, pinching my cheeks.

Now I had to find something else to wear. I hadn't packed another Indian outfit. All I had left were jeans and T-shirts.

Desperate, I looked in Kitty's daughter's closet. The doors slid open to reveal saris, salwars, dupattas, stoles in all colours: lavender, fuchsia, chartreuse, orange, pink – all embellished with fake gemstones, or silver embroidery, sequins, beads and tassels. The outfits were sealed in individual plastic bags, like items in a shop. I couldn't bring myself to tear off the plastic, plus Kitty would surely mind if I borrowed her daughter's clothes. I had no option but to wear the lunchtime outfit that Kitty had asked me to change out of yesterday. I wore the blouse and pants, ran a brush through my hair, and taking a breath to clear my head, walked out of the bedroom.

'Ah, there she is,' said General Malhotra, beaming. 'Our sweet little bride.'

They'd gathered on the terrace where the unpunctual moon wafted up from behind the branch of a tree. Parul walked over to me, holding a sieve as if it were a steering wheel. I remembered that I was supposed to look at the moon through it and then at Veer's face, breaking my fast with a sip of water. Parul approached with that alarmingly beatific smile of hers. All of sudden, the smile melted off her face. In its place was a glassy, surprised stare. She blinked, once, twice.

'Noomi,' she said, looking me over, furrowing her forehead. '*What are you wearing?*'

Everyone craned their necks to see. I looked down at myself, wondering if there was a button missing on my top, or a tear in the seat of my pants that I hadn't noticed. But there wasn't.

'My kurta got stained,' I shrugged. 'Didn't pack a spare. This was all I had left in my suitcase.'

Parul made a little squeak of disappointment. 'But you're supposed to be a ... a bride!'

'I'm sorry,' I said. 'I didn't know there would be so many occasions for fancy Indian clothes.'

'Didn't your mother advise you on what to pack?' Kitty arched her eyebrows.

'My mother doesn't advise me on anything.' I was going to say something ruder, but I felt a hand on my shoulder.

'Let's move on,' Veer said. 'Noomi doesn't know all these little things yet. Let's finish this ritual, so that you ladies can eat.' He held my hand, smiling. 'You must be starving.'

'Oh, how sweet,' Parul said. 'We're very used to it. I don't even notice that I'm fasting.'

'Well, I do,' I said, grabbing the sieve from Parul's hands. 'Come on Veer, let's see if this makes you look any more handsome.' I held the sieve up to Veer's face, then moved him aside and looked at the moon. I lifted a glass of water and drank it greedily, spilling it all over my shirt.

'Well done, Noomi,' said Mr Malhotra, clapping. 'Your first fast is a great success!'

'Not yet,' Parul interrupted with a small, girlish giggle. 'There is one last thing.'

'What?'

'Noomi, you must touch Veer's feet.'

'What!'

'It's tradition,' Parul pointed at Veer's feet in case I didn't know where to find them.

A pause. 'I'm sorry,' I said.

'Sorry?' Parul smiled and frowned at the same time.

'Yes, I'm sorry. I can't do that.' I shook my head.

'And I don't want her to,' Veer added hastily.

Another pause. I fixed my gaze on a floor tile with thin, lacy cracks; I could feel everyone's stares on the back of my neck. A green lizard, taking advantage of the distraction, slithered across into a bougainvillea. If Parul asked me again, I'd take the first flight out of Delhi.

'Okay,' Parul said. Although she was clearly annoyed, her tone remained as pleasant as ever. 'How about you touch Veer's daddy's feet, then?'

How about I lock myself in the bedroom and drink to oblivion? Veer's family literally wanted me to grovel at their feet! If I'd been less insecure – if I wasn't desperate to believe that Veer and I had something worth grovelling for – I would've walked out. I should've walked out.

'Okay,' I said. Sounds of relief from the crowd. I went to my future father-in-law and touched his feet.

'God bless,' Veer's father said. I straightened back up with a smile. He grabbed my face in his two hands and planted a wholly undesired kiss on my forehead, then pulled me in for a hug.

'Okay, okay, great,' Kitty said, sarcastically clapping. 'Dinner is served. Come on everyone.'

We came in from the terrace through a pair of gracious French windows. The dining room was lit with ochre lamps. The moon's watery light cast faint shadows across the marble floor.

Dinner was laid out on the glass dining table in massive silver dishes. Kofta curry, fried okra and eggplant, a salad with almonds, walnuts and raisins, vegetable pasta with a white sauce, and vegetable biryani. The maids circulated with pooris and parathas. There were also gulab jamuns, dark as bruises, glistening jalebis, and kheer with slivered almonds.

'So proud of you, Noomi!' Mr Malhotra exclaimed. 'Our good little bride-to-be.'

'And with a good little appetite,' Kitty said, glancing down at my plate. A server offered me a fresh, hot poori; I waved it away. Kitty went on, 'Dear, if you keep eating, how will you fit into your wedding outfits, hmm? Which reminds me.' She grabbed Parul's hand. 'I want you and Parul to stay back after dinner. We're getting clothes made for you. It would be good if you picked the designs yourself.'

'Thank you,' I said, surprised at the nice gesture. 'You really don't have to do that.'

'I'm not doing it for you. Veer is my eldest nephew, I want to do this for *him*,' Kitty sneered. She liked to sow her words with seeds of rage, I noticed, like a diligent farmer hoping for a bumper crop.

Once the other guests left, Veer, his father and Monty stayed for a drink on the terrace, while Kitty, Parul and I sat down at the dining table, which was now cleared of dishes and wiped down. Kitty spread out magazines and piles of fabric, beads, sequins and plastic gemstones.

'So, I thought, we could take this,' Kitty said, holding up a sequined swathe of fuchsia silk. 'And add these to the neckline and to the collar,' she smiled, tossing egg-sized fake blue and silver gemstones on to the cloth.

'Wow, Didi! That's a great idea. You're so creative,' Parul said.

'Yes. Very nice,' I said, although the idea of wearing fake jewel-festooned outfits made me want to die.

'And then, I thought,' Kitty went on, sounding pleased with her fashion-designing skills, 'we could make this' – she held up a bit of satin with giant sunflowers – 'into that type of Anarkali.'

She pointed to a picture in a magazine. 'Although Noomi is short,' she bit on a thumbnail, 'so I don't know if it will suit her.'

'No, no. It'll look very nice, Didi,' Parul shook her head. 'Noomi can wear high heels.'

I was going to have to wear these outfits, giant sunflowers and all, at the wedding, in public. I smiled and nodded, smiled and nodded. Somewhere inside me, a little animal screamed.

AFTER IT WAS ALL over, I crept into the bedroom and locked the door. From my suitcase, I took out my vodka bottle and set it gently, like a lover, on the canopy bed. The house was silent. Everyone had gone home or to bed. What might happen if I called off the wedding, and spent my life locked up in a room with only alcohol, cigarettes and books? I twisted off the bottle cap, poured three fingers of vodka into a glass and drank it down. The horrid evening fell from my skin like leeches dowsed with salt. I can handle it, I thought, pouring myself another. I'd have to become two people – Noomi Wadia and Noomi Malhotra.

My cell phone buzzed and Veer's name flashed on the screen. 'Hi,' I said unenthusiastically.

'Hey, what's wrong? Why do you sound so sad? You were amazing tonight,' Veer shouted over loud, pulsating music. 'You were brilliant. My parents were super impressed. Good job!'

'You're welcome,' I said, frowning. 'Wait, where are you? What's with the loud music?'

'Well, Mom sent me to the market to order flowers for Auntyji, you know, to say thank you for tonight, and I ran into some friends,' Veer shouted. 'They were drinking at 4S. Anyway, they dragged me to this nightclub. Don't worry, I'll be heading home soon.'

'Wait, why didn't you come pick me up?' I said, feeling angry. 'I could do with some alcohol.'

'Nooms, I can't pick you up so late at night,' Veer said. 'The family would think it inappropriate.'

'What's wrong with taking me out?' I yelled into the phone. 'We're engaged.'

'Don't be idiotic, Noomi,' Veer said.

'Fuck you, Veer,' I said. 'And fuck your family. This is like being married into a convent. I'm a nun now.'

'I'll let that go,' Veer said in his calm, corporate-guy voice. 'You've had a rough day. But never talk about my family like that again, okay? Now, tomorrow I'll pick you up at...'

I cut the call. The vodka bottle sloshed about as I carried it by the neck into the bathroom and took my cigarette pack out from where I'd hidden it in a laundry basket. I took a swig and sat down on the floor. My cell phone lit up through the thin cotton of my pocket. I took it out and looked at the screen.

A text from Veer: PLZ DONT BE ANGRY. ILU. C U 2MORO.

'Fuck you,' I told the message. I looked through my call list, desperate to speak to someone who'd get how upset I was. Usually, the person I'd call at times like these was Veer. I called my father, even though it was 1 a.m. and he was probably asleep.

'Hello?' Jeh sounded as if he'd been raised from the dead. 'Noomi, is everything okay?'

'Everything is terrible.'

'What happened?' Jeh asked. And I could tell that what he meant was: What did you do?

'I'm at Kitty's house,' I said, even angrier. 'Nothing happened, okay? Relax.'

'You sound like you've been crying.'

'I'm not crying,' I said, weeping. 'The evening was a disaster.'

'What's wrong, Piglet?' Jeh asked. 'Talk to me.'

'Dad, Veer's family, they're insane. His aunt wouldn't stop criticizing every fucking thing I do. And I was starving all day, and then they wanted me to touch Veer's feet!'

'Noomi, Noomi, you sound hysterical,' Jeh said. I imagined him pulling at bits of his hair, the way he did when he worried. 'Just keep them happy. You won't see them after the wedding.'

'So, your advice, as always, is to lie down and take it?' I raised myself up off the floor.

'Peace at all costs,' he said. 'Peace at all costs. That's always been my motto.'

'Fuck peace! Who gets to have peace? Why is it never me?' I screamed. My damp soles skidded around on the floor. I slid forward. 'I'm asking you to have my back, and instead you're telling me to bend and grovel.'

'In life, you have to be like a coconut tree. It bends, so it won't break. Veer's a good man. Don't be so self-destructive, Noomi. Try to please his family. Play the game for a bit.'

'Go back to sleep. Sorry I bothered you.'

'Promise me you'll behave,' Jeh pleaded. 'I don't want you to miss this chance at being happy with someone who loves you.'

'I'm leaving in the morning. There's no time to misbehave,' I said. 'Good night.'

'But...'

'Good night.'

I put the cell phone on the sink counter and pushed it away; it caromed across the granite top and crashed against the mirror. I looked at myself, my swollen eyelids and my crushed mouth. I was ugly. The vodka bottle was almost empty. I lay on my side on the floor, a towel under my head, taking small sips to make it last longer. The hard marble hurt against my hip bone. At some point, I must've passed out. When I woke up, the light outside the bathroom's small rectangular window had become a powdery, pre-dawn blue.

Still drunk, I stood under the shower for as long as I could stand the hot water. I brushed my teeth and sprayed perfume all over my naked body, hoping it would mask the smell of vodka that seemed to escape from my pores. I placed the empty bottle inside my suitcase and laid my clothes on top of it. I looked around to check if there was anything else that I needed to hide. So much time and energy spent hiding, lying about who I was. I'd left my cell phone in the bathroom. It began to ring, rattled to the sink's edge and fell off. The screen cracked. *Veer calling*, it flashed.

In the car on the way to the airport, I pretended to nap. Veer didn't seem to be eager to talk about last night; he was busy on his laptop, already in work mode. If he smelled vodka on me, he didn't comment. I didn't ask him what time he got home from the nightclub. I didn't care. My mind formed a picture of what being married to Veer would be like. I looked out the window. Delhi slid past in a nauseating blur. I groaned and closed my eyes.

A MONTH BEFORE VEER AND I were married under a pavilion set up in my grandparents' garden, Lily Mama and I sat together on the veranda on a winter afternoon, the sunshine sweet and soft, and pored over a goldsmith's sketches for my wedding necklace, a gift from my grandparents. I held a stone, the size of my pinkie nail, up to the light. It was full of green fire. I brought it closer to my eye.

'Remember,' Lily Mama scolded, 'emeralds are brittle stones. They'll crack easily.'

'Where did you get these?' I asked, setting the emerald down gently on the blue velvet cloth.

'They were my mother's,' Lily Mama smiled. 'I set them aside for your wedding on the day you were born.'

Love squeezed my heart. Lily Mama was good at hiding how much she cared for me. From our sofa on the veranda, Lily Mama and I looked out at the garden in comfortable silence. A green bird, the size of a ping-pong ball, with opalescent wings and a ruler-straight tail, landed on the terracotta birdbath by the rose bushes, admired its reflection for a moment, and then flew off.

'Uff-oh, this new gardener has vowed to ruin my roses,' Lily Mama said. She trundled off into the lawn, barking orders at the gardener in her broken, mangled Hindi, looking pure in the yellow morning sunshine. Like a fat, gracious angel. A greater coucal – a crow pheasant – hopped on to the lawn, copper wings burnished in the sunlight. Its eyes were tiny red flames in its oil-black head. It took off as I approached, letting out a whoop-whoop-whoop. In remote parts of the country, like the village Shanta Bai grew up in, the coucal's call was a bad omen. But I'd always thought of it as a sign of good luck.

I'd once pointed it out to Lily Mama and said, 'Look, my lucky bird.'

'He won't belong to you forever,' Lily Mama had said. 'Luck is a wild, untameable thing.'

That same day, I remember being in the kitchen when Lily Mama showed Asha how to make Jeh's favourite dessert, malida – made of wheat, ghee, cardamom, almonds and sugar. I watched as Asha slivered the almonds with a long knife and tossed them into a sizzling pan of ghee, while Lily Mama watched, arms crossed. 'No, no, you're supposed to wait until they're golden brown. You're doing it all wrong.' I saw Asha's eyes begin to tear up, her smile collapse under the weight of criticism. At one point, the knife slipped out of her hands and clattered to the floor near Lily Mama's feet. 'Well, come on, pick it up,' Lily Mama said. 'Pick it up!' she roared, and Asha dived to the floor. As she picked up the knife, it flashed in my eyes. My mother too was a brittle gemstone; she too cracked easily.

The coucal flew into the bamboo thicket, where I found him perched on a grey stone. Puffing up his throat, the bird let out a few whoops. I bowed. He flew off without returning the greeting.

'Did you put aside gemstones for the other baby? He's dead, so,' I said to Lily Mama, coming out of the thicket, 'can I have those as well?' I blinked until my eyes adjusted to the sunlight, putting one hand over my forehead like a visor to cut the glare.

Lily Mama was bent over a rosebush, big bottom in the air, pulling dead leaves out with her hands. She turned and said, 'What?' then went back to stripping the rosebush.

I strolled up to her with my hands clasped behind my back. 'Some years ago, Shanta Bai told me my mother had a second baby, born when I was six years old. He didn't survive.' I studied Lily Mama's marble face. Something bright and green flashed in the corner of my vision. I turned to watch a flock of parrots alight on a bare tree and become its leaves. They took off again when the dogs ran helter-skelter on the lawn, barking.

Lily Mama straightened up and squinted at me. 'He looked so much like you,' she said. 'Such a tiny thing.' She cupped her hands and brought them together. 'Asha was out of control. Screaming, shouting.' She looked down at the grass. 'His little lungs couldn't work. He lived only for a few days.'

I remember when my mother would lie still on the bed and let me paint her arms and legs with my Camlin colours set. I made flowers on her arms, vines twisting around her long, beautiful legs. I had very few happy memories with Asha after the age of six. I took Lily Mama's hands, plump as madeleine cakes, in mine. 'I'm sorry, Lily Mama,' I said.

Lily Mama smiled. 'Pudding,' she said, 'you're going to be okay. I can sense it.' The tailorbird flew down to the birdbath again. I took the emerald out of its velvet bag and held it out.

'Look,' I said to the bird, 'this colour is you.'

'Noomi! What did I say about being careful with those gemstones?'

Startled, the tailorbird took off, a jewel flying away in the pale winter sky.

THE GROOM'S PARTY WAS late to the mehendi, as they would be to everything. Veer's aunts and uncles walked through our front door carrying a basket of gifts. My family rounded up the herd of relatives and handed them presents. Jeh borrowed money to pay for the jewellery and saris for Parul, Kitty, Badi Mummy, and watches for Mr Malhotra and Bade Papa. I wasn't happy, but Jeh said weddings and funerals were occasions where one placed family unity ahead of individual feelings.

Smiling, Parul ushered me to a sofa. 'Sit,' she ordered. I sat. As the relatives watched on, she placed a velvet case on my lap. 'For our new daughter,' she said, opening it with a flourish to display a gold necklace and earrings, and a set of gold bangles with dodgy-looking diamonds. 'Now,' Parul said, 'let's see how our Malhotra jewellery looks on you.'

Parul unclasped the necklace with Lily Mama's emeralds and laid it on a table. She hung the thick gold rope around my neck. Veer's Auntyji, smiling, pushed a red fabric bundle of clothes, bangles, sindoor, bindis, etc., into my arms. I should've smiled more, pretended to be grateful for all the fuss. That afternoon, I understood that violence could be transmitted by the most innocuous-seeming acts. When Parul took off my grandmother's gift, I felt like I couldn't protest, or I'd come off as rude in front of all the fawning relatives. She took away my necklace, and along with it, my voice.

THE NEXT DAY WAS a break between the party to welcome the groom's side and the wedding itself. I dragged Jeh away from the lawn where he'd spent all morning on a chair, smoking cigarettes, the butts of which he'd pill up and put in his pocket, as he yelled instructions to a boy stringing up lights on the tall trees or chatted with the caterers. We escaped from the house without telling anyone and drove out to Seminary Hills. Jeh and I had this secret pathway through the forest that we used to walk, starting at the foot of those hills. I parked in our usual spot outside Our Lady of Lourdes Grotto. Back when I was little, the parking lot had a wire enclosure to one side where the priests kept fat pink pigs like the ones in Enid Blyton stories. Not like the nightmare hogs lolling about in the garbage around town, all bristled and mean. These pigs even let you pet them. The highlight of my childhood Sundays used to be walking up Seminary Hills and petting the Catholic pigs.

Leading away from the grotto, hidden behind a brick wall, a narrow footpath climbed up the hill and twisted around the back of the Gymkhana Club's tennis courts, went through a shallow ravine, ran along the toy-train tracks by the deer park, then skirted around the Parsi cemetery, and ended down at the Japanese Garden.

I lit a candle and placed it at the feet of Lourdes Mata, as she was known locally, who stood on a pedestal with a baby Jesus in her arms. She looked exhausted, the way mothers of small children often do. From the corner of my eye, I caught Jeh praying sincerely, eyes closed, lips moving. I took his hand. His fingers, fat and warm, laced with mine.

'Come on,' I said. 'It's starting to get a bit warm out here.'

Jeh paused at the beginning of the path to type a text on his Blackberry. He looked so lionhearted in his khaki shorts, like a middle-aged boy scout. I snatched the phone. He gaped in surprise.

'No phones allowed,' I said, colliding into him with my shoulder.

'Disrespectful,' he said, with a good-humoured smile.

We trudged up the dirt path. For the first time in months, I felt like things might turn out okay. The day was beautiful, everything felt perfect, except the path was steeper than I remembered. Sweat slid down my temple; I wiped it with the back of my hand. My stomach gave a loud gurgle.

'One foot in front of the other, Piglet,' Jeh said as I started to lag behind. When I was a child, he'd lift me up by my armpits, if I got tired, and perch me on his shoulders. We'd continue our walk up the hill. I'd pull leaves, large as elephant ears, from the teak trees as we went under their branches.

'Look,' I said, pointing at the cloud-mobbed sky. Brown kites, wings outstretched, were circling above our heads like planes in a holding pattern. 'Are those eagles?'

'Hmm,' Jeh said, holding up a pair of binoculars to his face. 'See the white breast? And those black wing tips? Brahminy kites.' He let out a low whistle. 'I haven't seen these many in a very long time. They're dying out because of all the pesticides farmers use these days.' He was part of a group that met once a month at the Gymkhana Club. 'Literally falling out of the sky sometimes.'

Jeh sat down on a rock. The kites wheeled around in the sky like sentinels for a god. A strong breeze lifted the dead leaves from the floor and made them dance. I placed my hand on

Jeh's shoulder. We studied the kites. All was silent except for the rustle and creak of the forest.

'Why are you so fascinated by these birds, Dad? I asked, squeezing on to the rock next to him.

Jeh gripped the hand I'd put on his shoulder. 'Do you know about Baba Amte's ashram?'

Once, at the lake, a herd of white-tailed chital deer ran past us on both sides, startled by the scent of a predator. Jeh had hoped it was a tiger. After they'd gone, Jeh and I sat in the car, waiting to see if a tiger would appear. I wanted to go home. 'Don't be scared, Piglet,' he'd said. 'I won't let anything happen to you.' But the tiger never showed up.

'Baba Amte, the old man who rescues animals,' I said, 'and then sets them free?'

'That's the one,' Jeh said. 'When I was a little boy, my father took me to the ashram on my – what was it? – my tenth birthday. He said he wanted to show me something. I remember being excited. He wouldn't tell me what we were going to see. "It's a birthday surprise," he said.'

I thought of the old pictures I'd seen of Jeh as a boy. His little overbite and his side parting. Lily Mama used to dress him like Pinocchio, in small shorts and suspenders. 'I'm guessing the surprise was a Brahminy kite?' I asked.

Jeh nodded. 'Baba Amte's foreman brought a Brahminy kite, wearing a hood, into the courtyard,' he smiled at me. 'When they took off the hood, the bird was startled, her pinion feathers ruffled up, as if she hadn't expected to be surrounded by staring people. Her eyes, they were wondrous. I saw an intelligence far broader, far more ancient than our own. It stole my breath.'

'What happened next?' I asked, transfixed.

'Well, I started crying,' Jeh shrugged. 'Such a remarkable gaze. I was overwhelmed. My father thought I was frightened. He said, "Come on Jeh, don't be a sissy. Be a man." But I couldn't stop.'

'Zal Papa was a very modern father, clearly.'

Jeh gave me the binoculars. 'Take a look,' he said. 'What do you see?'

'Umm. Kites and sky.'

'Exactly,' Jeh said. 'We see just the kites. But the kites see us, and they see the trees, the hill, the grotto, the city. We are a small part of that huge world. A mere speck.'

'What's so great about being a speck?' I said, feeling sad all of a sudden.

'Well,' Jeh said, shifting his weight from one side of his bottom to the other. 'It's comforting, isn't it? To know that you are a speck. That all this' – he gestured to the trees, the sky – 'can carry on, *will* carry on, without you.'

'I suppose.'

Jeh sighed. A rich, contented sigh. 'I feel so much lighter, now that you've found Veer.'

'He's not a speck on you, though,' I said, resting my cheek on Jeh's shoulder. 'I still need you.'

Jeh absent-mindedly brushed my face. 'In my next life, I want to be born a bird. I want to be free.'

ON THE NIGHT OF my wedding, tea lights turned the trees into shimmery creatures swaying to some secret music. An unexpected chill descended on the garden, making the guests pull on shawls over their wedding finery. The air smelled like marigold flowers and rose water.

Standing in front of my mirror, I rubbed my arms to warm up. My midriff was bare. My hair was yanked tight across my scalp and bundled with hundreds of bobby pins that bit into my head like tiny teeth. A maang-tika sat on my forehead, its delicate chain across the middle parting in my hair. A dupatta with gold roses was draped over my head. I looked down at my hands full of henna, my wrists full of red-and-white bangles like shackles.

Three knocks at the door and Jeh popped his head in. 'All decent?' he asked. 'Can I come in?'

'Come in, sit for a minute.' I frowned. 'I haven't seen you since yesterday.'

'Everything is running smoothly,' Jeh said. He walked into the bedroom and sat on my bed. 'Not bad work by dear old dad.' He smiled, laid his ankle across his knee and shivered his foot.

Struggling to keep my dupatta on my head, I nodded. 'Great job. Help me pin this.'

Jeh held the dupatta in place, smiling, while I fastened it with another thousand gold pins.

'Is Mom giving you any trouble?' I asked. 'I'm sorry. This wedding has to be a farce for you.'

Jeh placed his palm gently on the top of my head. 'No farce as long as you're happy, Piglet.'

'We've been acting like everything's fine for the Malhotras. That's ... They're awful. Maybe Veer and I aren't right for each other, Dad. I don't think I can walk out there tonight.'

Jeh held my shoulders. 'You're not marrying the family.' His smile in the mirror was, like a wineskin, filled with love. 'Don't give up now. It'll be over before you know it.'

I turned back to the mirror. 'I should finish getting ready,' I said, dabbing my mascara.

'I'll send Ammu to bring you out when the baraat arrives,' Jeh said. I watched his reflection leave. He paused for a moment at the door, arranged his features, and stepped out.

THE NEXT KNOCK WASN'T Ammu, but Asha, who pushed the door ajar and manoeuvred herself around it. 'Hungry?' she asked, holding up a plate. 'I brought you a nice fat aloo paratha to eat.'

'How can I eat?' I said, showing her my hands. 'I have mehendi all the way up to my elbows.'

'Oh,' Asha said, looking down at the paratha as if it might provide an answer. 'Shall I feed you?'

'No thanks,' I said, smoothing my clothes. 'I'm much too nervous. I'll eat after the ceremony.'

'Come on,' Asha said, tearing off a morsel and bringing it right to my face. 'Let me feed you.'

The smell of alcohol clung to her like a sloth. 'Stop it,' I said, pushing the edge of the plate away. 'You'll get food all over my lehenga.' I closed my eyes. 'Please. I need to get ready.'

Asha slammed the plate down on my dressing table. 'You are,' she began, 'such a rude, ungrateful person. I am trying so hard to be a loving mother to you – and all I get is your hate.'

'You always do this, Ma. Every important moment in my life, you manage to make it all about you. You've not given me much to be grateful for,' I said, sitting on the bed to exchange slippers for high heels. 'But I suppose I should be grateful to be alive. Not all your children were that lucky, na?' Cruelty was a language that I had learned at my mother's knee.

In movies, when someone is stabbed or shot, there's a moment when their eyes open wide in wonder, as if death were a magic trick. That's what Asha's face was like. She took the plate from the dressing table and tried to break it over my head. I caught her arm, and taking the plate away, threw it on the floor, where it shattered.

'Are you fucking crazy, Mom?' I said. 'It's my wedding day, and you're trying to kill me?'

'There, now you see how that feels,' Asha said, tilting her head to one side. She lifted her hand, as if she was going to slap me. 'You are cruel. I hope you lose a child. You have no idea how I struggled. I almost died in that hospital. Did you know that?'

'Look,' I said, making a placatory motion. 'I can't get into this right now.'

A knock at the door. 'Noomi?' Ammu had been instructed to bring me out when the baraat arrived. 'Uncle wants you at the mandap in about fifteen minutes. Aunty,' Ammu turned towards my mother, 'you need to be at the front gate.'

Muttering under her breath, Asha yanked a tissue out of the box on my dresser, scrubbed her cheeks and walked off. We watched the bedroom door swing close with a loud bang.

'How do I look?' I asked turning to Ammu shakily. 'This is one of Kitty Auntyji's lovely designs.'

'A bit like those dolls we used to play with,' Ammu grinned. 'Sanskaari bride Barbie.'

'Shut up,' I said, smiling in spite of myself. 'You're jealous you can't wear an outfit which makes it look like your zamindar husband regularly bankrupts his farmer serfs.'

'Thakurain chic,' Ammu giggled. Eyeing the shattered plate in the corner, she looked at me. I shrugged. Ammu smiled and kneeled on the floor to arrange the fall of my lehenga. It was a loving gesture, something I imagined a mother would perform.

'Thank you,' I said, on the verge of tears.

We heard the music as Veer's baraat got closer and closer. My heart thumped along with the dholak, as I sat stiffly on my bed, waiting, like dessert, to be brought out at the right moment. At the front gate, my family stood with garlands for the groomsmen. Veer would be brought down off his horse – so that my mother could paint a red tika on his forehead.

'Look what I have,' Ammu grinned, pulling out a cigarette from her purse.

'Oh god, yes,' I said. 'Quickly, before I have to go out and face my new in-laws.'

'Cigarette before the firing squad?' Ammu raised her eyebrows. 'So dramatic, Noomi.'

'Hurry up and light it.'

Ammu lit the cigarette and gave it to me, pinched between thumb and forefinger.

'I can't have the smell on my clothes,' I said, tilting up my face. 'Give me a few drags, please.'

Ammu put the cigarette to my lips. The tip glowed brighter when I inhaled. I could feel the smoke creep into the empty places in my stomach. I couldn't remember the last time I'd eaten. The baraat sounded louder. The dholak made my heart go pitter-patter, pitter-patter.

'Are you happy to finally become Mrs Malhotra?' Ammu asked.

I winced at the sound of my married name and took another drag from the cigarette.

'People act strange at weddings, you know,' Ammu said. 'There's pressure to put on a show.' She crushed the cigarette under her heel. 'It'll feel much better once it's just you and Veer.'

'I hope you're right,' I frowned.

A folk song, filled with quivering women's voices, was the cue for me to walk out, under a net of flowers held overhead, to Veer waiting at the pavilion. The flower net was held up by male relatives: Adil, and some distant ones whose names eluded me in my nervous state. I couldn't help thinking that if my brother had lived, he would probably have been holding up a corner. Perhaps he would've had a lover watching him from the crowd of wedding guests, who'd have been teased about being next. I imagined Jeh feeling proud of the way people talked about him.

Veer and I exchanged our milni garlands to oohs and aahs, and posed side by side for photographs. Then we were guided to where the pandit sat cross-legged, impatient to marry us. The pavilion was silver fabric gathered with orchids, dusted with tea lights, and crowned with rococo arrangements of carnations, lilies and long, twisted silver twigs.

The priest, humming his Sanskrit prayers, set the sandalwood fire ablaze, so that the serious and sober business of getting married could get started. Puffed rice and sandalwood chips were tossed into the fire so its smoke got thick and fragrant. Soon, my face began to feel hot, feverish – sweat gathered on my forehead. After a while, the garland of fragrant roses felt like a steel cable. The priest told me to bend my head. Veer took a ring filled with sindoor and rolled it over the parting in my hair, making a red mark. He placed a mangalsutra around my neck. The entire ceremony took an hour to complete, and by the end of it, we were married. Yoked together by stoles, Veer and I were made to touch everyone's feet. Crushed under the weight of my clothes and the garland around my neck, tired from the smiling and bending, I felt a rush of relief when they untethered me from my new husband. I ran back to my room to wipe off the sweat from my face before our reception.

I LAY DOWN, SAVOURING THE coolness of my pillow and the comforting smell of my sheets. A writer I loved once said that dressing up a bride was like polishing firewood. I'd never fully understood that sentence until today. 'I am firewood,' I said to the ceiling. Summoning all my willpower to stand up, I took a deep breath, looked at my room, my beloved objects, photographs, the poems on my mirror, for what felt like the last time, and left. I found Veer in the driveway, looking handsome, and a little bit lost, as if he'd wandered into the wedding and they'd asked if he'd like to be the groom. We were taken to a car whose bonnet had been decorated with a mountainous bouquet of purple orchids.

The streets in Kamalpur empty out after sunset. Our car paused at a red light, beside a van filled with children. A girl with gravity-defying pigtails stared at me, her nose pressed white against the glass, her face lit with awe. She curled her fingers in a wave.

'So, Mrs Malhotra, how do you feel?' Veer asked cheerfully.

'Don't think I'll change my name,' I said, waving back at the girl. She stuck her tongue out.

'Okay. We don't have to get into that right now,' Veer said. 'How do you feel? Happy? Sad?'

'Are you happy?' I asked, sticking my tongue out at the girl, who giggled.

'The whole thing has gone off perfectly. My parents are so proud of us,' Veer gave a satisfied yawn.

'Yes, but,' I said, taking his hand, 'didn't you feel like we lost control over it all?'

'It was overwhelming,' Veer nodded. 'But it made my parents happy. That's what matters.' He searched my face to see if I agreed with him, worried that I planned to throw a tantrum. 'Are you wearing comfortable shoes? We'll be standing for a few hours, you know.'

'*Of course* I'm not wearing comfortable shoes,' I snapped. Then I felt guilty. 'I'm sorry. I'll be fine once this' – I pointed at the club's entrance, decorated with lights and flowers – 'is over.'

'Almost at the finish line.' Veer gave my hand a squeeze.

WHEN WE ARRIVED, THE guests had already started to line up. Veer's father led us to a stage decorated with gold fabric. The guests began their procession, entering on the right with an envelope of money or a silver dish – or in some annoying cases, a heavy kitchen appliance – smiling for a photo and exiting stage left. Some felt put upon to make a comment. 'Congratulations! You've been promoted from bahu to mother-in-law!' said a woman to Veer's mother, who stood beside me, palms joined. 'Your status has gone up in the world!'

For two hours, I stood, smiling, shifting from one aching foot to the other. My lehenga felt like it was made of lead. I stole looks at Veer in his dress shoes and brushed wool suit, effortlessly charming all the aunties. I didn't want to smile at anyone ever again.

I searched the crowd for my parents. Jeh weaved, like an autorickshaw driver in heavy traffic, through the twisting buffet line, receiving envelopes full of money, shaking hands. Asha wasn't with him. I looked around a woman trying to get a closer look at my jewellery and scanned the crowd for my mother. A few minutes later, Asha rushed up onstage, holding her sari above her shins. The line of guests scattered like marching ants as she broke through and grabbed me, sobbing. I could smell the vodka on her breath, in her hair, on her skin. She buried her head in my clothes, I heard a rip in my red-and-gold dupatta.

'You can hate me all you want,' Asha blubbered, pawing my face, kissing me. 'But I'll always be your mother.'

I scrubbed my mother's kiss away with my hand. This made her grab my face and plant more kisses. Soon, my entire forehead was covered in lipstick marks. The Malhotras looked appalled, but also puzzled, as if Asha had sprouted tentacles from her head. Veer stared at the floor. An embarrassed giggle escaped my lips, then I began laughing uncontrollably. Shrieking, really. More people came walking towards the stage. They stared. The bride? Laughing? Unthinkable. Brides were supposed to be serious, mournful. From under her tears, Asha looked at me. Then, she began to wail louder and louder, like an ambulance. This made me laugh even harder, with no idea what I found so hilarious. Maybe it was my in-laws' faces as they slowly realized Asha was drunk. It felt like Jeh and I had pulled off a massive scam.

In the midst of this chaos, Jeh rushed up on to the stage and pried Asha off. He led her down from the stage, muttering excuses and apologies. I looked at Veer and giggled, enjoying the light shade of salmon pink flushing up from under his shirt collar. We were let go to mingle with the guests. I went to a sofa and slumped on it. A waiter brought over some food and a glass of water. I drank it off. The food was standard club buffet fare. I pushed it around with a fork, wishing with all my heart that I could have something real to drink. Veer sailed by, carrying a plate to a table occupied by his friends.

'Mrs Malhotra,' Ammu came up, smiling, holding hands with Shiv. She plonked down next to me, looking more than a little tipsy. 'Do you feel different now that all is official and state sanctioned?'

'I feel tired,' I said. Her sweat smelled like rose water. And alcohol.

'Congrats, Noomi. And my compliments to your dad. This wedding has been super fun,' Shiv grinned.

'Someone had a bar in the trunk of his car in the parking lot,' Ammu laughed. 'And was playing loud Punjabi music with the windows rolled down. We had a dance party.'

'Apparently my mom found that bar,' I said. I stood up. Buds of pain shot up into my feet.

'Hey, wait, where are you going?' Ammu called after me.

'To get Veer,' I said over my shoulder. 'I'm done with this wedding.'

VEER SAT WITH A bunch of his old college classmates around a table under a lit-up palm tree. A waiter went back and forth with drinks and snacks. These men were his pakki yaari – brothers from another mother. I waved for Veer's attention. He smiled, waved back, then turned, rolled his eyes, laughed, and resumed talking to his friends. I waved with both hands; he seemed determined to ignore me.

'Veer,' I said, 'could you come here for a minute?' Veer's friends stopped talking and stared, smiling, in my direction. I felt like a clingy child.

'Oye hoye,' said one, raising his glass. 'Paapey's married less than half an hour and already in the hot seat. That's got to be some kind of record.' The others laughed and clinked their beer bottles. Veer dragged himself from his chair like a teenager. He threw his napkin on the ground.

I tapped one foot on the grass. Hot seat. Fucking idiots.

'Can we go?' I said. 'I haven't slept. If I don't get some rest, I'm going to have a breakdown.'

'In a while.' Veer squeezed my arm hard. 'Let me finish eating dinner with my friends.'

'I want to leave *now*,' I said.

'I can't right now, okay? The guys are all flying back tomorrow. You know how important they are to me.' Veer tipped his head up and let out a frustrated sound. 'You're being so selfish. Grow up.'

'I'm selfish?' I said. 'It's our *wedding night*, and you're more concerned about your friends' feelings,' I put all my contempt into the word 'friends'. I pulled on his arm. 'Don't you care if I'm happy?'

'Noomi,' Veer said, pulling away. 'This is not just *your* wedding, okay? It's also a celebration for our family, our close friends. They've worked so hard to make it special. Stop being such a brat.'

I swallowed the knot in my throat. I was lost in an undiscovered country; there was no one to speak my language here. I'd thought that once we were married, Veer might put me first. Instead, I felt like my eight-year-old self, watching from her garden hideout, as Veer walked back to his friends.

Two hours later, in the car heading to the hotel, he leaned over to kiss me. I turned my face away.

'What the fuck is your problem?' Veer's voice went a bit shrill when he felt embarrassed.

I stared out the window. 'This was the worst night of my life,' I said, rather dramatically.

'Oh god, grow up,' Veer said. He rolled down the window and lit a cigarette.

'I need to be alone now. Will someone from your family be waiting for us at the hotel room?'

'Maybe, I'm not sure,' Veer said, shrugging. He took a long drag. 'Knowing my mother and her love for doing things the "right way", probably yes.'

'Veer, please, tell your mother we'll see her in the morning?'

'Okay,' Veer agreed after a pause. He took out his cell phone. 'Hi ... yeah, Mom? Everything's fine. Are you ... are you waiting for us, you know, at the hotel room? It's just ... Noomi says she's feeling very tired.' Another pause. 'Uh, okay,' he said and cut the call. 'Sorry sweetie.' Veer turned to me. 'Mom's excited to give you some gifts ... or something like that.'

Parul was there to greet us in front of our hotel room. Standing on tiptoes, she held the sides of Veer's forehead and kissed it, while I bent down to touch her feet.

'Kitty Auntyji decorated your room. Isn't it lovely?' Parul led me by the hand to the hotel bed strewn with red rose petals. I began to feel nauseated. 'And this,' Parul said, holding up a sari wrapped in cellophane with a big red bow, 'is for my new daughter-in-law! We are so...'

I sat down on the bed, tore off my dupatta and tossed it to the floor. Slowly, with shaking hands, I began plucking out the hundreds of bobby pins stuck in my hair.

'Oho! Why is she crying?' Parul asked Veer, looking worried. She reached out her hand and then drew it back, as if I might bite her. 'Was it something I said?'

'She's tired.' Veer came up to me, stroking my head like I was his pet. 'She needs to sleep.'

'Oho, beta, don't cry, smile! Come, please, give me a smile. You look much prettier when you...'

I cried – louder and louder – until, giving up, Parul went away, closing the door behind her.

PART THREE

'Remind me again now, how long have you been married?'

'About two years.'

'And you're happy?'

'I'm not ... miserable.'

'He's not abusive: emotionally, physically?'

'No.'

'And he has a good job? He can support a family?'

'Yes.'

'So then, explain it to me one more time, why do you want to end this pregnancy?'

Dr Roosi Mistry was a kindly old Parsi gentleman who liked to steeple his fingers and chew on his lower lip. He listened to my decision with the trademark indifference of a long-time Mumbaikar. Then he put on his gold spectacles and looked again at my sonogram, which showed a small blob – the size and shape of a kidney bean.

'I'm depressed,' I said, stacking the plastic ovaries and uterus on his table as if they were Lego blocks. 'I'm not in any condition to become a mother. I can barely look after me.'

That was half the truth. The other half was that I couldn't – no – I *wouldn't* stop drinking. Not for a baby. Stark sobriety for a whole nine months and change wasn't in the realm of likelihood. And Veer wasn't helping. If we weren't out getting smashed, he'd spend his evenings nursing a beer or two on the sofa, watching TV. If I tried to start a conversation, ask him about work, tell him about something from my day, he'd give me this look – I placed it between surprise and irritation.

Sometimes I'd call his cell phone and he wouldn't pick up or call back. I began to haunt our Bandra apartment – unseen and unheard. I walked around the house in my pyjamas and drank vodka out of a coffee mug. The only time Veer appeared interested in me was when we were around other people. Like the time his boss came home for dinner. The boss had just married. Sitting in our small living room, drinks in hand, he and his wife stared at the towers of books all over our flat. Veer, puffed up with pride, explained that I was a writer.

'She even gets published in foreign journals,' he'd said, taking his boss's glass to pour him a fresh drink.

'Well,' I smiled, 'I got a poem published once, in *Granta*. But that was probably a fluke.'

'Noomi's read every book in this house,' Veer said, plonking down on the sofa and holding up his whisky glass to indicate the shelves. 'She spends more time between pages than in this apartment.'

'Well, it's good to keep busy,' Veer's boss's wife said. 'Since you don't have any children.' She took out a fancy phone from her purse and showed it to us. The wallpaper was a picture of a boy and a girl in matching pyjamas. 'These two are my whole life,' she smiled and blew a kiss to the phone. 'My niece and nephew, Arya and Aarav. I can't wait to have two of my own.'

'Having a few book-children would be nice,' I said. 'And probably more rewarding.'

The boss's wife looked at her husband, who looked at Veer, who looked at me. I stepped into the kitchen, and on the pretext of frying up some kebabs, took a swig from the bottle I kept under the sink. When I came out, the boss was talking about their summer trip to Italy and Paris, while his wife was taking a series of selfies with my books in the background.

The boss and his wife left around midnight, Veer went to shower, and I helped the maid clean up. Later, I stuck my head into the bedroom. He was lying on his side of the bed, staring at his phone.

'That was nice of you,' I said. 'To praise my writing to your boss.'

'Uh-huh,' Veer said, swiping his finger on the screen.

'Do you want to read the poem?' I said, stepping into the room. 'The *Granta* one? It's online.'

Veer's eyelids flickered up and down as he scrolled on his phone. He wasn't paying attention.

'Veer,' I said, walking up to him. 'Veer?' I shook his shoulder rather violently, 'Hello?'

'For fuck's sake, what?' he snapped. 'I'm in the middle of a really interesting article.'

'Never mind,' I said, turning away from him. 'I'm going to make myself another drink. Night.'

'Good night,' Veer said. 'Tell the maid that I want breakfast at 8.30 tomorrow. Eggs.'

I'LL NEVER FORGET THE look Veer gave me when I said I'd made up my mind to have the abortion. One of unfettered relief. We scheduled the procedure for two weeks before we were supposed to visit my in-laws in New Delhi. Veer missed half a day of work to come to the clinic.

'It's okay,' Dr Mistry said smiling wryly, scribbling on a pad. 'India's population is too large anyway.'

I gave a weak laugh and balled my kurta in my sweaty fists. 'I've never had one.'

'Will it hurt?' Veer asked, looking a little pale.

'Not really,' Dr Mistry said. 'A chemical termination feels like period cramps.' He looked again at the scan. 'Only a bit more painful.' He took my clammy hand in his two warm, dry hands, shook them, and then stood up. 'Follow me,' he said, shuffling out the door. Veer was told to find a seat in the waiting room.

Dr Mistry never accepted a patient unless she was married, and even then, he didn't examine his patients himself. He handed me off to a lady doctor in a starched blue sari and lab coat. 'My associate, Geeta, will do the procedure,' he said, walking out immediately. 'Good luck!'

Dr Geeta checked my pulse, blood pressure and temperature. She made me lie down on the table, and covering me with a sheet, instructed me to take off my underwear. Then, without preamble, she inserted two fingers into my vagina.

'Cervix is nice and *spawngey*. You are definitely pregnant,' she said.

'I know,' I said, looking up at the tube lights embedded in the ceiling, wincing in discomfort.

'You're having a girl?' Geeta asked, pushing down hard on my belly. 'Is that why you are wanting to terminate?' She smiled, and one by one, squeezed my nipples.

'What? No ... I don't know. It ... it doesn't even have a heartbeat yet,' I said, looking at her.

'Okay,' Geeta said, putting on another pair of gloves. 'Many times, we are doing termination because the families are wanting a boy instead of a girl.' She bobbled her head, smiling. 'Of course, we cannot reveal the sex, because that is illegal,' she assured me. 'But other ways are there, to find out.'

'I don't want a boy or a girl,' I said, fighting back sour tears. 'I don't want a baby at all.'

'Of course,' Geeta continued as if I hadn't spoken, 'with IVF, nowadays they can simply pick male embryos, like choosing eggs from a grocery basket.' She smiled and pushed two suppositories into me. After I'd worn my underwear, she gave me another two pills to swallow with water that had a faint sulphur smell to it.

'It will start in a few hours,' Geeta said. 'You'll have somebody with you?'

'My husband is with me,' I replied.

'Have him or your maid prepare you a hot water bottle. And take this painkiller. Good luck.'

In the waiting room, Veer was flipping through a magazine, shaking his leg. I went over and touched his shoulder. He shot out of his seat.

'How badly did it hurt?' he said, hugging me. 'You look surprisingly all right.'

'It hasn't started yet,' I said, pushing him away. 'Don't squeeze me, I'm feeling sick.'

THE SEA WAS SMOOTH and glistening, like a tub of Vaseline. As the cab crossed Worli Sea Face, Veer told the driver to turn right. The car slowed to a stop by a greyish building, stippled with bands of sea light. Veer gathered his laptop bag and prepared to get out of the cab. He kissed me on the forehead. 'See you later,' he said.

'What the fuck! What are you doing, Veer?' I asked, grabbing his shirtsleeve.

'My boss wants me to meet this new client,' Veer said, slowly disentangling his arm.

'The doctor said I shouldn't be alone right now. When the cramps start.'

Veer said that I wouldn't be; he'd called our maid and told her to stay over. And besides, I looked fine to him. Couldn't I manage for a few hours? 'I'll see you soon, baby. I love you.'

The cramps began as the cab climbed up our lane. By the time we arrived at my apartment building, the pain was like a small animal clawing the inside of my body, trying to get out. I had to have the watchman help me into the lift. The maid left me curled up on my bed with a hot water bottle. I took the painkillers and went into the bathroom to sit on the toilet. A few minutes later, I felt something slide into the pot. I looked. A betta fish of blood and tissue floated peacefully in the porcelain bowl. The pain abated. In its place were relief and exhaustion. I took an ice-cold shower to rinse off the sweat. With my hair wet and dripping, I turned the AC up as high as it would go, got under the covers, and fell into a dark, dreamless sleep.

A WEEK LATER, VEER took me out to dinner in a tepid attempt to cheer me up. By the time we arrived at the restaurant, I was already so drunk, I could barely taste the expensive seafood served on platters decorated with orchids. Next came shots at a strobe-lit nightclub in a Juhu hotel, where I danced shoulder to shoulder beside a woman with a tattoo of roses on her cleavage. Veer peeled me off just as I was starting to have fun, saying it was getting late. He had to work the next day. I didn't want to leave – he dragged me outside by my arm. On the street, we smoked cigarettes and fought while waiting for an autorickshaw. Veer was the kind of easy-going guy who picked up friends the way the wind picks up leaves. Only I knew how to burrow under his skin like a tick. When I couldn't get the ugly reaction that I wanted from him with my words, I slapped him across the face.

'Stop, or I'll hit you back,' he said, catching my hand. He twisted my arm behind my shoulder.

A policeman strolled over, his wood lathi scraping along the road. In Marathi, he asked Veer what was going on. Veer replied, in Hindi, that it was none of his business. The policeman looked at Veer as if he'd insulted his mother. A sly meanness crept into his face. He turned to me and tapped my bottom like he was testing the ripeness of a watermelon.

'Come on, go home. You North Indians are ruining this city,' he said in Marathi. 'Go back to UP.'

'I'm from Delhi, motherfucker,' Veer said.

The policeman assessed Veer's six-foot frame, and probably realizing that he'd get pulverized in a one-to-one, slowly put his walkie-talkie to his mouth. The situation was turning dangerous. I placed a hand on the policeman's arm and gave him a dazzling smile.

'Please ignore my brother,' I said, tottering precariously on my heels. 'He's mentally not all there.' I took whatever cash I had in my purse, folded it and slid it into the policeman's palm. He took the money, then stared at me as if waiting for me to beg some more. I obliged him by shedding a few tears.

The policeman left, swinging his lathi. I flagged down an autorickshaw. We stopped once and bought kathi rolls, then ate them, as the auto jostled us over the potholed lanes. Then we stopped again and bought cigarettes from a boy on a bicycle.

'Why'd you tell that thulla that I was your brother?' Veer asked, wiping his mouth with the back of his hand.

I pushed a strand of hair off my damp face, taking a drag from my cigarette. 'That's what it feels like nowadays,' I said, 'like we're siblings.' I flicked ash to the rickshaw's metal floor. The driver had 'Don't call me bhaiya' scrawled in bright paint across the back flap.

'You were coming on to that woman tonight,' Veer said.

'Was I? I don't remember that. Oops,' I shrugged. 'Sorry.'

'It was hot,' Veer said, slipping his hand under my shirt.

We got home as the sky turned sunburn pink. The watchman looked not at all surprised. In the bedroom, Veer pulled me towards him. We kissed, fumbling with each other's smelly, sweaty clothes. The red betta fish floating in the toilet bowl swam into my head. I pushed Veer off of me. His face showed that he was tired of my being miserable all the time. He pulled the covers over himself and slept off. I wanted to say something but didn't know how to put into words what I'd felt, so I turned away from him and closed my eyes.

WE FLEW TO DELHI a week later. Thanks to a protocol only for high-ranking government officials, my in-laws received us as soon as we stepped out of the aerobridge. Parul had worn pearls – pearls! at seven in the morning! – while Mr Malhotra had on a beige suit with a peacock-hued cravat. I smiled at them, feeling a little bit like how one feels at the dentist's waiting room – as if a vaguely but also assuredly unpleasant encounter lay ahead.

'My children!' my father-in-law said, his arms open. 'Welcome, welcome home!'

A young man appeared from behind him with a bunch of pink and white roses tied together with a giant pink bow. His face was quite serious, as if giving bouquets of flowers were part of his official government duties. I took it from him with a polite, bobble-head nod-and-smile. 'Thank you very much,' I said.

'See, the flowers perfectly match Noomi's fair complexion,' Parul said.

As I knew I was supposed to do, I bent down to touch my in-laws' feet.

'Oh, so nice, god bless you,' Parul said. 'May you have a long and happy life.'

'Come, come,' my father-in-law said, ushering us out. 'Veer, I want to show you my new car!'

From the number of lackeys surrounding us, it was clear that Veer's dad, by way of a recent high-profile posting, had reached the pinnacle of his career. Mr Malhotra was escorted by four men carrying Kalashnikovs to a bulletproof SUV. Delhi-wallahs, perennially enamoured by power and its trappings, dived out of their way, all the while staring goggle-eyed. A driver jumped out of the SUV and ran around to open the doors for us. Veer sat up front like a kid. I squeezed in the back. A chap with a Kalashnikov sat in the cargo seat, the muzzle of his gun disconcertingly close to my head.

Since it was Independence Day, the SUVs in our cavalcade had tiny Indian flags. They elbowed aside civilian cars, two-wheelers and cyclists on the way to the heart of Lutyens' Delhi, a nest of Raj-era bungalows with Raj-era lawns dotted with Raj-era peacocks. Throughout the hour-long journey, Veer enthusiastically praised his father's new car, pressing all the shiny buttons, making the side mirrors flap back and forth like elephant ears when we stopped at security checkpoints. When we drove into the bungalow, a band started up next to the portico. Whom was this show-sha intended to impress? A daughter-in-law like me held the lowest rank. And yet it felt like this was all for my benefit.

The house was abuzz with young men in white uniforms who brought out tea and government canapés: canned pineapple skewered with cube cheese, baked beans on tiny pieces of toast. Two secretaries with their wives waited in the foyer, arms full of flower bouquets. After they handed all the flowers to me, we made small talk: How was your flight? Doesn't Mr Malhotra's car drive well over our horrible Delhi roads? How kind of him to come personally to pick you up!

'Noomi darling, could you please take this around?' Veer's mother said. We'd settled on the rattan sofas on the marble veranda that overlooked the lawn. Parul pointed a delicate finger to a plate full of paneer cubes with toothpicks sticking out of them. 'Offer it to everyone. Start with Dad.'

I'd sat down with a cup of tea and a sandwich. The flight was an early one; we hadn't eaten anything before boarding. 'Can't one of the others do it?' I pleaded. 'I'm starving.'

'Noomi, it would be *so nice* if you could serve everyone. You are our new bahu.' Parul smiled.

'Bhaiya,' I called out to a young man on the lawn. He jogged up to the veranda. 'Could you show this around to our guests, please?' I handed him the tray of paneer and smiled at my mother-in-law.

'No, Noomi,' Parul said, shaking her head at the young man, who backed away. 'It has to be you.'

Parul always sounded soft and pretty – it hurt my head to match her cooing voice to the talons in her words. I tried to catch Veer's eye, but he was chatting with my father-in-law's two secretaries, senior and junior, who were always hovering around him like attentive mosquitos – while their wives were to be reliably found in whichever room of the house Parul was. Parul cleared her throat and nodded at the tray of canapés. Out of options, I beamed dutifully and showed it around, suddenly desperate for a smoke.

ONCE BREAKFAST WAS OVER, we were led to our guestroom that had a king bed piled with frilly pillows, a basket of fruits, and a neatly organized his-and-her dressing area. The bathroom had his-and-her toiletries, plus a small bag full of make-up for me. Eyeliner, pink lipstick and a packet of red bindis, all still wrapped in plastic. I locked myself in the bathroom and found a metal trash can, turned it over, stood on top, and blew cigarette smoke straight into the exhaust. If my in-laws ever found out that I smoked, it would be awkward. They didn't even know Veer smoked. He became a different person around his parents – formal, circumspect. He treated me like a boss would his new intern. His eyes lost their soft, warm light, as if they were the windows of a shop that was temporarily closed for business.

Sometimes, I thought about what made me stay married to Veer. Maybe it was the idea that having a leaky roof over your head is better than being in the rain. Or maybe it was those moments when we were alone, doing mundane stuff like eating dinner or watching a TV show, and a sense of peace would descend over me like clouds on a mountain. There was this one morning in New Delhi when Veer and I snuggled deep under a fluffy winter blanket. A space heater was next to the bed. Periodically, I'd poke one foot out to warm it. We didn't want to talk or have sex. We lay inside the blanket like two hibernating creatures, too content to even get up for coffee. I put my head on Veer's chest and listened to his heart. Happy memories are like cash in the bank.

'What's taking you so long?' Veer said, knocking on the bathroom door. 'We need to unpack.'

I hopped off the trash can, threw my cigarette into the commode, flushed. I spritzed perfume in the air. The butt didn't go down. 'Just a minute!' I called, flushing again.

Veer had dumped out his suitcase on the bed. 'Hey, where are my yellow socks?'

'I don't know,' I said. I picked up a pile of shirts and found him a pair of argyles from under them. He didn't say thank you.

'Were you smoking in there?' he asked.

'Yeah,' I said, and pushed all of his clothes to one side to lie down.

'Noomi, you know you can't smoke here. You know that.' Veer frowned. 'And you can't nap right now either. Get dressed. Dad wants to take us all to the Golf Club for brunch.'

I turned over on to my stomach and put a pillow over my head. 'Ugh, no thanks,' I said.

Veer lobbed a pair of socks at my butt. 'Seriously Nooms, get dressed.'

'Can't I close my eyes for a bit while you put away your stuff?' I asked from under the pillow.

Veer smacked my bottom. 'Feisty cat,' he said. 'I like your bum.'

'Okay, fine,' I relented. I looked for an outfit that was right for the snootiest country club in Delhi. 'Shouldn't you put your clothes in the dressing room closet?' I asked Veer with my hands on my hips. 'Your parents strike me as the type who value neatness.'

'Oh, Dad's flunkies will fold them up,' Veer said. He slipped a shirt with a polo pony over his head, popped the collar, then stepped into a pair of blue jeans. 'They usually come in and put all my clothes away in the closet.'

'Oh good,' I said, bundling my clothes at him. 'My salwar kurta needs to be ironed and hung.'

'Well,' Veer said, spritzing cologne. 'Remember, these are all young men. They might find it weird to handle a woman's clothes. Sorry, sweetie. You'll have to manage on your own.'

'Are you serious? You get five-star service and I'm supposed to do everything myself?'

'It's not just you,' Veer said. He sounded as if I was being difficult again. 'Mom always manages her own clothes. She'll teach you to iron your salwar and all the other stuff.'

'Argh!' I said, and walked off. 'You owe me for putting up with all this bullshit.'

AT THE GOLF CLUB, we were seated at a table overlooking a slim, long green dotted with Mughal ruins, ancient tree canopies and the occasional peacock. Around us sat South Delhi – the women in oversized sunglasses with designer handbags on their tables, the men wearing polo shirts and mirrored aviators. Everyone looked fresh from the salon. No one smiled at or even made eye contact with the waiters. With movie stars and politicians jostling for a spot on its waiting list, the club wasn't a friendly place. I recalled a news story about a nanny who'd accompanied children to the Golf Club for a birthday party and was told she couldn't enter the main dining room as her clothes looked like 'maid's attire'.

'Bloody Marys for the men,' Mr Malhotra said to a waiter and thumped Veer on the back. 'I want to have a drink with my son.' He turned to us, 'Parul, what would you ladies like?'

'Nothing for me,' Parul said, smiling. 'Only some warm water with lemon.'

'Yes, good idea, warm water with lemon for me too,' the senior secretary's wife said quickly.

'Same here,' said the junior secretary's pretty, plump little wife.

'I'll have a Diet Coke,' I said.

The senior secretary's wife threw me a smile. 'Diet-shiet? When we were younger, there was no such thing as a Diet Coke. Are you concerned about your figure? Now that you're married, you must put on a little bit of weight.' She smiled. Parul had introduced her as Mandira.

'But you can call me Mandy Aunty,' she'd said between air-kisses.

'If you want to put on some weight, Nooms,' Veer said, 'this is the right place.' He studied the menu. 'These kakori kebabs look outstanding! I wonder if they'd let me have the recipe.'

'Veer is an excellent cook,' I said, smiling at the secretaries' wives, senior and junior.

'Oh,' Veer's father said from across the table, looking at his son, worried. 'You mean after a long day, you come home and cook?' He looked at me. 'Why doesn't Noomi do the cooking?'

'Well, I don't do it every day. We have a maid who comes in to make rotis and sabzi. But it relaxes me,' Veer said. 'It's a hobby of mine. I like trying new recipes once or twice a week with Noomi.'

'Haw-haw, look at this son of mine,' Mr Malhotra said to his secretaries, who obediently began to chuckle. 'Cooking? A hobby? Now, *eating* – that's a worthwhile hobby!' He laughed. The secretaries laughed.

'Why would I want to put on weight?' I asked, turning towards Mandy.

'Oh-ho, because a little bit of weight helps to' – Mandy mimicked rocking an infant – 'you know. Look at Tanya here, already in the family way.' She gestured towards the junior secretary's wife, who gave me a shy smile.

'Well done,' Veer's father said. He thumped the bespectacled junior secretary, who beamed, his glasses sliding down his nose. He called, 'Waiter! Another round of Bloody Marys.'

'I don't think I'm ready for children,' I said, looking down, folding and unfolding my napkin.

'You mean,' Tanya was alarmed, 'no children ever? But then who will look after you in old age?'

'It's a child, not a pension fund,' I said. Tanya looked embarrassed, so I softened my tone. 'I don't think never. Just not right now. I'm not ready yet.'

'Nonsense,' Mandy scoffed. 'Who is ever ready for a baby, silly? Don't you agree, ma'am?'

'By god's grace,' Parul said staring heavenwards, 'all will happen when it is the right time.'

'Ma'am is too nice to say anything,' Mandy said, 'but I'm toh a very frank person.' She held her palm up and shook her head. 'Nowadays youngsters don't want to make their parents happy.'

'Aunty,' Veer's voice floated over to us from the men's side, above the restaurant's chatter and din. 'That is nobody's business but ours. Mine and Noomi's.' He smiled and took a sip of his drink.

This didn't sit quite well with my father-in-law. 'What do you mean it's nobody's business?' he said and began to vibrate like a teapot about to whistle. 'It's my business! And your mother's! It's all our business!' He was so angry, his comb-over slid to his forehead. I waited to hear what Veer would say. But Veer merely took more sips of his Bloody Mary. My heart sank into my shoes.

'What are you yelling about, bhai?' Kitty Ahuja had walked in, dressed head to toe in Burberry, her ears dripping with diamonds. Monty, her husband, followed behind.

'Brother-in-lawji,' Monty said, shaking his hand. 'Great to see you. And beautiful Parul Rani, too.' He pulled up a chair for himself without offering one to his wife. I noticed that his shoes had discreet heels to make him appear taller. 'Chubby, take a seat with the ladies.'

'Let's all make some room for Kitty Didi,' Parul said. As the wife of the junior secretary, very pregnant Tanya was about get up, until a waiter ran over with a chair for Kitty.

'We can't stay,' Kitty said, looking at the chair. 'We have plans. But I came over to invite you for lunch tomorrow.' She looked over at me. 'Oh, Noomi, I didn't notice you.'

'Hello, Auntyji.' I stood up to touch Kitty's feet, assuming that's what she wanted. 'Nice to see you.'

'Oh god, what're you doing?' Kitty said. 'People will think I'm some kind of old-fashioned behenji.'

'Sorry,' I said, feeling stupid. I sat back down and resumed fidgeting with my napkin.

'Parul,' Kitty said, making large eyes at my mother-in-law. 'Train her better.'

'Ma'am is doing her best,' Mandy said, loyally.

What would Mandy say, I wondered, if I went to the men's side of the table, picked up their pitcher of Bloody Mary, poured myself a drink, gulped it down, and threw the rest on her?

'Okayji, we must be off,' Monty said. He stood up. The men shook hands. Kitty gave Parul a hug. 'Chubby and I can't keep our friends waiting. Please be at our place tomorrow, 12 noon sharp.'

I'D SNUCK A BOTTLE of gin in my suitcase, and gin always made me feel like shit the next day. I woke up with a headache and a racing heart. In a few hours, it would be time for Kitty's lunch party. And there was a problem. Kitty liked to turn everything into an occasion; one quick way to do that was to impose some sort of theme. She loved themes. Today, she wanted us all to dress in yellow.

'I have nothing yellow to wear,' I said to Veer, guzzling a bottle of ice-cold water.

'You're hungover?' Veer said disapprovingly. 'Noomi, you promised you wouldn't drink on this trip.'

'Why do you get to drink, then?' I said.

'I'm drinking?' Veer looked around him. 'Where's my glass?'

'Who drank those Bloody Marys at the Golf Club, huh?' I crossed my arms and stared at him.

'That's different,' Veer said, sounding irritated. 'I was bonding with my father.'

I rolled my eyes. 'What do I do about this fucking theme?' I asked, squeezing my forehead. 'Where am I supposed to find something yellow to wear?'

'Borrow something from my mom,' Veer said. 'She'll have lots of outfits in yellow, I'm sure. She's a big one for bright colours. Now stop bothering me until it's time to leave. I need to send out this email.' Light from his laptop glinted off his glasses. He banged on his keyboard. 'Go get dressed.'

A fit of nausea walloped me in the stomach. 'I think I might be dying,' I groaned.

'Go throw up, then,' Veer said. 'Don't drink gin if it makes you sick.'

Over the toilet, I stuck two fingers into my mouth and heaved up a string of bile. I flushed, closed the lid and sat on it, taking my phone from the edge of the sink. I called my father.

'Hi baby!' Jeh said, answering on the second ring.

'Hi Daddy,' I said. 'I miss you. What's going on? We're in Delhi and I am hating it.'

'Oh, that's right. I forgot. Are you behaving yourself?'

'Yes.' A pause. 'No.'

'Oof, Piglet.'

'I don't want to get into it. Tell me, what have you been up to?'

'Well, nothing much. We might have a small thing at the fire temple, for Parsi New Year.'

'Oh, nice,' I said. 'That's this weekend, right? Why don't Veer and I come? We can all be together.'

'I'd love that,' Jeh said. 'Would you be able to find tickets on such short notice?'

'My father-in-law will be able to get us train tickets, I'm pretty sure,' I said, staring at my splotchy face in the mirror. I would need lots of make-up to hide the bags under my eyes. 'I'll ask Veer if he can take a few more days off.' I wondered how long it would be before someone began telling me to get ready. 'Is Mom being good these days?' I asked.

'Asha found a therapist. She's been going, uh, once a week. One sec.' Jeh began coughing, and then wheezed like he couldn't breathe. 'Sorry,' he continued. 'Yeah, she's doing a lot better, actually.'

'What the hell was that? What happened to your breath? Are you okay?'

'Yeah, yeah.'

'Have you seen the doctor?'

'Don't worry about me, I'm fine,' Jeh said. 'I have to remember to take my heart medication.'

A sense of doom crawled up my arm like a furry spider and closed its spidery legs around my throat.

There was a tap on the door. 'Noomi, are you ready?' Parul trilled. 'I brought a few outfits for you to try on. I'll leave them here on the bed.' I heard her walk away. 'Hurry up, dear!'

'I'll be right out.' Into my phone, I whispered, 'I have to go. Love you.'

'Love you, Piglet.'

I chose a high-collared mustard silk kurta, with flowers embroidered down the front. Standing in front of a mirror, I slipped the kurta over my head. It fit me surprisingly well. The colour added a touch of gold to my face. Apart from the itchy embroidery and the fact that it was a little too warm for the August humidity, it was a nice outfit.

'You look beautiful,' Veer said, shrugging on his jacket. 'See? Nothing to worry about.'

'I guess so,' I said, smiling at my reflection.

THE WEATHER WAS MILD and cloudy, if not exactly cool. Kitty had her French windows opened on to the terrace of her condo, which overlooked a broad, leafy street. The clouds parted once in a while and a friendly light danced on the glass dining table with its massive arrangement of flowers. Whenever the kitchen door swung open, one heard the clatter of pans and a hissing pressure cooker. Seated on the sofa, in a silk kurta and expensive sandals, Kitty spoke in blocks of fast sentences about a wedding she'd recently attended. 'Oh, they must have spent a bomb,' she said, putting a hand up to her forehead. 'Pakistani girl, very pretty. Fair, tall. My friend Lavi's daughter.' She turned to Parul, who looked fascinated.

'Anyway, what was her name?' She stared at the ceiling. 'Ah, Heena, that's it. She took me upstairs. I had to use the powder room. And on the bed' – Kitty made a shape with her arms – 'there were a dozen Toosh shawls, each one probably costing more than a Gucci dress, okay? Heena says to me, "Dekho Aunty, this is my trousseau. It's my ambition to buy a Toosh shawl in every colour." I smiled at her, but to myself, I thought, what a dumb ambition,' Kitty rolled her eyes. 'My children would never want anything so stupid. I'm so proud of them both. They're too busy with their careers.'

'By god's grace,' Parul said, 'Karan and Dimple are a great credit to you and Monty Jeejaji.'

'Thank you,' Kitty settled like a cat in a spot of sunshine. 'Only I wish they'd hurry up and marry.'

'Umm, Auntyji, when will lunch be served?' I asked. Dizzy and sick, I looked over at Veer, who was standing with his father and the secretaries senior and junior, listening to Monty expound on some whisky that he was pouring into their glasses. I thought I was over my hangover. Evidently not.

'We'll eat when the men are done with their drinks,' Kitty said coolly.

Without food, my hands began to shake. Sweat pooled in my armpits. I wished I'd taken something to settle my stomach. A maid brought around a tray of coffee. I took a cup, and filled it high with milk and sugar. But the coffee made my heart race even more. 'Excuse me,' I said to Parul, and walked over to Veer. I yanked on the tail of his jacket. He didn't turn. I tapped his shoulder. Still nothing.

'Hey!' I said and poked him hard in his ribs. 'Am I invisible?'

'What?' Veer snapped. The men fell silent. I looked away, embarrassed.

'I'm not feeling well,' I said in a small voice.

'Okay, give me a minute,' Veer said, and then turned around. I waited, but he kept talking.

'Chubby,' Monty said, holding a bottle of beer in one hand and a tall, frosted glass in the other. 'We are getting too drunk. I think you should serve us some food. Brother-in-lawji, what do you think?'

'Yes,' Veer's father said, clinking glasses with Monty. 'Ladies, please put lunch on the table.'

'Don't bother yourself, Didi.' Parul shot up before Kitty could move. 'Noomi and I will make sure that lunch is served. You just relax and chat with your guests.'

'Thank you, Parul,' Kitty said. 'You're more like a sister than a sister-in-law.'

'Oh, not at all, Didi,' Parul said, blushing like a teenager. 'It's our pleasure to help.'

Since Kitty only went to her kitchen when she had to give orders, it was no surprise that she'd spent little money or time on making it a comfortable place to work. The ventilation came from a small window near the ceiling, fitted with an exhaust. The stoves and oven were old and leaky. The kitchen seemed permanently steamed up from the various bubbling pots on the stove – maa ki dal, saag paneer, biryani, vegetable korma, etc.

I pulled at my kurta's high collar, suddenly feeling extremely dizzy.

Parul ordered the dishes placed on the counter, where a flurry of hands filled them up. The cook made rotis and flipped them on to a plate, while the maids marched out with the dishes.

'Noomi, could you take that bowl of dahi out to the guests?' Parul said, pointing to a crystal bowl filled with ice-cold yoghurt. 'And then come back inside to help with the rotis.'

A damp breeze from the French windows greeted me as I brought the dahi over to the dining table. A coolness spread slowly across my back; I realized that I'd sweated through my kurta. The embroidery caused an unbearable itch. The urge to scratch it almost made me drop the bowl in my hands. The dahi wobbled in a way that made me feel sick. I was about to put it down and rush to the bathroom, when my father-in-law gestured for me to come over to him.

He was seated at the head of the dining table. The only sound in the dining room was of marrow being sucked from bones, the smacking of lips, the licking of fingers, a few appreciative burps from the men whose dinnerplates were a salmagundi of yellow, brown and green. As I bent to serve my father-in-law, pain hit my head like a cudgel. My mouth flooded with spit. Drops of sweat collected at the back of my ears. Without any warning, I snatched the yoghurt bowl from my father-in-law's hands and retched into it. Around me, I heard the sound of chairs being pushed away. I looked up to see disgust pasted upon everyone's faces. 'Sorry,' I muttered. Cradling the sour-smelling bowl in my arms, I hurried into a bathroom to dump my sick in the toilet, ignoring Veer's bewildered questions from the other side and Parul's offers of help.

'WHEN YOU LOCKED YOURSELF in the bathroom, my mom got quite excited,' Veer said. 'She kept asking me if you weren't pregnant.' He gave me a sidelong look. 'All afternoon, she was like, "Are you sure, Veer? Are you very sure?" Isn't that funny?'

The Delhi–Kamalpur Shatabdi began lurching into the station. I pulled the dirty train curtain from the window to feel the sun's heat on the tempered yellow glass. A porter hopped into our compartment dragging all the station-smells inside – sweat, urine, spices, oil, smoke.

'You should've told her about the abortion,' I said. 'That would've shut her up.'

'Right,' Veer snorted. 'Didn't you hear my father going off at the Golf Club? I wish you didn't drink so much, Noomi. My parents aren't fools, you know. They'll figure it out eventually.'

'There's nothing for me to do but drink,' I said, leaning my forehead on the warm glass. It felt like there was a small child inside of me, always howling inconsolably. When I drank, she fell quiet. Then I was free, like a mother who'd put her infant down for a nap and could spend a few hours alone. I remember how my mother would enter a party on the verge of tears, and then, as if by magic, I'd pass by her an hour or so later and she'd be laughing, a drink in hand, her face glowing like a lamp.

Veer asked the porter to carry our bags; the man said it would cost a hundred rupees per suitcase. Veer never bargained with someone poor. The porter took off his gamcha from his neck and coiled it into a pillow. He squatted so that we could pile our suitcases on his head. Then he stuck out an arm for Veer to hang a duffel bag. Our platform was far away, ninth from the exit. He walked ahead of us gracefully, swaying for balance, like a dancer. A rat ran across the platform and I leaped to avoid it. We briefly lost sight of the porter in the crowd. I was alarmed. Then he reappeared, a dark strip of sweat down the back of his soiled red shirt.

The exit was swarming with cars, taxis, autorickshaws that picked up passengers, tossing up clouds of ochre dust. A flow of pedestrians weaved through the traffic. I spotted Jeh's car, a Maruti Gypsy, and directed the porter towards it. Jeh was sitting in the driver's seat with the door open. I jogged up and gave him a hug. He hadn't shaved; his bristles poked my face. He smelled, not in an unpleasant way, of dead leaves. He was never the first to let go of a hug. I felt calm envelop me like a shawl.

'I'm so happy to see you,' I said, smiling. 'Where's Mom? Is she waiting for us at home?'

'I sneaked out without telling her,' Jeh grinned. He gave Veer's hand a shake. 'I wanted to be the first one to welcome you and Noomi home.'

'Thanks, Dad,' Veer said. 'Noomi has been talking non-stop about coming home. She missed you a lot.'

'Dad, after lunch today, let's take Veer on our old walk in Seminary Hills. I want to show him where we watched the kites build their nests, remember?' I hugged him again.

The porter put the luggage in the back. Jeh gave him a large tip. 'Here you go, boss.' He smiled.

I pushed Jeh and got into the driver's seat. 'I'm driving. You'll take forever to get us home.'

With Jeh next to me and Veer crammed in the back, I drove the jeep out of the station lot, careful of the crowds of pedestrians. At an intersection close to home, we stopped to let a funeral procession pass. Mourners carried a corpse covered in flowers on a bier over their heads. A man shouted, 'Ram naam satya hai.' As if in reply, a coucal whooped from a neem tree. Street dogs barked.

I killed the car's motor and turned, drumming the dashboard. 'So, what's today's plan again?'

'Lunch is at Lily Mama's,' Jeh said, lighting a cigarette. 'For dinner, we can go to a restaurant if you want.' It only took a puff for him to start coughing. His skin had turned a worrisome grey.

'Dad,' I said, and plucked the cigarette from his mouth. I tossed it out of the window. 'You're fifty-three years old and you smoke more than I do.'

As the last stragglers from the funeral walked past, the havaldar in charge of the intersection blew his whistle and motioned for the traffic to move. I honked at a sputtering autorickshaw blocking my way. Traffic began to unsnarl. I looked in the rear-view mirror at Veer. He'd been very quiet.

'Hey babe,' I said. 'You want to stop and buy some flowers or something for Lily Mama?'

'Later,' Veer said. His folded-up legs looked cramped in the back. 'I need to get out of this car.'

Milo, Dad's dog – a fat, joyful golden retriever – began barking as soon as he heard our car. Milo was a glutton for affection. He'd sidle up to anyone for a pet. Once you stopped petting him, he'd scooch closer and closer until you started again. He ruined our clothes with his slobber, and then followed us up the stairs, whining. He knocked over vases and ashtrays with his furiously excited tail.

'This numbskull follows me everywhere,' Jeh said, pulling Milo's neck so his ears waggled.

Asha emerged in an orange kaftan, trailing cigarette smoke. She came towards us, stretching out her arms. 'Your father didn't even tell me before he left to pick you up,' she said. 'You didn't bother to call me to say you were coming, but I've been so excited. I couldn't sleep last night.'

'You were asleep when I left,' Jeh said sheepishly. He crouched and gave Milo a belly rub. Milo's pink tongue hung over the side of his open mouth; he moaned like he was going into labour.

'Don't start guilt-tripping Dad as soon as he walks in the door,' I said, wheeling in my suitcase to my bedroom. 'I'm sure we'll have lots of time to catch up, Mom.' I turned, waiting for Veer to follow. He went up to Asha and folded his arms around her.

'Hi Mom,' he said, planting a small kiss on her cheek. 'You look good, I like your kaftan.'

Veer never made Asha feel as if she didn't matter. A few months ago, when Asha wanted his advice for a project at the orphanage, Veer went through her presentation, slide by painful slide, offering input on how to improve it. The orphanage was a world where Asha was the sky. It was where, Jeh said, she spent most of her time these days. In conversations, she brought up the orphanage when she was feeling insecure or looked down upon. The children had become her little proxies out in the world.

THE LAMPS IN LILY Mama's drawing room looked like drop earrings – she'd found them at chor bazaar. The window curtains were stained with yellow sunlight. A painting of Shiva and Parvati hung above a dining table inlaid with mother-of-pearl chrysanthemums. As children, when we knew that Lily Mama and Zal Papa had retired for the afternoon, Adil and I would climb on the table and pretend the painting was a secret map. I'd point up at the mountains behind Lord Shiva's head, 'That's where the treasure's buried.' Memories only recreate the past. I tried to recall the good ones, but bad memories, like dirty water after a storm, kept flooding back. Still, I was happy to be home that afternoon, and with my family. Not even a few habitual barbs from Zal Papa could put me off.

'Noomi dear, I hope you're keeping your lord and master happy.' Zal Papa leaned back, hands on his knees. A mug of beer sat on a side table, within easy reach. His grey beard looked freshly trimmed. Zal Papa's eyes held love that was lit up by little sparks of anger.

'Ask him yourself, when he returns with my beer,' I said, perching myself on Jeh's knee.

'Aren't you a little old to sit on your father's lap?' Lily Mama chuckled. 'And also heavy?'

'She'll never be too old to sit on my lap,' Jeh said hugging my waist. 'Even when she's a mother.'

'Kids aren't on the timeline yet,' Veer said, sauntering back from the kitchen. He gave me a beer.

'Thanks babe,' I said. Veer looked as if he'd given me the beer against his better judgement. I tried to reassure him with a smile. He turned away. It struck me that I might lose him if I didn't stop drinking. Oh well, I'd worry about that tomorrow. I took a sip and began to feel good.

Veer pulled his chair close to Asha. 'Mom, you've been quiet this afternoon. Everything okay?'

'I'm watching,' Asha said, pointing her chin at Jeh and me, 'the daddy–daughter act. Very charming.' The orange chair she sat on didn't match Lily Mama's beige sofas. Asha was wearing her orange kaftan from this morning. As if she'd wanted to camouflage herself. She crossed her legs, dangling a slipper off of one foot. In her hand was a glass of lemonade full of ice cubes. Asha was being good, while we drank beer. I could feel the resentment rising from her like heat from an oven. It played out like this: at first, sobriety, then seething, pulsating anger, and finally, relapse. I hoped that Veer and I would be gone before the final stage.

Lily Mama inspected Asha the way I'd seen her look at the aphids eating her rose plants. 'Asha dear,' Lily Mama said, 'your kaftan needs a slip. I can practically see your underwear.'

With just that, it was as if Lily Mama had gone behind Asha's chair, tipped it, and sent her crashing to the floor. Asha gathered her kaftan in her lap, muttering something about a faulty lining. It irritated me to see her cut down so effortlessly by my grandmother. I looked over at Jeh, hoping he'd speak up. At the same moment, I realized that he wouldn't, and if it were me in

Asha's place, Veer wouldn't either. I'd wanted to marry someone like my father – and I had.

'Want to know something weird? Veer's mom's never worn a skirt in her entire life,' I said viciously. 'She thinks her calves are too scandalous. Imagine.' I took Jeh's beer and poured it out into my glass. A muscle in Veer's temple twitched, but he stayed quiet. He hated it when I spoke about his mother like this, as if she were some kind of village prude. 'I'll get you a new one,' I said when Jeh grumbled about his beer. Kissing him on the cheek, I stood up and went into the kitchen.

A pot of dhansak sat spattering on the kitchen stove. I took a ladle and swirled it in the dal, until I found a cube of mutton to pop into my mouth. Shanta Bai appeared from Lily Mama's pantry and slapped the back of my hand. 'Wait until lunch is served,' she frowned. I smiled and gave her a hug.

'What do you think about my nowra?' I asked, smiling. 'Does he look like Chunky Panday?'

'Changla,' she nodded. 'Little bit soft-spined,' she added after a few moments' consideration.

'True,' I said, looking in the fridge for a beer. There was a chocolate cake with 'Welcome home Veer and Noomi!' frosted on its face. I dug a finger into the icing and licked it.

Back in the living room, my grandparents were ready for lunch. Asha's chair was empty.

'Did Mom leave already?' I asked Jeh, secretly relieved. 'Doesn't she want to eat with us?'

'She had a headache,' Jeh said. 'Went to lie down. Asked me to bring up a plate for her later.'

I shrugged, looking at Asha's empty orange chair. 'Shall we have lunch then? I'm hungry.'

'Shanta Bai! Lunch!' Lily Mama said. Zal Papa sat, as usual, at the head of the table. Veer had the place of high honour on his right. I sat between Lily Mama and Jeh. Shanta Bai's dhansak arrived in a huge bowl, hot and delicious. Its aroma cast a reverent silence around the dining table.

'Hey Dad,' I said, breaking the spell. 'Don't forget. We're taking Veer on a walk after lunch.'

'Haven't forgotten,' Jeh said and turned to his father. 'Daddy, would you like to come with us?'

'Where, darling?' Zal Papa sprinkled salt on his food and then threw a little bit over his shoulder.

'You know, the old walk, up Seminary Hills.'

Zal Papa shook his head. 'Oh no, that slope is too steep. My heart can't take the strain.'

'We'll have to go soon,' I said, looking out the window. 'It looks like it might rain today.'

'It'll be nice to see the kites again,' Jeh smiled. He turned his head to stare out the window.

Then we heard a coucal calling from the trees, 'Whoop-whoop-whoop!' Its cry seemed otherworldly. Shanta Bai hurried over to shoo it away. 'Hut! Hut! Hut!' she shouted, leaning out so far I was afraid she might fall into the garden.

MY HEART WAS BEATING too fast when we reached the summit of the hill with the kites. Jeh was bent, his hands on his knees. He said he was feeling a bit out of breath and sat down on the rock.

'Dad, are you okay?' I asked, noticing a tinge of blue on his lips, his pale face.

'I'm fine,' Jeh said. 'Just winded.' He smiled. 'Shanta Bai should make her dhansak less rich.'

'Perhaps we should rest. Why don't you sit here? I'll catch up with Veer.'

'Good idea,' Jeh said. 'I wanted to have a good look at these kites anyway.' Scrunching up his face, he took a pair of binoculars from a pocket and put them up to his eyes. 'You go ahead,' he said with a reassuring smile. 'I'll catch up in a bit.'

'We'll wait for you down at the ravine,' I said and hurried after Veer, who'd lost interest in the birds long ago and walked on. The ground crunched under my shoes. I looked forward to discovering the little bruises I always got on my legs from the scrubby brush. Veer had stopped to tie his shoelaces. He grinned as I caught up with him, even more out of breath. Competitive guy. Then he craned his neck and looked around me. A shadow of worry crossed his face.

'What's wrong with your dad?' Veer asked, sounding alarmed.

Before I could turn around, Veer sprinted back up the hill, scudding with his new sneakers over loose rocks and dirt. I ran after him. Jeh had fallen from the boulder and lay on his back, hands and legs apart, like the Vitruvian Man. I dropped to my knees in the dirt beside him. Veer pulled out his cell phone and began punching in numbers.

'Is he having a heart attack?' I watched my father's mouth open and close like a fish on dry land.

'No network here,' Veer shouted. 'I'm going down to get help.'

'Dad ... can you speak?' I asked. 'What happened?'

Jeh stared at the sky in amazement, as if the kites had, through the patterns of their flight, given him the answers to a difficult riddle. His eyelids fluttered when I said his name. Cold rain fell inside my T-shirt. My brain stopped working. I forgot which side the heart was and did compressions in the wrong place. As he died, my father let out a sound that I can still hear at night sometimes, when I'm alone. The earth held his still body in her gentle, brown palm, like a small offering.

The rest of the memories from that day appear to me like scenes from a movie I'd watched long ago. Veer running up with two (or was it three?) priests from the seminary, cassocks flapping; driving on the wrong side of the road to get to the hospital; the sick sound of a defibrillator; Asha, rocking back and forth, back and forth, on a chair, praying loudly, something I'd never seen her do; Lily Mama, standing next to Jeh's bed with his hand in hers.

'Tumka deemag nahi chalta hai kya!' she screamed at the nurse in her awful Hindi. Is your brain not working? This is my son. Don't cover his face! Are you stupid? How will he breathe?

Zal Papa, sitting on a dirty plastic chair, looking like he'd watched his house burn down, pieces of ash fluttering everywhere like butterflies. 'Jeh, Jeh,' he said, as his old hands slowly found their way to his old face. His shoulders moved with sobs.

I closed my eyes. Zal Papa crying out my father's name was the sound of my world ending.

FATE STALKS OUR LIVES like a tiger from downwind. But she is patient and won't act before it is time. Two days ago, we'd walked behind my father's body. A day earlier, he'd smiled. Alive. Awake. Now I was driving to a crematorium to take his ashes. It was late afternoon. Shadows on the tar road had begun to stretch out like soft wax. The humid August air smelled of decay, of earth.

I put my hand out the window and sieved the cottony breeze. How did I get here? I looked back on the years sewn together by the presence or the absence of a bottle in my mother's hands – in my hands.

The crematorium prided itself on accommodating both traditional and modern funerals. There were pyres: long cement blocks, some with embers glowing, and there was also the electric crematorium, tucked away inside a shed. It was cool and dank with the smell of cement like at a construction site. When he saw us walking in, a thin man with soot up to his elbows opened a hatch and used a trowel to noisily scrape out ashes into a rough iron bowl. Bones were mixed in with the ash and made a solid clunking sound as they fell in. Ash flew out in thin licks into my nose.

'Careful, the bones are still hot,' the man warned as he put the bowl on the floor.

There was Jeh, then, in that bowl.

I took a bottle of sedatives out of my handbag and swallowed two. The man brought a scraggly little garland, incense and a square of red cloth. He tossed the flowers and incense into the bowl, laid the cloth on the floor, put the bowl on it and tied the corners. He held out the bundle to me – my knees started to buckle. Veer took it. Balancing the bundle on his hips, he held me up with one arm.

'It's okay,' he said.

As the man with the sooty arms had begun to feed Jeh's corpse to the furnace, I wanted to stop him, shake his shoulders and say: You should know who he was before he turned into this waxen doll with cotton stuffed up his nose. He'd always play Sinatra's 'My Way' to sing along when he was drunk. His favourite flower is the mogra – the night jasmine. In school, for an entire year he split his pocket money with a friend whose dad lost his job. He loved chocolate. He'd eat rice straight from the cooker, packing it into his palm. He loved the colour red but never wore it. He liked to hassle babies until they cried because he thought they looked cuter that way. You need to know all this about my father. What you're about to do is as intimate as the moment his mother gave birth to him.

To balance breaking from Parsi traditions by honouring Jeh's wish to be cremated, instead of buried in the Parsi Aramgah, Zal Papa wanted all the funeral rituals and prayers – no shortcuts. A shamiana was set up in the lawn for the guests who'd begun to stream in since morning, once the news spread about town that Jeh had died. Funerals aren't that different from weddings, I thought, with the fire, the prayers, the people who wanted to offer condolences instead of congratulations.

'Jeh was always caring,' said an elderly neighbour. 'When I was sick, he'd visit the hospital every day. He found out I needed a blood transfusion and rolled up his sleeve without any hesitation.'

'When I needed a loan for my new business, no one would help me, until Jeh used his goodwill with the banks. He put a roof over my family's head. I owe him everything.'

They cleared the hall of furniture and laid out a rug. In its centre burned a sandalwood fire inside an afarganyu, a brass fire urn. Around it sat five priests in muslin robes – mouths hidden behind masks to keep their breath from polluting the sacred fire, whose fat, fragrant smoke made our eyes burn. They hummed prayers that, like bees, flew around our heads in a swarm, surrounding, blurring the outlines of our mournful bodies. They hummed and hummed and hummed for hours. Then they stood up. Like surgeons after an operation, they changed out of their robes and dumped them in a cloudy pile. They slipped shirts over their bellies and turned back into ordinary men.

A maid brought tea, fresh fruits and biscuits on wooden trays. There was a gathering to celebrate Jeh's life, followed by long farewells. Then, a silent house. I squeezed shut my eyes, swollen and pink from the smoke. A desire to get blind drunk took over me, and my shame quieted it down.

THE WORLD WAS ENDING. And it felt like thumbs pushed into the soft cartilage of my throat. My breath came out ragged, fighting up from my chest. The road that I was driving on seemed to sway back and forth like a bough. Sweat dripped from my upper lip into my mouth. My heart scampered about.

'You're dying,' said my mind. 'This is what death feels like. This is it.'

I swerved my car to the side of the Sea Link bridge to cries and insults from cars charging across the suspended freeway. The noise was deafening. A taxi slowed down next to me. A man rolled down his window halfway, wearing sunglasses the shade of dragonfly wings. I thought he was going to ask me if I needed help. 'Crazy bitch! Learn to drive!' he yelled, and then motioned for his taxi driver to go.

It was late August. A year since Jeh died. The sea was grey and motionless, like an unfinished cement floor. The low-tide stench made it hard to breathe – worse than the drying bombil fish smell that hung over Sassoon Docks. The sky was full of big-bellied clouds, so low one could almost touch them.

I took out my cell phone and searched for a number, then pressed the call button, hugging my chest with one arm, praying that Natasha wasn't busy with another client.

'Hi? Noomi?' Natasha sounded a lot older on the phone. Not that I knew her age; she never revealed any personal details during our sessions. I'd received a shock the first time I'd walked into her office. A therapist should have a few grey hairs, right? This one was alarmingly youthful. I'd nicknamed her Jung. She'd stood up and extended a small, neat hand. I shook it, looking sceptical. Still, there was something honest about her eyes when she smiled.

'I'm hah-ing a panih attah,' I mumbled. My mouth felt full of marbles. I hoped Jung could understand what I was saying over the din of seabirds and shrieking traffic.

'You're having a panic attack?'

'Yeh.'

'Where are you right now?'

'Sea Lick.'

'You're on the Sea Link?'

'Yeh.'

'What?'

'YES,' I said. 'And,' I sat back in my car, 'I'm having trouble breathing.'

'Be mindful of the breath,' Jung said. She always said *the* breath, instead of *your* breath, as if I had nothing to do with my own breathing. 'Let the panic flow through you, in and out. Once you start feeling better – which you will, Noomi, I promise you – drive your car back across and get in a cab.'

'Can I come over?' I said, wearing my seatbelt. There was a short pause. I heard something being rearranged, some papers being shuffled.

'Okay, I have a cancellation at 1.30. If you leave now, you'll make it.'

'I COULDN'T TURN ON the bridge,' I said, plonking my purse on the tiled floor and collapsing on the comfortable, bowl-shaped rattan chair in Jung's office.

'We only have twenty minutes, okay?' Jung said. Her tone was what one might use with a toddler who was threatening a tantrum, gentle yet unyielding. 'Maybe we can have two sessions next week?'

'I'm not in town next week,' I said. 'Flying home to Kamalpur for the first anniversary of my father's death.' I lit a cigarette. 'They're having one-year prayers,' I continued, blowing out smoke, waggling the cigarette about in a circle. 'I don't know the details, yet. The entire family is going to be there.'

Jung looked at me. 'It's been a year since he died.' She tilted her head. 'How do you feel?'

'It's ... hard to believe I won't ever see him again. Ever,' I said, pulling on the cigarette.

Jung made what I thought of privately as her therapy-dog face: her eyes big and soulful, her brows furrowed, her head cocked to one side. 'How do you feel?' she asked again.

I shrugged. 'I suppose I should feel sad. I should be grieving or something.'

'You talk a lot about how you should or shouldn't feel. How do you actually feel?'

'I feel ... exposed, somehow. Like a turtle without a shell. I wake up feeling afraid.'

Jung uncrossed her slim, churidar-clad legs, shifted her weight and recrossed them. 'What are you afraid of? Do you know?'

'I don't.'

'Could it be possible that,' she said, 'your panic attack today was related to going back home?'

'Umm, yes, obviously,' I said, and enjoyed seeing Jung disguise her irritation at me under a smooth mask of professionalism. 'I have to deal with my family at home. I have to deal with my mother.'

'Will Veer be joining you?'

'He'll fly in later. He can't get out of his important work commitments.'

'And how do you feel about that?'

'Hmm. Angry.'

'What makes you angry?'

I let out a plume of smoke and rubbed the back of my neck. 'I don't know. I'm fucking angry. I'm either angry or scared. At least when I'm angry, I'm not scared.'

'Would you say,' Jung clicked her ballpoint pen, 'that Veer loves you? Or that you love him?'

I considered the question. 'I don't know,' I said. 'I've never understood the idea of romantic love. I know that when I hear a good song, discover a new dish or a recipe, or watch a great movie, pet a cute dog – the first person I want to talk to about it is Veer. Is that love?'

Jung made another small note. 'Let's talk a little more about your panic attacks.'

'Last night, I put my head on Veer's chest. His heart was beating, but I felt terrified it would stop. The fear made me sick.' I puffed on my cigarette. 'So, I got out of bed and got really, really drunk.'

'Have you been drinking a lot as a way to cope with this?'

'I've always liked to drink,' I said. 'But now I drink so that I can feel like the universe isn't malevolent. And because it's the only way I can be around people without wanting to scream at them.'

Jung gave a smile. 'I had a teacher who loved George Eliot. Have you read *Middlemarch*?'

'Not yet,' I said, sliding down in my chair.

'We lived in Juhu, and my school was in South Bombay. I had a long commute home. So, my teacher gave me *Middlemarch* to read on the bus. There's a line in there that I painted on a strip of silk and made into a bookmark: "What loneliness is more lonely than distrust?" I think that's what made me want to become a therapist. To help people learn how to trust.'

'That's the first time you've ever told me anything about yourself,' I said.

'Well,' Jung shrugged, 'I only share things from my personal life if I think it might help you.'

Sadness is a lake. If you explored its depths, it swallowed you whole. Anger – on the other hand – is a cliff. Standing on its edge, life seemed smaller, further away. But cliffs are lonely, dangerous places.

IT WAS POURING, THE night I returned to Kamalpur. The rain fell in straight lines like a running stitch down the roadsides, cleaning them of trash: plastic bags, cigarette stubs, a rat, a gelatinous condom. Adil had to take the long way back home from the airport. The flyovers had turned, by the evening, into sky rivers. I put my feet on the car's dashboard. Pressing my toe to the glass, I drew a face in the condensation.

'Could you not do that?' Adil said. 'Seriously, I just bought this car.'

'So touchy,' I said, slowly putting my feet down. 'New car, huh? Business is good, I see.'

'It's great,' Adil said. He switched the indicator on to turn. Tick-tock, tick-tock. His face was spotted with the shadow of raindrops. Tick-tock went the little green arrow. 'By the way,' he said, looking at me, 'I'm not sure you know this, but we had to fire Mr Murthy.'

'You fired Daddy's secretary?' I stared. 'Old Murthy? Why Adil? He was always so nice.'

'It didn't work out,' Adil said, looking at me. 'He refused to adapt to my style of doing business.'

'But he's been with the company for thirty years,' I said. 'He still sends me birthday cards.' I drew an angry face in the window. 'Dad was so fond of him. Mr Doubting Thomas Murthy.'

'It's not personal, Nooms,' Adil said. 'I took over Uncle Jeh's work in the company. I need to have a secretary that I can get along with. Isn't that fair?'

After Jeh died, Adil had taken over his role in the family business. He claimed that he'd done it for Zal Papa, who couldn't speak my father's name without breaking down. Having Adil around was the only thing that kept him together. They made Adil, who was only twenty-four, a director, and gave him Jeh's old office. And his staff. They also took Jeh's car away from Asha – as the company owned it – and gave that to Adil as well. Asha and I had no say in the matter.

HOME. 125 BANYAN ROAD. The house Zal Papa built. Upstairs, a garland of marigolds adorned the door. I reached up and plucked one off. I pressed it to my nose, breathing in its familiar watery scent. It told me that Lily Mama had been upstairs today, to make sure my bed had been made with freshly laundered sheets, the floor swept, and that all my favourite foods were in the fridge.

I began taking clothes out of my suitcase and laying them on the bed. There was a tiny knock at the door. Asha poked her head in with a little smile. She walked in and sat on my bed, right on top of my clothes, and picked up a T-shirt to fold, although it was already folded. Her hands shook a little.

'The maid told me that you were in your room,' Asha said, smiling too much. 'I'd waited up for you.'

'The roads were flooded,' I said, pulling out a pair of slippers from my suitcase. I threw them on the floor with a loud slapping sound that made Asha jump. 'We took a detour.'

'I thought you'd at least come into my room to tell me that you're home.'

'Didn't think you'd care.' I shrugged and yanked a pair of pants from under Asha's bottom.

Asha stretched her arms out to me in a way that reminded me of how, as a small child, I'd reach up to her for a hug, right after she had slapped me for making noise, or for annoying her with too many questions, or 'back answering' in front of strangers. Children will seek comfort from the same people who hurt them, like a dog wagging its tail at the man who beats it with a stick.

'Prayers start at seven in the morning tomorrow,' I said, giving Asha a mechanical hug, suppressing a frown at the alcohol hidden in her breath. 'Zal Papa will be angry if we're late.'

'I promise not to be late,' Asha said, and left.

A memory flooded my mind. A bright orange sun and the creaking of a playground swing. Asha was late picking me up from school. My teacher in fourth grade – I'd forgotten her name ... Miss Sharma? Miss Kumar? – sat on a bench in the playground, propping her head up with a fist. Birds chittered in the trees. The sky was glowing with winter light.

'I've never had a parent be five hours late to pick up a child,' my teacher said. 'Where could your mom be?'

'Don't worry, miss,' I'd said. 'She'll be here soon.' I swung higher and higher. The goal was to touch the setting sun with my foot. I loved the butterflies in my stomach each time I came down.

When Asha arrived, she was drunk and apologetic. She hugged me and breathed vodka into my ear. 'So sorry, so very sorry,' she said to my teacher. 'I was busy at work. Lost track of time completely.'

I could tell my teacher did not believe her. But she was tired and wanted to go home. She looked at me, and I gave her a nod to say: I'll be okay. 'Please make sure this never happens again,' she said, staring at my mother.

'I promise not to be late again,' my mother pinched her neck and smiled. 'Mother promise.'

We got into the car. Asha threw my bag in the back, lit a cigarette, and pushed a tape into the deck. A pop song played through the speakers. Chirpy, upbeat music. 'I'm sorry, baby. Tell me, how can I make it up to you?' she said.

'Let me try that,' I said, pointing to her cigarette. 'I want to see why you like it so much.'

'What?' Asha snorted. 'No way. Cigarettes are dangerous for kids, stupid girl.'

'Then why do you smoke when I'm around? I'm breathing it in, aren't I?'

'That's different,' Asha said, looking irritated. 'Don't be cheeky.'

'Let me try, or I'll tell Daddy you left me at school for five hours.'

Asha shifted gears and looked at me. Trees and cars whizzed past. The sky was bluish purple.

'Come on,' I pleaded. 'One little puff.'

Asha narrowed her eyes. 'Okay,' she sighed, handing the cigarette to me. 'Don't tell anyone.'

'I promise.' I licked my lips and took a tiny puff. I began coughing immediately. 'This is so disgusting!' I said, passing the cigarette back to my mother, and spat away the taste.

Asha let out a brassy laugh. 'Serves you right,' she said. 'Now you know better.'

I began to laugh. We were friends now. Partners in crime. 'I'll never smoke again,' I said, pinching my neck the way I'd seen her do. 'Mother promise.'

We hit a stretch of empty road. Relaxing in her seat, my mother sped up. She flipped the tape in the deck to side A. I stuck my head out of the window. There were butterflies in my stomach. I'd discovered the pleasure in falling down very far, very fast.

As with anything the Wadias got involved in, the prayers began precisely on time. The priests in white robes sat around the fire, murmuring gathas for Jeh's departed soul, and the health and well-being of his family. I sat cross-legged on the floor, my back against the hard wooden leg of a chair. After an hour, I felt myself rising like a balloon over my own body, until I bumped up against the wedding-cake ceiling of Lily Mama's stately living room.

Lily Mama had on a pale blue sari, its diaphanous pallu covering her head. Her face was beautiful, inscrutable, like a marble statue. On the other end of the sofa sat Zal Papa, his face the opposite: all emotions and twitching muscles. Too scrutable. He looked smaller, as if grief had shrunk him. His collar seemed too big for his neck. Friends commented that he'd lost his enthusiasm for meddling in other people's business. In fact, nowadays, they said, Zal Papa barely stepped out of the house.

Binny sat between my grandparents. Her husband, Cyrus, Jeh's older brother, joined heads with Adil, whispering something to do with the priests' fees. Binny gave Zal Papa's arm a comforting rub. Tears glazed his face every time the priests said Jeh's name.

I'd heard that Binny had been planting tiny seeds in Zal Papa's head and gardening them diligently. They'd begun looking for a wife for Adil, and he would need a house to start a family. He'd already taken over Jeh's role in the family business, so why not his flat too? Asha didn't need three huge bedrooms now that she was all by herself. Besides, their marriage had been a sham. Everyone knew. Jeh was too weak-willed to ask for a divorce. Everyone knew. One might even go so far as to say that Asha was the reason Jeh's heart gave out – because of her constant drinking, her breakdowns, her tantrums. Everyone knew.

I looked at my wristwatch. It was half past noon. The watch was a gift, Veer had bought it for me for our first wedding anniversary. He'd taken me to the shop to choose it. The salesman tried to nudge me to get a more feminine style. 'That's not her,' Veer had told him with a grin. He'd be here in two days' time. I had to keep going until then. From behind me, I heard a little sound. Asha had covered her mouth with her dupatta. Tears dripped on to her hand. I wasn't sure if it was sadness, or if it was smoke from the fire that made our eyes hurt. Perhaps both.

Sheila Sehgal arrived with Sid once the prayers had ended, at the head of a retinue carrying food. The only person Sheila hugged was Binny. They'd been close friends since high school; good-looking girls who knew they amplified each other's good looks. Sheila swished past Asha with a nod, swooping her hair over one shoulder. Gracefully, she touched my grandparents' feet. Sid did too. He and Adil hugged, the way young men hug, smashing into each other.

The next to arrive were Ammu and her parents. Ammu took my hands in her own, and I noticed a diamond the size of a chickpea on her ring finger. My mouth fell open like that of a ventriloquist's dummy. 'That's quite the rock on your hand,' I pointed out.

'Yeah, I got engaged.' Ammu shrugged, shyly running her fingers through her fine hair.

'When? Why didn't you say anything?' I said, staring at her, taking in her face. 'Who is it?'

'I didn't know how to,' Ammu said. 'To be honest, I'm a little embarrassed.'

'Is it Shiv?'

'Of course it's Shiv.' She laughed.

'You'll be so happy,' I said, a band of jealousy tightening around my heart.

'Oh, we'll do fine,' Ammu said, grinning, tucking a wisp of hair behind her ear. 'I want to talk more, but you should go see to your guests. I have to say hello to your mom. We can chat later.'

Ammu approached Asha, touched her on the shoulder and pulled her in for a hug. Ammu's life was like a well-rehearsed play. Actors showed up on cue; everyone knew their lines, exits and entrances; there never seemed to be any doubt about which scene followed the one before.

I should've been happy for Ammu, but I wasn't. In a mood to irritate, I slinked off. Sid was at the lunch table, debating hard between an aloo or a gobi paratha. He saw me and smoothed down his hair. I imagined him as an old man still preening for every woman who gave him a second look. I smiled at Sid and didn't need to turn to know that Sheila was boring her eyes into my skull.

'The food looks really good,' I said, though it looked horrible and oily. 'I'm so hungry.'

'Well, you know, Mom always finds the best cooks,' Sid said, slapping an aloo paratha on his plate. 'Anushka says that she's never tasted maa ki dal like at our house.'

'Where is Anushka?' I asked, looking around. 'How come she's not here with you?'

Sid tore a piece of paratha and chewed on it thoughtfully. 'Where's your hubby?' he asked.

'He'll be here by Friday,' I said. 'It's the middle of a work week, you know, Sid. Everyone doesn't have a corner office in Papa's factory.'

'I've heard your husband is a corporate big shot. Do you guys have an amazing place in Bombay?' Sid said, scratching his stubble. 'Where's Veer from again? Agra ... or Lucknow?'

'Delhi,' I said. 'His dad's a high-ranking government official.'

'Oh?'

'Oh yeah, he's got like, an office in Raisina Hill and everything,' I said, hating how I sounded.

'Really,' Sid said, pulling the word long like silly putty. 'You've moved up in the world, huh?'

I wondered if Sid practised in front of a mirror until he found the most disaffected way to say things. 'Yeah. So anyway, where's Anushka?' I said, pulling out a spoon that had slipped into some curry.

'Anushka is at her parents' house,' Ammu said, strolling over with a plate. 'Isn't that right?'

'Nuskhi is pregnant.' Sid smiled at Ammu. 'She's at her parents' until the baby comes. It's a boy.' He relayed this fact as if it was relatively uninteresting and placed an arm around my shoulders. 'Hey, since we're all in town, let's celebrate with a little get-together. What are your plans for tonight?' He looked at me.

'Adil's dropping by at around nine. Why don't you tag along? You should come too, Ammu. I haven't hung out with you in a long time.'

'Oh no, I can't make it tonight.' Ammu smiled. 'I have plans to video-call with Shiv after work.'

'How sexy,' I said. I looked around for my mother, and saw Sheila and Binny on the sofa, tittering like wicked sisters from a fairy tale. Asha sat alone. Fury boiled around in my head like a cumulous cloud.

'Noomi, don't be crude,' Ammu said, flustered. 'We're just going to talk.'

'Sounds good,' I said to Sid, pouring out a glass of nimbu paani. 'I could use a real drink.'

'See you tonight,' Sid said, cocking a finger gun at me. 'I have to get back to work. Ciao.'

ADIL DIDN'T SEEM TO like that I'd accepted Sid's invitation. 'It doesn't look right,' he said. 'The first anniversary of your dad's death, and you're going out drinking? What will people say?'

'Fuck what people say,' I snapped, pulling on my cigarette. The car stopped in front of Sid's massive front gate. 'Why do you get to go out and meet people, and I don't? He was your uncle, after all.'

'Don't act so naïve,' Adil said. 'You know there are different rules...'

'For men and women,' I said, cutting him off. 'Yes, yes, I know. I also know that if I don't have a drink soon, I'll die,' I said. 'I need to be sedated between long stretches of reality.'

Adil parked next to Sid's sleek white car in the driveway. The chowkidar directed us to the gazebo. Sid looked rich and free of care in his Gucci loafers. Industrial-strength hair gel protected his Johnny Bravo pompadour against the oppressive monsoon humidity. Sid was always a generous host. The alcohol was top-shelf: Japanese whiskies, artisanal gins. Loud and expensive speakers played Punjabi hits, which Bollywood churned out faster than Sid's factory did low-grade cement.

Since I was neither very rich nor very pretty, I wasn't supposed to talk much. That was okay. I was happy sucking on drinks overfilled with ice. Adil lit Sid's cigarettes and laughed a bit too loudly at his jokes. The topic of conversation was, as usual, money – who had it, who did not. Women came up often as well. Acquaintances' wives and girlfriends rarely escaped without having their social media pictures pulled up on a phone, their body parts neatly dismembered and appraised for value.

'Women are like Bombay real estate,' Adil said, swirling the ice cubes in his drink. 'At twenty, they're a Colaba penthouse. At twenty-five, a three BHK in Bandra.' He grinned. 'At thirty and beyond, well, then we're looking at Andheri or Juhu. Not bad, but no status symbol either.'

I kept my face politely blank. Men seldom leave a trace of the sweet boys they once had been. When Adil and I were children, our garden would be overrun with swallowtail butterflies in the monsoon. Once, a large blue one had landed on Adil's shoulder. When it didn't fly off, he named it 'Buttsy'. Adil showed Buttsy to us. 'Look, I have a pet!' he said. Then, lifecycle over, Buttsy died. Adil, who was, I think, six or seven at the time, cried and cried. We picked Buttsy up by its dusty wings and placed it in a matchbox.

At the funeral, Adil insisted that we all say something nice about his butterfly.

'What're you then, Noomi?' Sid said. 'A PG in Matunga?'

'Fuck you, Sid,' I said.

'Relax,' he said, stretching his legs out on the sofa. 'I'm teasing you. Of course, you're lovely.'

Adil looked from Sid to me and said, 'Think it's time to head home.' He grabbed his car keys from the coffee table, stood, stretched out his arms with a yawn. 'Come on, Noomi. We have to get up early for prayers.' With his palm on the glass door, he turned, wondering why I hadn't stood up.

'Chalo, Noomi,' he said and jerked his head towards the lawn. 'Let's go home. Chop-chop.'

Sid poured out tequila shots. I drank one down and felt it burn pleasantly in my throat. Three gin-and-tonics later, I was still thirsty. 'Go ahead,' I said to Adil. 'I'm not sleepy at all.'

Adil jangled his car keys like a jailor. 'You'll never get up on time tomorrow.'

'Stop acting like my babysitter,' I said. 'I'm the older cousin, remember?'

'Adil, chill the fuck out,' Sid said, handing me another tequila shot. 'I'll drop Noomi home.'

A look crossed Adil's face – as if this was what he'd feared would happen. 'Fine,' he said. He pushed open the door and loped off across the lawn. I tossed back a tequila shot and watched his outline get smaller and more indistinct, until the garden, and the night, swallowed him whole.

NEXT MORNING, MY HEAD hurt with a steady, dull throb. My mouth tasted like an ashtray, my sweat reeked of alcohol. I wobbled over to the bathroom to splash cold water on my face. While wiping off my streaky mascara, I turned and threw up, heaving into the toilet. My heart pounded nastily against my chest. I brushed my teeth and flung my toothbrush in the sink, mashing the heel of my hand into my eyes. Last night was bits of memory that didn't fit together, like a jigsaw puzzle left in the rain.

Adil left, Sid and I moved on from tequila to sharing a joint. We began talking about the past. The talking led to kissing. It was almost romantic. Then Sid said: Wouldn't it be a thrill if I blew him, right there in the open? He unzipped his pants and pulled out his penis. It looked like a fleshy stamen with denim petals. It was nauseating. I thought of corpse flowers that give off a rotting stench when they bloom. Suddenly, my father's waxy face, just before they'd cremated him, appeared in my head.

'Sid,' I said, moving away from him. 'I want to go home.'

Sid grabbed my wrist and pulled my hand towards his penis. 'Okay, get me off and I'll take you home. I haven't had sex in months. Anushka won't let me touch her. Come on.'

'I'm serious,' I said, 'I'm going to be sick.' Vomit erupted from my mouth right on to Sid's lap.

'What the fuck,' Sid said, grabbing a napkin to wipe off the tequila-smelling puke.

He looked so disgusted, it made me giggle.

This made Sid very angry. He grabbed the back of my neck. 'You think this is fucking funny? You're a worthless piece of trash. Girls like you are born with a "use me" sign around their necks.'

'Sid, let go,' I said. 'Please.'

'No,' he said. 'You're going to blow me.'

He pushed my face down. I didn't know what else to do, so when I got close enough, I bit his thigh. Sid let go of me with a yelp. I whipped my head up and hit him in the nose. There was a sick wet sound and drops of blood spilled all over the white couch.

Clutching my forehead, I went through my handbag and found my phone. I scrolled through the list of last-dialled numbers. Five missed calls to Veer at 3.17 a.m. Then a call back from him. I shut my eyes. What had I told him? Static. I took a deep breath and dialled his number.

'Hey Nooms, you're up already?' Veer sounded concerned, but not worried.

'Umm, yeah,' I said, sitting down on the bed. 'Did ... did we talk last night?'

'Yeah, I was going to call you, but I thought you'd sleep in late. You sounded pretty upset last night,' he said. I closed my eyes. Veer had thought he wouldn't have to deal with me until later. 'You said you missed your dad. Then you started crying, saying your family's going to kick your mom out of the house, or something like that? You weren't making a lot of sense.'

'I need something to help me stop drinking. Antabuse or some other pill, Veer. I can't control it.'

'That's a bit dramatic, no?' Veer said. 'Everybody overdoes it once in a while, Nooms.' I heard a car honking in the background. 'I'm sure you can learn to control yourself.'

'I can't, okay?' I said, wiping away tears. 'Veer, I think,' I sat up straight, 'I think I'm in real trouble.'

'You're being hysterical,' Veer said, his voice calm and dismissive. 'Listen, I've got to hang up. But I've changed my flight to tomorrow. I'll be there soon, okay? Take it easy. Stay out of trouble.'

Veer cut the call. My stomach made a sound. I went to the kitchen to cut up some fruit and took it back to my bedroom with a glass of water. Passing by Asha's door, I looked in. Her bed was neat, bare, like it belonged to someone dead. At least one of us had made it to the morning prayers.

I turned on my laptop and typed 'Can you die from a hangover?' in the search bar. The answers were crazy. I searched for Alcoholics Anonymous. Taking a bite of an apple, its flesh a little tart, metallic, I looked through AA locations: Worli, Panvel, Byculla, etc. Too close by, too far away, too crowded. I clicked the minimize button, sighed, slammed shut the laptop, and stretched out towards my phone. Jung's number was in the emergency contacts list. I pressed call. It rang and rang but no one picked up. I texted: 'Need help. Can you prescribe Antabuse? If yes, send a prescription via email.'

A knock at the door. Asha, dressed in white, smelling like sandalwood smoke. She walked in and sat at the foot of my bed, crossing, in a deliberate way, one leg over the other. I shifted uncomfortably.

'What is it?' I said finally. 'Why are you looking at me like that?' I crossed my arms.

'They were all asking about you,' Asha said, dropping her gaze to look me over. 'Adil told us what happened last night.' Asha shook her head. 'You were out of control, he said. You broke Sid's nose.'

I tried putting my recollections of last night in the proper order. Adil had come back. He'd helped me off the floor, his hands like a forklift under my armpits. What else, what else? Oh god. I'd thrown up on Sid's sofas and gone out into the garden, screaming for my father. Oh fuck. And then Sheila had come running out in a nightgown, yelling on her cell phone.

'Do ... do Lily Mama and Zal Papa know?'

'Know?' Asha snorted. 'When he found out, Zal Papa yelled at me. Like I'd made you into this ... this person.' Asha's eyes began to glaze over. 'You could think about me for once, Noomi. They'll kick me out of the house for sure, now that Jeh isn't around to protect me.'

If making everything about yourself was an art, Asha had mastered it. I wanted to be angry, I wanted to scream, 'What the fuck's your problem!' but she looked so frightened, like a child. I swallowed my rage and squeezed her hand. 'I won't let them do anything like that,' I said. 'This is your house.'

'Zal Papa wants to have a talk with you – once he gets up from his afternoon nap,' she said.

I remembered sitting in Zal Papa's office with Jeh, watching him bully, cajole and wear down my father into sending Asha away. If Zal Papa wanted something to happen – it happened. Suddenly, fear held me in its spidery embrace. Everything started to blur. I couldn't breathe.

'What's wrong?' Asha said, grabbing hold of me.

'Nothing,' I said, shaking.

'Noomi, talk to me, what's happening to you?' Asha shook me.

'Panic attack,' I choked, slumping sideways. The fear-spider wrapped all its legs around me.

Asha pulled me to the warm spot where her collarbone met her neck. 'Shh, everything's okay.'

'Stop it,' I said, pulling back. 'You're making it harder for me to breathe.'

'You need to sleep it off,' she said, hurt but trying to hide it. She took a sheet of pills from her purse. 'Here, take two of these.' She handed me the glass of water on my bedside table.

'Thanks,' I said. I didn't ask her what pills those were; if they could help me sleep, I'd take a hundred.

'Shall I leave the rest here? Just in case?' Asha asked. 'I'll leave them here, okay?'

I put my face on a pillow. Slowly, the knots in my neck and back came loose. The spider let go. I covered myself with the duvet and welcomed sleep like an old friend. The last thing I heard was Asha shutting the bedroom door with a small click.

MY DREAMS TEND TO be rather clichéd, as if my subconscious were operated by a washed-up novelist who'd run out of good plots a long time ago. In this one, I struggled to finish a math test, but the ink kept evaporating from the page. I was drunk, and it was hot in the cramped classroom. Being drunk in a dream is weird, because all dreams are based on drunk logic. The numbers on the test kept jumping about, like grasshoppers. I sweated alcohol through my clothes. My papers were snatched away. The final bell sounded like a telephone.

It turned out to be my cell phone.

'H ... hello?' I answered the call in a dry-mouthed whisper.

'Noomi, I saw that you'd called me a few times. Is everything all right?' Jung said.

'One second.' My eyelids felt glued together. It took me a moment to recall that I was in my room, at home, in Kamalpur. I heard birds squabbling in the trees outside my window.

The setting sun dyed my walls orange. I squinted at my phone. It was past 7 o'clock. I was late to meet my grandfather.

'Can I call you in a bit?' I said, getting up. 'I'm late for a meeting with my grandfather.'

'Sure,' Jung said. 'But before you hang up, I called because I can't prescribe you any medication. I'm not a psychiatrist. Even if I could, I wouldn't recommend Antabuse.' A brief pause. 'You don't need to punish yourself like that.'

'Why not?' I yelled, boiling in frustration. 'Do you even know how hard it is to stop drinking?'

Silence.

'Fuck,' I said. 'Sorry. I'm anxious about this meeting.' I flung a pillow to the floor. 'I don't know what my grandfather wants to talk about. Mom keeps saying that he wants her out of the house.'

'Noomi, go look in the mirror. You're not an eight-year-old any more,' Natasha said. 'You grandfather can't treat you like one. He doesn't have the same power over you as he did when you were a child.'

'Ugh, okay,' I said. 'Except he can. And he does.'

'You're back on Monday, right?'

'Yes, I hope so.'

'Well, I have a cancellation on Tuesday. Would you like to come in?'

'Yes. Thanks.'

'Okay, great. And Noomi?'

'Yes?'

'Please don't yell at me like that.'

'I know. I'm sorry.' I grabbed my forehead. 'I'm really, really anxious.'

'I'm here for you, but please don't do that again, okay?'

'Okay.'

I swung down to pick up the pillow I'd thrown. Under my bed, I saw Milo's little red ball, glowing like the tip of a cigarette. My cheek pressed against the floor, I stretched my hand out for it. Milo had loved Jeh. Every night, he used to run out barking his head off when he heard Jeh's car at the gate. Jeh would push open the passenger door and Milo would hop in. Together, they'd drive into the garage. A few months after Jeh died, Milo was run over by a car. The driver wept as he helped the chowkidar carry him inside. We thought that when Jeh stopped coming home, Milo went out to look for him. We laid poor, sweet, greedy Milo to rest in the garden with a candy bar in his paw.

Tossing the red ball from one hand to another, I went down the hall to Jeh's bedroom. It looked like Jeh was still alive. Lily Mama had it cleaned and had the bed made every day. She was at war with Asha about Jeh's old things. On the day he died, Jeh had laid a shirt on a chair to be ironed; it was still there. So were his slippers. The book he'd been reading was still on his bedside; he'd used his glasses for a bookmark. The book's cover said it had won many prizes. I went to the closet and wrenched it open. The smell of Jeh's cologne pulled my face into his clothes. I sat in it and closed the doors.

ZAL PAPA WAS WAITING in the glass sunroom he'd installed in the veranda – to 'enjoy his garden in air-conditioned luxury'. The room was built soundproof, not by accident. Lily Mama had a bad habit of shouting at the gardener, at her maids, at the drivers, continuing to shout long after they'd hurried away. Zal Papa liked reading his newspapers in peace. He was sitting at a table, turning the pages of a file with one hand while keeping the other on his knee. Next to him, with fingers steepled over a stack of papers, was my father's older brother, Cyrus. I dragged up a chair and sat down.

'Glad you took time out of your busy drinking schedule to meet with me.' Zal Papa looked up at me. 'I'll get right to it.' He stabbed at the file with one finger. 'This appears to be Jeh's will.'

'Okay,' I shrugged.

'But it isn't signed,' Cyrus added.

'So then who cares,' I shrugged again. 'You don't want to carry out his wishes anyway.'

'You better be respectful,' Zal Papa warned, 'or I'll take off my chappal and thrash you.'

'Noomi' – my Uncle Cyrus's nasal voice made it sound like he was always complaining – 'your father had a lot of debt, mostly because of your wedding and some because of Asha's stints in expensive rehabs. He passed away before he could pay the company back.'

'Yes,' Zal Papa began to blubber softly. 'And now, my Cyrus is kind enough to wipe out that debt.'

'Thank you, Uncle,' I said, without feeling gratitude. Whatever he had done, I was sure that it wasn't only for my benefit. Until now, Zal Papa had dismissed his elder son for being too soft. Too weak. As a boy, Cyrus had been very attached to his mother. Before school each day, he'd sit on Lily Mama's lap at the breakfast table. 'What're you, a bloody pansy?' Zal Papa yelled, pulling him off to give him a whack. Jeh, on the other hand, was Zal Papa's little man. He picked fights with the boys in his class, he played football, he played rugby, he walked about in the garden, shirtless and potbellied, claiming, 'I'm Sandow!' When Jeh was around four, Zal Papa got knocked unconscious by a loose roof tile. Lily Mama took the boys to see him in the hospital. Cyrus, sobbing, held on to his father's hand, while Jeh said, frowning curiously, 'Bloody fellow is dead or what?'

Zal Papa wanted Jeh to 'be a man' and control his wife. Asha's public struggles with addiction and depression emasculated him, in Zal Papa's eyes. Made him seem lacking the ruthlessness required to be respectable. This was the greatest disappointment of Zal Papa's life.

'We understand the word "respectful" a bit differently,' I said, looking over at Zal Papa. 'You mean "respect my authority". But I think' – I opened my palms on the table – 'respect means treating a person with dignity.' I flipped them downwards. 'Why do I have to treat you like an authority for you to consider treating me with dignity?'

Zal Papa leaned forward in his chair. 'Really?' he said with a bitter smile. 'Your demand that we treat you with dignity makes me laugh, when you behave like a madwoman. Where was that dignity last night, huh? You're lucky the Sehgals didn't decide to call the police on you.' He jabbed the air with his forefinger. 'Your behaviour reflects at all times on the family.'

'That's ridiculous,' I said.

Cyrus cleared his throat and shuffled papers.

'We've discussed it,' Zal Papa continued. 'It's best that you don't come back home to Kamalpur unless your husband comes with you. We cannot take responsibility for you any more.'

'What? You can't banish me from my own home!' I banged the table with both my hands.

'As long as I'm alive, what I say goes!' Zal Papa screamed.

'Please, Daddy,' Cyrus said, indicating the will. 'Let's get back to why we called this meeting.'

'Go on, son,' Zal Papa said, patting his back. 'You tell her.'

Here it comes, I thought, bracing myself. They were going to kick Asha out.

'Noomi,' Cyrus said with a new note of authority in his voice, 'in this will, which is unsigned, Jeh said that he would like to leave his flat to you and Asha.' He opened his palms and tipped his head to one side. 'We don't think it was his final intention. We know he wasn't happy with your mother.'

'Should've never married Asha. Should never have,' Zal Papa blubbered suddenly. 'My son.'

'Daddy, calm,' Cyrus said with a hand on Zal Papa's shoulder. He turned to me, 'Firstly, the house still belongs to Zal Papa. And frankly, we don't want Asha having a claim on the property.' He smiled.

'But she can stay in the upstairs apartment, right?' I asked. 'You're not kicking her out?'

'Of course,' Cyrus frowned. 'Why would we behave so unfairly towards your mother?'

I held up my palms, looking at them both. 'You can do whatever you want. Who's around to judge?'

'Noomi!' Zal Papa stopped his weeping to glare at me. 'I've had enough of that smart lip.'

'You need to grow up, my dear,' Cyrus said. 'There's no one to indulge you any more. Jeh's dead, and that's not my fault.' He gave me a look that was sly yet opprobrious. 'In fact, if anyone is to blame,' he pointed, 'I'd say it was you and your mother who hassled him to death.'

I'd had enough. Rising from my chair, I said, 'My father loved me more than any other person in his life. You can paint it otherwise, but it would be a lie. I don't have to listen to this bullshit.'

'Where do you think you're going?' Zal Papa demanded. 'Take these papers and destroy them.'

'Destroy them yourselves,' I said. 'I'm going out for a drive.'

'Fine,' Zal Papa said. 'But don't get into any trouble, understand? I won't hesitate to kick you out.'

When I was very little, Zal Papa would throw me up in the air and catch me, saying, 'Come on little pigeon, flap your wings!' He'd toss me high, again and again. I landed back in his arms, laughing until I couldn't breathe. 'One day,' he said, kissing the top of my head, 'one day you'll learn to fly, my little bird. And then we'll never see you again.'

Ignoring the stares of men, whose only job, it seemed, was to hang about the blue-lit shopfront of Lakshmi Wines, I paid the cashier for a nip of vodka along with a soda, and then hurried, holding the bags to my chest, back to my car. I had to honk at the fool who'd double-parked his motorbike behind me until he came jogging up, staring as if I had horns growing out of my head. I flipped him off and enjoyed his look of surprise, before manoeuvring to join the crushing flow of cars, buses and rickshaws. The market at 8 o'clock on a weekday meant traffic was more convoluted than the plot of an art-house film. Three bony cows decided to plonk down in the middle of the street, tucking their hooves under them. Rather than shooing off these sacred animals, traffic flowed past them like a river around a boulder. Begging children weren't granted the same kindness. They had to leap out of the way once the lights changed, or risk losing a limb.

At the traffic signal before the turn home, an old man selling plastic sunglasses rapped on my window. He put on a bright pink pair, offering a sad but funny contrast with his old, lined face. I waved him off. The thought of going back home became more and more unbearable, the longer I waited for the lights to change. Instead of turning right, I drove up the jewel-green Seminary Hills, past the deer park bordered by the tracks of a toy train. With their heads close to the ground, the deer licked blocks of pink salt, ignoring the calls of children who thrust fistfuls of grass through the chain-link fence, hoping to tempt them close enough to pet.

At the corner of the deer park was the red mica road, lined with teak trees, that led to the Parsi Aramgarh. I drove on, listening to the dirt crunch under my tyres, and stopped in the parking lot overlooking an overgrown gulley. Why was I here? Jeh had been cremated; I didn't have a grave to visit. The soda fizzled as I poured half of it out on the dirt. I topped the rest up with vodka. I lit a cigarette and studied the showy sunset in front of me.

The cemetery had a caretaker – an old Parsi man who always wore white pyjamas and a sadra – who didn't seem to be around. Keeping the bottle close, I went through the wrought-iron gate and began to wander among the gravestones. Look at me, I thought, drunk in a graveyard. Seventeen-year-old Noomi would be proud. The cemetery, with its beautifully carved headstones, was of another era. Most of the graves dated back to the Raj. There were some children's ones, heartbreakingly small. I saw a simple marble one chiselled with the same name as my grandmother: *Lily Amber, August to October 1912, A Sunbeam Gone Too Soon.* Stray dogs lolled on some of the graves like guardian spirits. I whistled to one and he trotted over, tail wagging, and allowed me to pat his back.

I'd heard that you had to wait a year before installing a tombstone, as the grave needed time to sink. I saw a fresh one with a wooden marker bearing the number 125. That was our house number. 125 Banyan Road. I could pretend this grave belonged to Jeh. I sat cross-legged by its side.

I sat drinking from my plastic soda bottle until the sky looked like carbon paper with stars poked into it. Clouds began to gather. Then it started to drizzle. I looked up. Raindrops fell into my eyes, blurring my vision. I got up from the wet ground, brushed off clumps of soil stuck to my jeans, and began to pick my way back through the graves in the dark.

The half-finished vodka was waiting for me on the passenger's seat – a loyal friend. I started the car's engine and took little sips straight from it while I found my way home in the rain.

I never liked the taste of alcohol, and I associated its smell with my mother. What feels familiar is always comforting, in its own terrible way. The rain looked like it was pouring out of a bucket. In any other town, I'd have had an accident – but thankfully this was Kamalpur, and at 11 o'clock, the streets were empty. At the front gate, I killed the car's engine, letting it gently roll down the driveway in the hope that no one would find out I was home. Zal Papa would be asleep. Lily Mama might be watching late-night TV. If I could get upstairs without being noticed, I'd be fine.

The garage's harsh tube light hurt my eyes. I squinted at my reflection in the car window. Colours appeared and disappeared, like weeds under the surface of a river. On the ceiling a lizard, the colour of chapati dough, blinked twice. I tossed the vodka bottle into a trash can at the foot of the stairs.

Climbing up the stairs to my parents' flat took some effort – it was as if my legs had turned to lead. I reeked of smoke and vodka, of rain and sorrow. I looked forward to taking the blue pills and falling into a long, dreamless sleep. The light in my bedroom was on; the door was ajar, making a yellow column in the dark hallway. I stepped inside to find Lily Mama sitting on my bed. Standing over her – looking a little bit like a priest in a frilly nightie – was Binny.

'Where were you?' Lily Mama said. 'We were worried that you'd had an accident in this rain.'

'I had ... I was,' I cowered at the door like a scared dog. I sighed, 'I was at the Aramgarh.'

'You smell terrible.' Lily Mama scrunched up her face. 'I can smell you all the way from here.'

'Noomi,' Binny said, sounding like a bad soap actor, 'have you been ... drinking?'

'Can we talk tomorrow?' I dumped my handbag on the floor and headed to the bathroom.

'Explain *now*,' Lily Mama said, catching hold of me. 'Be honest, have you been drinking?'

The bedroom door creaked opened. Sliding herself around was Asha. 'What's going on?' She looked at Lily Mama, then Binny, then at me. When my eyes met hers. Asha seemed to know instantly.

'Asha, return to your room,' Lily Mama roared, pointing. 'I'll handle this.' She was easily riled up – hard to calm. Binny had been working on Lily Mama's rage, tending to it like a coal engine's boiler. I hoped Asha would stay. If there was ever a time for my mother to be her stubborn self – this was it.

Asha left, closing the door behind her.

'You are a disgrace to my son,' Lily Mama said. 'He loved you so much. He had such hopes for you. And you are hellbent on turning into *her*.' She pointed at the door that Asha closed behind her. 'He deserved better than you both.'

'Leave me alone please,' I grabbed my head. 'Leave me alone or I swear...'

'I *swear*?' Lily Mama mimicked. 'What do you swear?' She looked like she wanted to say more, but instead, stared at the ground. Binny put a hand on her shoulder. After a moment, Lily Mama looked up and said, 'You should be in a hospital. It breaks my heart to do this, Noomi, but I think you might, not tonight perhaps, but soon, do irrevocable harm to yourself.'

'What?'

'Noomi, dear,' Binny said. 'You've been behaving bizarrely since you landed in Kamalpur. Do you know that Sheila called me last night, absolutely hysterical? You were screaming so loud the neighbours came over.' She began walking towards me, lamplight filtering through her nightie, her carroty legs silhouetted against my bed. 'A few nights under a professional's care couldn't hurt.'

'I am fine,' I said. 'Don't touch me!'

'Enough!' Binny said. 'We've had enough of your havoc. Look at your poor grandmother. Have you ever seen her cry like this?' Her grip was strong. 'You're going, whether you like it or not.'

The bedroom door flew open once again. Binny, who'd put her hand on the knob, was knocked flat backwards on her ass. Asha rushed in and put her body in front of mine. 'You're not taking her,' she said, her voice low, yet firm. 'They don't treat women like human beings in those places. Binny, Lily Mama, you both need to leave our house at once.'

'Asha, I told you already – stay out of this,' Lily Mama said, bustling across the room. 'You're making it harder for me to do this.' She took Binny's hand and pulled her up with an unfeminine grunt.

Asha showed them her cell phone with the number already punched in. 'I will call the police.'

Something that felt like love, or perhaps gratitude, for my mother welled up inside my heart.

'You can't drag the police into a family matter,' Binny said. Her plan was quietly backfiring. She'd banked on Asha's obedience, on her lack of any maternal instinct.

Asha held the door open. 'You have a minute to leave this house,' she said, her voice like iron.

'Come, Lily Mama,' Binny said, taking my distraught grandmother's arm. 'They are beyond all help.'

'Noomi,' Lily Mama said, crying, 'please, I'm begging you. Let me help before it's too late.'

'This isn't over,' Binny said. 'I'm going to tell Veer all about what happened tonight, Noomi.'

'Go ahead. Veer is *my* family,' I spat. 'Mine. He's not going to trust anything you say to him.'

Asha and I watched Binny and Lily Mama leave. Once they'd gone, Asha accepted a hug from me but didn't give one back in return. She turned and trudged down the hall – looking tired, so very tired.

'Thank you, Mama,' I said. 'For coming back.'

'I'll tell Shanta Bai to warm up your dinner,' Asha said over her shoulder.

Rain sizzled outside my bedroom window. I shucked off my smelly clothes and crawled into bed. My cell phone lit up and began to buzz. Annoyed, I picked it up. A text from Veer.

WAT U UP TO BABE? LUV YOU. FLIGHT AT 7AM. SEE U TOM.

I tossed the phone to the floor. Tomorrow. Tomorrow hovered over my life like a guillotine. Under the sheets, my bare legs felt cool, smooth. Hoping for some kind of peace, I slipped a hand past the waistband of my underwear and tried to unravel the coil of my body. But alcohol works like an anaesthetic between your legs too. I gave up, feeling disgusted. You need to sleep, said a voice. A nice, deep sleep will soothe your heartache. I groped around on my bedside table for the blue pills that Asha had left, and then I began to take them all, one by one.

IN MY DREAM, I was back at the cemetery parking lot. Jeh and I sat on the waist-high brick wall that separated the lot from a cliff-drop into a forest gulley. Dawn broke operatically, singing arias of pink clouds and golden-orange sunrays. Unafraid that my legs were dangling over what appeared to be an infinite fall, I put my head in the dip of Jeh's shoulder. The smell of him, Old Spice and sweat. It struck me afresh how much it hurt to miss him. I took his hand and felt the familiar rough-dry skin of his palm. When Jeh spoke, his voice was exactly his.

'So,' Jeh said, smiling his Mona Lisa smile. 'Here we are.'

'Yes, but where are we?' I said, tears streaming down my face.

'You should know,' Jeh pointed to the sky and the gleaming forest below. 'You've built all of this.'

'What about that spot?' I pointed towards a place covered by the shadow of a vast, dark cloud.

Jeh smiled. How much I missed that smile. 'That,' he said, 'is an undiscovered country.' He wiped the corners of my eyes and said, 'Piglet. Your life wasn't meant to be easy. It'll get better, though. We're so much more than the sum of all the things we've done,' Jeh said, stroking my hair.

'I want to go back home,' I said. 'I don't want to die. Please.'

Jeh turned to me, his face shining. 'Give me your hand.'

THE BED I WOKE up in smelled unfamiliar, like cotton sheets washed with industrial soap and left to dry in the sun. A rough woollen blanket was pulled up to my midriff. I realized I wasn't at home.

'Noomi.' Veer's face swam into focus. He held my hand. Behind his head, I saw that I was in a room with plain white walls, with bars on a window, and a framed poster on the door of a kitten holding on to a branch, its hind paws dangling in the air, that said: *Hang in there!*

'What happened?' I asked. My head throbbed powerfully. I tried to bring my hand up to my face but couldn't – I was hooked by a catheter to an IV slowly dripping liquid. Panic spread in my chest. I breathed fast, as dark spots mushroomed in my vision. 'Where the fuck am I?'

'It's okay,' Veer said, stroking my head. 'You'll be fine. They found you in time.' I saw my reflection in his glasses. My hair was a mess. My eyes were small and bloodshot. I looked like a sick, sad child.

'Where am I?'

'This is a hospital room,' Veer said, pressing his palm to my face. 'Here, drink.' He brought me a glass from the nightstand. The cold water felt like razorblades going down my throat.

'Why can't I swallow?' I said, sitting up and grabbing my throat with both hands. 'It hurts.'

'Lucky for us, Shanta Bai brought dinner to your room last night,' Veer said, putting the glass on the stand. 'She said you were snoring in a strange way. When she tried to wake you, your head lolled on your chest. She immediately went and got your mom. Asha searched your bed and found the empty pack of sleeping pills. They shook you awake and made you drink a lot of saltwater. Then Asha put a finger down your throat and forced you to throw up.'

'Is my mother here?' I said. Dizziness struck my head like a hammer.

'Shh, shh, lie back down,' Veer said. 'She's staying at her friend Rhea's. I'll call her for you.'

Asha's voice sounded as if she was calling from outer space. I could barely understand her, so I said that I took too many pills by accident and I'd talk to her later. She seemed eager to believe me.

'That wasn't the truth,' I said handing the phone back to Veer. 'I didn't take those pills by accident.'

People trapped in a burning building will sometimes jump out the window, preferring to leap to their death rather than be eaten slowly by raging flames. After I'd taken one pill, I convinced myself to take another, another, another, like some kind of dare, until I could no longer lift my hand to my mouth. Then there was nothing except the noise of the rain.

'Why Noomi?' Veer lifted his glasses and pinched the bridge of his nose. 'I don't understand.'

The door opened with a little knock. A nurse in a white sari and canvas sneakers walked in to check on my IV. Mrs Malhotra isn't allowed more than one visitor at a time, she said, doctor's orders.

Mrs Wadia was waiting outside. Could Mr Malhotra let her have a turn?

'No problem,' Veer flashed his corporate guy smile. 'I'll see you soon, sweetheart,' he said to me.

'Veer ... Binny,' I said, grabbing his wrist. 'Has she ... has she been talking to you?'

'We'll talk about it when you're feeling better,' Veer said.

'Please,' I pulled him closer. 'Tell me what she said.'

'Please stay calm,' the nurse said, fixing a new bag on my IV. 'Or I'll have to add a sedative to this.'

'That won't be necessary,' Veer snapped at her. 'Finish whatever you're doing and leave us.'

The nurse spoiled her neat, pretty features by making a face. She finished her task and left.

'Be careful,' I said to Veer with a smile. 'She might put an air bubble in my drip.'

'Don't waste your time with Binny,' Veer said, holding my hand again. 'I told her to fuck off.'

'Thank you,' I said, my vision blurry with tears. 'Thank you, Veer. I really mean it. I love you.'

I LEFT THE HOSPITAL three days later. Veer flew back to Bombay with a promise that he'd return for me. Lily Mama tipped the hospital staff a ridiculous amount. That was her love language.

The first thing I did was call Jung. She said that she was sorry I'd felt alone enough to take those pills, and glad that Veer had shut Binny's discord-factory down. The next thing I did was to spend the day emptying out Jeh's closet and giving his clothes away to a home. All except for the shirt laid out on the chair.

That I saved. Asha came home from Rhea's place and – predictably – flipped out.

'How could you?' she said. 'You should've asked if I wanted to keep anything!'

I gave her Jeh's shirt, folded, ironed and wrapped in paper. 'Here, this is for you.'

Asha looked at me like a dog running after a car that stopped – she didn't know what to do.

'Thanks,' she said, holding the packet. 'Although I wish you hadn't laundered out his smell.'

'There's something else I want to give you,' I said, handing Asha a file.

'What's this?' she frowned.

'This was Dad's will. Read it. You'll realize that he always loved you,' I said, holding the papers out.

Asha put the shirt under her arm and took the file; her hand dipped slightly from its weight.

'How are you feeling?' she said, looking at me. 'I was scared I was going to lose you.'

'I'll be okay,' I nodded. 'We are more than the sum of all the things we've done.'

As promised, Veer flew back to pick me up, and we were set to return on Sunday.

The hour before we left, I spent walking around the garden. I stopped by the wall against which my little hut used to lean. The stone was cool, rough, like my father's hands. I rested my head on it, feeling a stab of pity for the little girl who used to hide by herself in this place.

They'd dug Milo's grave under the pink champa tree. Jeh had swiped the champa as a sapling for Lily Mama from the traffic island on M.G. Road. Pink champas were rare. I plucked a few flowers to place on Milo's grave, and put my hand in the earth to feel it thrum as it worked to take back his body.

The car honked in the driveway. They were done loading the suitcases. I stood up, put the rest of the flowers in my bag, and gave the garden a last, long look.

When Lily Mama put her hand on my head to say goodbye, I felt a twinge of heartache, like pain in a phantom limb. Zal Papa asked me when I would come back – *with Veer* – to visit. I lied, 'Very soon.'

On our way to the airport, I asked if we could stop for a moment at the cemetery. I took out the pink champa flowers, crushed and bruised from being in my bag, and scattered them on grave number 125. I should've brought mogras, as those had been Jeh's favourite. But then I saw a terracotta bowl, the kind Lily Mama used as birdbaths. It was full of mogras – white flowers whose small size belied a strong, mesmerizing scent.

'I'm sorry,' I said to the stranger's grave. I turned and walked away, thinking about what Lily Mama had said to me in the hospital. After Veer left, the door was held open by a ward boy and Lily Mama had shuffled in. She sat in the chair that Veer had pulled up to my bedside.

'Did you know that Jeh was born in this hospital?' Lily Mama had said. 'Sometimes I wish he could be born all over again. So I'd get a chance to do things differently.' She unclasped her purse and pulled out a black-and-white picture from it: Jeh wrapped in a swaddle, looking like a baby elf. 'He was early, and so little,' she parted her forefinger and thumb. 'After I'd nursed him, Zal walked around the hallway with Jeh, saying to any nurses or doctors who passed by: "Say hello to my new pocket edition son."'

'Daddy was always his favourite,' I smiled. 'Was he a good child?'

Lily Mama treated me to her Mona Lisa smile. 'Mostly,' she laughed. 'But he could be very bad too. One time, he jumped up on to my aunt's dining table and swung on the crystal chandelier with a belt, shouting, "Me Tarzan!" The whole bloody thing came crashing down – the crystal sounded like chattering teeth.' Lily Mama covered her smile with her hand. 'Jeh hid like a cat. I looked in all the bedrooms. "I won't get angry," I said, to get him to come out. And he did, after many hours. He was tiny, you see. He'd hidden under the bed, squeezed between suitcases.'

'Did you keep your word?' I asked. 'Or did you punish him?'

'Oh yes,' Lily Mama, said, chuckling. 'I thrashed him with the same belt.'

'Why couldn't you have lied,' I said, feeling sad, 'and not told me that?'

Lily Mama winced. It looked, oddly, like the beginnings of a smile. 'There are times,' she said, her voice breaking softly, 'when we do awful things, believing we're acting out of love.'

The door opened. The nurse poked her head in. She had a broad middle part, a streak of red sindoor through it. 'Madam, your driver is here,' the nurse said. 'Visiting hours are over.'

Lily Mama put her hand on mine. Large tears ran down her face. 'Don't scare me like this again.'

'I'm sorry, Lily Mama,' I said.

'When they took you to the hospital,' Lily Mama said, 'your eyes were rolling in your head. It was so frightening. I couldn't sleep. Finally, I looked up and shouted, "Jeh! Your daughter needs you!" Thank god your grandfather is half deaf, otherwise he'd have woken up and had a heart attack.'

'He did come,' I said, grabbing her hand as she was about to leave. 'We had a long talk.'

'He was always an obedient son.'

Lily Mama smiled. On her way out the door, she paused to straighten up a pile of my clothes on a chair. A lamp illuminated half of her face, while the other half remained in shadows.

PART FOUR

THE DOCTORS' HANDS MOVED like shadow puppets behind the pale blue surgical sheet, as they cut a smile into my belly. A half hour ago, they'd given me an epidural, so all I felt was a tugging below my navel. A strange pulse started beating inside my head and died out as soon as the baby appeared, mewling like a kitten. I tried to get a glimpse of her face on the other side of the partition.

The doctors sewed me together, chatting over my body like they'd run into each other at a buffet. A nurse said, 'You're doing great, Mama,' into my ear as she took my shrieking baby to wipe away the grey-white goop that covered her like model clay. I realized that Veer had been holding my hand when he dropped it and followed the nurse. I heard the sly click of a phone camera. Veer returned with a picture of a pink, scrunched-up face. Our baby looked displeased, groggy, as if we'd suddenly switched on all the lights in her bedroom.

'Six pounds, eight ounces,' Veer smiled.

'What sweet little rosebud lips,' I said. 'Can I hold her now?'

The kindly nurse brought the baby over in her peach-fuzz arms, wrapped up warm and dry. My daughter, unamused at being born, pinch-faced in her blue-and-white blanket, wearing a little hat. She undid the swaddling and put her on my chest.

This baby weighed as much as a cat, I thought and took one tiny hand. I smiled as her translucent jelly fingers curled around mine.

'Thank you for being perfect,' I whispered into her pink shell ear. 'Your name is Maya.'

'Noomi, come on, smile for the family back in India,' Veer said. He lifted his phone high above our heads for a picture. My face was like a puffy mushroom, my arms full of tubes, holding our daughter. 'I said smile! Argh, never mind.' He flipped the camera, got in with us, made a victory sign and took a number of rapid selfies. I managed to smile in at least a few.

Three years had passed since my father died, when Veer's company assigned him a short-term work transfer to New York. Even though I was four months pregnant, I was eager to go. If getting away was possible, then so, perhaps, was another life. One where I could be a good person, perhaps even a good mother. I'd held the pregnancy test in both my hands, waiting on our small balcony for Veer to come home. He arrived at the usual time, his shirt, crisp when he left in the morning, now wilted from the heat. He held two shopping bags full of new clothes.

'There was a sale on men's formal wear at Zara,' he shrugged. 'I'll need sweaters in New York.'

I turned towards him, holding out the plastic stick with two lines. 'I'm pregnant again,' I said.

'What?' Veer dropped his bags and strode up on to the balcony. He leaned one hand on the railing and covered his face with the other one. 'What? How? Are you sure?' he said, frowning at me.

'The lines don't lie,' I said, slipping the test into his shirt pocket.

'Ew, what the fuck, Noomi?' Veer took it out and held it between his fingertips. 'It's got pee on it.'

'I know,' I said. 'I'm the one whose pee it is.' I looked down to the driveway, where three little boys were playing cricket. Crows cawed in the trees, and the sea, always close, breathed and raged.

'So, what do you want to do?' Veer asked, frowning. 'Shall I make an appointment with Dr Mistry?'

One of the boys swung his bat and hit the red cricket ball so hard it flew up and into our apartment. Veer managed to block it from breaking our windows. 'Arey, watch what you're doing!' he yelled.

'Sorry, sorry, sorry,' the boys cried together. 'Please, bhaiya, we'll be careful. Give it back, na.'

Veer threw the ball at them. Then he looked at me, his face stamped with a question mark. 'So?'

'I want to have it,' I said, staring out at the sea. 'I feel,' I looked at Veer, 'it'll be different this time.'

Letting out a groan, Veer folded his arms. 'Are you sure?' he said, nodding at the boys. 'You want one of those? They seem to be a lot of work.' He squeezed my shoulder. 'You're not scared?'

'Terrified,' I said, smiling up at him. 'But I need,' I hugged my stomach with both hands, searching for the right words, 'I have all this, I don't know what to call it,' I shrugged, 'I guess, for lack of a better word, love. Love with nowhere for it to go. It's like,' I paused, 'like having lots of money but nothing to spend it on.' I leaned my head on the balcony door. 'I need a place to put all of it down.'

Veer was sceptical, but the lure of having an American child, one born with opportunities stuffed inside her like springy snakes in a prank Pringles can, won out. We packed up our apartment in Bandra and applied for visas. Feeling audacious, we researched rents, salaries and childcare costs.

I discovered that when you're pregnant, people love telling you horrible stories as if that might help. Lily Mama called every Sunday to see how I was doing. She'd recount the latest birth horror someone had told her over tea. 'You know Silloo Patel, my friend who lives in Civil Lines? Her eldest daughter had to be induced. But the umbilical cord got wound around the baby's neck, so she had to have an emergency C-section. Something went wrong, and now the poor girl can't pee or poop and has to go to physiotherapy for six months.'

'Lily Mama,' I said, 'why do you keep telling me these things?'

'Just be prepared for anything, love,' Lily Mama said. A pause. 'Remember what happened with your mother? I don't want you to be caught in that situation.'

'I remember,' I said. 'But please stop telling me these stories. You're not helping.'

I called Asha with the news of our impending move. Her response was infuriatingly predictable.

'Oh, so lucky you are!' she exclaimed. 'Going to America with your husband, having a baby. I wish something like that had happened to me. Maybe my life would've been different then.' She paused to let out a sigh. 'Now you'll be off, while I'm stuck here, getting sicker and sicker every day.'

'Mom,' I said, sitting down slowly on the sofa. 'The doctor said the new arthritis medicines will help, but only if you don't drink.' I picked up a mug of tea from the table.

'Don't lecture me, Noomi,' she snapped. 'I'm the one whose body is falling apart, not you.'

'Madamji, we are done packing up the bedroom.' The young man the moving company had sent that afternoon came into the living room, sweating, wiping the back of his neck with a handkerchief.

'Thank you,' I said, and gave him a tip. I wondered if he could make out that I was pregnant. I felt like a smuggler, sometimes. I imagined the foetus as a big bag of contraband goods under my T-shirt.

'You need to sign this,' the man said, holding out a paper stuck to a dirty board.

'Mom,' I said into the phone, 'I've got to go.'

'When are you leaving?' Asha said.

'Tomorrow.'

'Call me when you get there.'

'Okay,' I said, getting up to look for a pen.

'I'll miss you.'

'That's nice.'

'Aren't you going to say you'll miss me?'

'I'll miss you,' I said robotically. 'Now I've got to go.'

'Call me when you board the flight.'

'I'm not calling you when I board, Mom,' I said. I found a ballpen in the kitchen drawer and signed the paper, holding the phone under my chin. 'Thank you,' I said to the man once more.

'What did you say?' Asha's voice had that edge I remembered from childhood, the one it took on before she gave me a slap. 'Speak up, I can't hear you. Will you call me when you board?'

'Yes, okay,' I sighed. 'I'll call you when I board. Now please, let me hang up.'

'Tch, tch, tch, so lucky,' Asha said. 'Such a lucky girl.' I imagined her slowly shaking her head.

'Bye, Mom,' I said, and cut the call.

We landed in JFK on a glum, rainy day in July, a week before I turned thirty. Veer invited his cousin, Diya, Kitty's daughter, for dinner at a mall in Paramus, as we were staying in a hotel there until we found an apartment in New York City.

'The Cheesecake Factory, really, when there's all of Manhattan to choose from. You guys are fobby, I must say.' Diya took a sip of her drink, leaving red lipstick on the brined rim. For all her nose-upturning at Cheesecake Factory, she sure seemed to love its margaritas. This was her fourth.

'You'll have to show us around Manhattan, Diya.' Veer gave her a toothy smile. 'I'm dying to see the Empire State Building, the Statue of Liberty and Times Square. And Central Park.'

Diya, whose buffed skin was the exact colour of a besan laddu, tousled her blonde-streaked hair, wrinkled her nose, and said, 'Only tourists go to all those places.'

'Well, that's what we are,' I smiled at her poisonously. 'A pair of fobby tourists.'

'Huh,' Diya pouted. 'Maybe you should try being less sarcastic with your husband's relatives.'

'Don't mind her. All hormones.' Veer slid his eyes at his cousin, winding a finger next to his head.

'I can't imagine,' Diya sniffed. 'Being so round and puffy mustn't be good for one's mental state.'

'I'm surprised you can't imagine, Diya didi,' I said. 'Being peri-menopausal must feel the same way.'

Veer, desperate to change the conversation, cleared his throat and offered to drive Diya back to the city in his new company car. 'Okay,' Diya said. 'But I don't have much faith in your desi driving skills.'

'If you can drive in India, you can drive anywhere,' Veer said, with bravado I knew he didn't feel.

They dropped me off at the hotel, and so I spent the remainder of my last baby-free birthday in a hotel room, watching television and picking at leftovers from a Styrofoam box. A year ago, being abandoned on my birthday would've sparked a brushfire of rage and resentment that could only be dowsed with vodka. But now, I was as sober as Mother Teresa. I wish I had some kind of epiphany to share, or that I'd found a great guru or a new philosophy to help me stay sober. The plain fact was that I had terrible morning sickness: the sight of alcohol made my stomach turn. It was like having a hangover. All the time. I'd learned that sobriety stemmed from being okay with feeling not okay.

But now that I wasn't drinking, I was bored. I got under the fluffy, clean-smelling comforter on the high hotel bed and turned on my laptop to browse the internet, etc. I'd become addicted to the dopamine reward of googling random questions that popped into my head. Why do cats sound like babies? Why is yawning contagious? Do all mammals love their offspring? Why do birds fly in circles? Why does schizophrenia not afflict the blind?

A notification bloomed in one corner of my laptop's screen. 'Sid Sehgal posted new photos.' Despite knowing better, I clicked on it. There was Sid, partying all over fucking Prague with Anushka. And ... Ammu and Shivraj? Since when did the four of them holiday together? A spike of jealousy grew out of my heart like an orchid. I studied their laughing faces and their white teeth. In every photo, Anushka did a duck face, threw up a peace sign, or stuck out her tongue. Ammu looked content with Shiv's arm wrapped around her waist. What was I supposed to post?

A selfie of me sitting alone in a hotel room in New Jersey on my birthday?

My phone buzzed with a text. It was Veer.

WAT'S UP? ALMOST HOME. LOVE YOU.

I typed, 'Don't look at your phone while driving, stupid,' and smiled at the next text: a blurry view of the Empire State Building, its spindle wreathed in a laurel of moonlit clouds. I posted it.

THE FIRST NIGHT AFTER giving birth, pressure cuffs had gently massaged my calves, a prophylaxis against blood clots. I had to sleep sitting up so as not to bust open my tender stitches, and dreamed my milk came in, but instead of milk, it was red wine. I put my baby to my breast only to find that she was an old woman with a fluffy skull. She suckled toothlessly. Her hands clawed the sides of my breast.

At dawn, I woke up to the squeak of trolley wheels as the blonde nurse brought Maya, in a clear plastic crib, to my bedside. I sat up straighter, wincing with pain, and stretched out my arms, which were attached to an IV of Motrin. I'd refused the Percocet on offer, afraid I'd never wean myself off. 'Plus, it makes you poop concrete,' the nurses said. 'The moms on Percocet are all very constipated.'

'Good to know,' I said.

The nurse placed Maya in my arms. She showed me how to insert my nipple into her mouth. Maya began to cry, her mouth pink and cavernous like the belly of a whale. After a couple of clumsy tries, she latched on. I sighed with relief, but a blood pressure machine on my right showed the numbers going up. A mother for less than forty-eight hours, I was already terrible at it.

After ten minutes, Maya got tired of sucking and fell asleep. My milk hadn't come in yet, but the nurse said that she'd still benefit from the teaspoonful of colostrum.

'The more she stimulates your ducts, the faster your milk will show up,' said the nurse, who, in my head, I'd named Dianne after Dianne Wiest. She had the same smizey face. 'When she's asleep, you should use a breast pump so that your supply won't dwindle. It's going to hurt at first. Your nipples will probably crack and bleed a bit. Tell your husband to buy you lanolin ointment.' The nurse wrote 'lanolin' in neat, Catholic-school cursive on a notepad, tore out the page and gestured towards Veer, who was snoring like a chainsaw on the narrow blue sofa next to my bed. As if he was the one who'd given birth. I threw a pillow at him.

He snorted awake and looked at me. 'What?' he said, blinking slowly.

The milk, when it came in, was like a firehose. Maya would choke, and then scream like I was trying to murder her. I had to nurse her while lying on my back to slow down the flow, with Maya lying on my stomach, her mouth plugged on to my nipple. We looked like a pair of sea otters. I'd read that otters link their arms while sleeping so that the sea doesn't sweep them apart. Maya only drank two ounces at a time, and then fell asleep with my nipple still in her mouth. I'd lay her down in the crib and pump the milk still aching in my breasts. I dated the bags and stored them next to the ice cream and frozen meat. Wasn't it sort of gross to keep my breast milk in the same place as the food, Veer asked. I told him to cook to free up the freezer space. He said he was too busy with work.

'We live in Manhattan now, babe,' he said. 'Order whatever it is you're craving.'

It turned out that the thing I craved was Shanta Bai's mutton dhansak. I decided to call my mother. I had to check on how Asha was doing anyway; the doctors had her on steroids for her arthritis. They made her face round, like a full moon. Sometimes we video-called, but only if I'd washed my hair and put on make-up, or else I'd spend the whole call listening to how I looked exhausted. Am I doing okay? Should she come visit? I didn't want my mother to visit. I called her randomly at night to make sure that she wasn't drinking. To my relief, she sounded sober. I asked her to put Shanta Bai on.

'Nooma,' Shanta Bai said, shouting into the phone. 'How are you my sweet darling girl?'

'I'm fine,' I replied, smiling. 'You don't have to shout, Shanta Bai. This isn't a trunk call.'

'How is Maya baby?' she asked. 'Is she a good happy child? Or a bad angry one, like you?'

'She is...' I paused, wondering what to say. 'She's her own person, I think.'

'Make sure you tie a black thread around her ankle to ward off the evil eye.'

'Shanta Bai' – I reached for a notepad on the table – 'tell me how to make your dhansak.'

After I'd written down Shanta Bai's recipe, we chatted for a while. I tried to describe my new life as best as I could. New York. The Upper East Side. Then Asha took back the phone.

'How is Maya?' she asked. 'Is she putting on weight? I hope you're making enough milk.'

'Too much milk,' I said. 'She's doing fine. And I'm fine too, thanks for asking.'

'Of course you're fine,' Asha snorted. 'You're a cockroach. Indestructible.'

'Yes, I'm a cockroach,' I said, rolling my eyes. 'Do you know that cockroach milk is one of the most nutritious substances on earth? It's better than cow's milk.'

'Oh yuck,' Asha said. 'That's so gross.'

I imagined her making the face she used to make when Jeh farted in bed.

'I realized something,' I said. 'I don't know if you ever breastfed me.'

'Sorry?'

'When I was a baby. Did you breastfeed me or did I have formula?'

'Formula?' Asha went shrill. 'God no! Only breast milk was good enough for your highness. You'd scream if I brought a bottle anywhere near you. You were exclusively breastfed.'

'Did you enjoy it?'

'Enjoy what?'

'Breastfeeding,' I said. 'Did you enjoy all that oxytocin release and what not?'

'It tied me down to home. I wanted to wean you quickly and get back to the kids at the orphanage. Now, they *really* needed me. But,' Asha sighed, 'you were stubborn – even as a baby. You weaned yourself off when you were ready.'

'I've always had my own back,' I said, feeling irritated. I looked at the picture on my bedside table. My mother and me in our garden. I have a toddler's hand outstretched towards a fat red rose, while she is smoking a cigarette with the hand that isn't supporting my diapered bottom. By her drowsy expression, I can tell it is very hot, and that Asha would rather be anywhere than with me.

'You're lucky,' Asha said. 'Maya seems like a sweet, easy-going child.'

'Unlike me, you mean,' I said.

'You said that – I didn't,' she chuckled.

'How do you know what she's like anyway?' I said. 'You haven't met her.'

'And whose fault is that?'

'Mom, we've been through this,' I said. 'The apartment isn't ready yet. I don't even have a guest bed.' I heard a cry. 'Okay, I have to go. Maya woke up. She needs to be fed.'

'Next time, at least make it a video-call so I can see my sweet baby.'

Maya was awake and making small pre-cry snuffles. Her head movements were animatronic, like ET. I smiled. 'Hi, Mayoo Jaan,' I said. She closed her eyes, frowning like she thought I was an idiot. I picked her up and put her to my nipple. It still felt bizarre to feed a person with something made from my body. It felt animalistic. When outside, I had to hide my nursing baby under a blanket. My mother's erratic moods had made me watchful as a child; now that watchfulness had a new purpose. Instead of my mother's face, it was my daughter's that I studied. Drooping corners of the mouth meant Maya would bring down the house if I didn't figure out what she needed immediately. Eye contact with grunts – poop was incoming. Hands flung above the head – contentment. A mouth in an O – wonder? Or gas? A red face and tight fists – anger. It was as if I'd been given an animal, a baby bear or a bird, eyes full of occult wildness, and been tasked to train it to be a person.

WITH MAYA STEADILY NURSING, I relaxed into my chair. My fear, before Maya was born, was what if the nursing made me too horny? My nipples were my number-one erogenous zone. Veer knew this. My ballooned, post-partum breasts excited him. The doctors said we should wait twelve weeks or so for my body to heal from the surgery. So, Veer suggested one afternoon, why not some heavy petting? Like teenagers. He was clearly unaware that giving birth had turned the valve of my libido to the off position, maybe permanently. I said we should wait, which made him sulk like I'd taken away his video games. Life in our cramped little apartment was unbearable as it was. I relented.

One Sunday, Veer hired a sitter to take Maya to a mommy-and-me class – enough time to get me in the 'mood'. As I took off my pyjamas, I thought: If Veer *really* wanted to turn me on, he'd clear the leaning tower of dishes in the sink, or wash the mound of laundry lying at the bottom of our closet.

'Nothing below the waist,' I warned as Veer crawled towards me on the bed, his erect penis pendulating between his thighs. Ribbons of afternoon light streamed in from the windows. A beam slanted across Veer's face, turning his eyes a honey brown. His abs looked like a candy bar. Veer worked out at the gym five times a week, while my belly sagged like a defeated boxer on the ropes. My breasts were of porn-worthy proportions with none of plastic surgery's gravity-defying perkiness. I lay on my back, hoping that it would at least make my boobs stand up like yurts.

From the state of his penis, it appeared Veer didn't mind my flabby belly, and for a brief moment, I was grateful that he still desired my tired body. Then gratitude was replaced with resentment, at the thought that he got to keep his abs. I was so annoyed that I didn't notice Veer taking my left nipple between his lips. Only when he jerked his head away and spat breast milk on to our sheets, staining them a translucent yellow, did I realize that my breasts had begun spontaneously erupting.

'What the fuck! Why are your boobs doing that?' Veer cried out, disgusted.

'Sorry,' I said, getting off the bed. Drops of milk spattered across the floor as I walked to the dining table. I sat down on a silk cushion that felt cold and slippery under my naked bottom, took out my pump, and began filling up bag after bag. Finally, my breasts became empty and floppy. Veer came over and draped a light shawl over my goose-fleshed shoulders, throwing me a sorry look as he gathered up the bags. He opened the freezer door, and a sigh escaped him like air from a bicycle tyre. Milk bags were stuffed in all the corners, wedged in the crevices between our frozen leftovers.

'Should you see a doctor?' Veer looked down at me with real concern. 'Is this normal?'

'Of course, it's normal,' I said. 'What would I tell them? Help, I'm making too much milk?' I gave him a look. 'You know how doctors treat women who complain about nothing.'

'What the hell should I do with all of these milk bags?' Veer asked, slamming the fridge door.

'I don't fucking know,' I yelled, covering my breasts with the silk cushion as I ran to the bathroom. I needed to shower away my rage and embarrassment. 'Make ice cream!'

'Perhaps we should call our family to come help,' Veer said a few minutes later from the other side of the bathroom door. I'd finished shampooing my hair, and had turned the water hot, letting it pummel my unhappy shoulders. 'Who?' I shouted, lathering under my armpits. 'Who do we call? I cannot deal with your parents right now, Veer.'

'Why?' Veer sounded exasperated. 'My mom loves babies. She would be amazing.'

'Are you joking?' I yelled, scrubbing hard. 'Have you forgotten the gift they sent with Diya?'

'What gift?' Veer asked.

I turned off the shower for a moment, 'They sent Maya a doll, Veer. A baby doll.'

'So?'

'Isn't it obvious?' I leaned my head against the tile. 'She's just been born and they're ready to groom her for future motherhood.' I wiggled a finger in my ear. 'It's so sexist.'

Three days ago, my mother-in-law had called me at 5 a.m. – a reminder to fast for Veer's long life that day. I'd put Maya down after her first feed of the morning. Parul wanted to 'wish me a good fast' and make sure I'd prepared the thali and the sargi meal. I shook Veer awake and handed him the phone, telling him to let his mother know I'd rather throw myself into the East River.

'You're acting crazy,' Veer said.

'Whatever,' I said. 'Your parents are not coming.' I turned the water back on. 'And that's that.'

'How about your mom?' Veer said, tapping what sounded like his wedding ring on the door. 'She's been dying to come see Maya. She keeps emailing me, asking for new pictures.'

'No!' I shouted, turning off the water again. My voice echoed off the bathroom tiles. 'No. I can't deal with her when I'm like this.' I wrapped a towel over my head, wrinkling my nose at the smell of my shampoo. I'd washed my hair with an Ayurvedic potion the colour and smell of tar that my mother said stopped hair fall. It hadn't, but I used it anyway. 'She can't see me like this.'

'She can't see you like what?' Veer said.

'Like,' I said, rubbing my body so hard it turned pink. 'Like I don't know what I'm doing.'

'You're being stubborn again,' Veer said. 'You're more like your mother than you realize.'

I came out of the shower feeling tired. Veer said he was off to the gym. We heard the sitter come in through the front door. Veer paid her before he left. I heard her laughing, a bit flirtatiously, at something he said. From the quality of Maya's wailing, I knew she was hungry. I threw on a dressing gown, took Maya from the smiling babysitter with a curt nod, and carried her back into the bedroom. Wearily, I felt the milk filling up in response to her howls. Maya gobbled up my nipple, thwacking at my breast with her fists. When that no longer entertained her, she grabbed the end of my towel turban. My damp hair tumbled over us like a black curtain, ragged as rain.

VEER DECIDED TO 'SURPRISE' me by buying Asha a ticket. After screaming at him for an hour, I gave up. Something was better than nothing, Veer said. When I saw Asha walking out of the airport terminal, rumpled clothes, sallow face, hair sticking up from the twenty-hour journey, my heart dropped into my shoes. She looked very ill. We hugged briefly. Pulling back, I studied her face, which I knew better than my own. A mother is the first mirror in which we see ourselves. But what if the mirror you look into is broken? You might see yourself always in pieces, no use to anyone, and take that as the truth.

When she saw Maya snuggled against me in the baby carrier, Asha's angry face melted into a smile. She lifted Maya out and took a deep whiff off the top of her head. It ambushed me, how much Asha would dote on Maya. She was a fairy-tale grandma, reading to her, burping her, changing her diapers. On sunny days, she'd carry Maya up to the picture window in our living room, which held a jigsaw-piece view of the New York City skyline, and whisper stories into her small ears. Two weeks with us, and Asha's face became clear and oval again. Her horseshoe-like dark circles disappeared.

With me, however, she was the same old mother, grinding me down with her anger, her dissatisfaction. Why haven't you lost the baby weight? Why don't you people ever cook? She'd tell stories that I'd heard many times already, snapping like a piranha if I didn't pay attention: 'So sorry I'm not interesting enough!' I felt her tapping at the walls of my new-found sobriety, trying to find a hollow sound. In a month, my mind began to retreat into its old self-destructive ways of thinking.

A week before she was supposed to head back to India, Asha lost her passport. So of course I had to drop whatever I was doing to help her look. As the hours passed and we couldn't find it, Asha started to wind herself up. She had this weird anxious tic, a sharp intake of breath, like a hiss. The more worried Asha got, the more it sounded as if there were a snake loose in the apartment.

'Will you calm down?' I said. 'The passport doesn't have legs, you know, it hasn't walked out of the house.' I went to the bedroom and threw off her duvet. 'It's got to be in your room somewhere.'

'I am calm, okay, Noomi,' Asha said, rifling through her handbag. 'Where the fuck did I last see it?' She pulled out a ballpoint pen, absent-mindedly put it in her mouth and chewed the end. I knew she was dying for a smoke. And a drink, most probably. 'Keep looking for it.'

I got on my hands and knees, and looked under the bed, irritated that I had to spend Maya's naptime looking for Asha's stupid passport, instead of taking a nap myself. My mother was a selfish, joyless, frustrating ... oh wait, there it was, the passport, stuck between the bed slats.

'Found it,' I said, standing up. A picture fell from between its pages. It was of a man, around my age. He was on a beach. His skin was a dark brown, and his teeth were white, a first-world white. Next to him stood a tall, blonde woman, holding a little girl with skin and hair the colour of clover honey. They looked happy. I felt a twinge of jealousy – wondering if Veer, Maya and I might look like that someday.

'Do you know who that is?' Asha asked, pointing at the man.

'No,' I said, studying the picture. 'Who is it?'

'That's Raju, the baby you picked up from our doorstep,' my mother smiled. 'A family in Amsterdam adopted him. That's his wife, Annelise, and their daughter, Swati.'

'They're beautiful.' I smiled and gave back the photograph. 'He got really lucky.'

'When you were growing up, no one cared about my orphanage kids. Not your father, nor your grandparents, nor you. But the work I did, it mattered, Noomi,' Asha said with a note of longing in her voice. 'You were always clinging to me. But I was never enough for you.'

'*I* was never enough for *you*.' I threw the passport at her.

I CALLED JUNG IN Bombay for advice on how to deal with Asha.

'Noomi,' she said, 'you don't have to be triggered by every single thing your mother says.'

'But how?' I said. 'It's the whole tightrope act. Asha's always out to prove that I'm a terrible person. I don't love her, I'm rude, I suffocated her career when I was a child. Then she turns around and starts complaining that I have so many pictures of my dad all over the apartment, but just the one of her.'

'It's interesting that Asha pointed out the lack of photographs, but never asked what she did to make you not want her photographs,' Jung said, being uncharacteristically to the point.

'That's true,' I said. 'She's never talked about the things that she did to us. It's only what was done to her that keeps coming up.' I hit the table with my palm. 'That's all she remembers.'

'Noomi,' Jung said, her tone softening, 'you're not a bad person because your mother says so. I want you to understand that. Remind yourself that you are good. Be gentle with you.'

'Thank you,' I said and paused to stifle a sob. 'I've been feeling so lonely since she arrived. I brought Maya into this world so I wouldn't feel alone in it – but having Asha here negates everything.'

'Asha's mind is shattered,' Jung said. 'Whatever it reflects will always appear as a distortion.'

If Veer was late, or travelling for work, Asha and I would eat dinner in front of the television, in part because we both enjoyed American TV, its mindless energy, and in part to avoid having to talk. On the news, lately, there'd been chatter about a hurricane – but not any old hurricane, a 'once-in-a-hundred-years' storm. Lovely word: Hur. Ri. Cane. It sounded like a poem. Viewed from a satellite, the monstrous storm looked like a flying Catherine wheel made of clouds and rain. Or like whipped cream swirling in a huge blue porcelain bowl.

Asha and I watched the news while Maya napped in a bassinet next to us, arms flung above her head. President Obama updated the reporters gathered around him in a scrum. He pursed his thin lips when they asked about the scale of the disaster, as if the hurricane were an ill-behaved guest.

'No-drama Obama.' Asha smiled, pressing the volume-up button on the remote. 'He reminds me of your father. Reliable. Relatable. Always does exactly what he says he's going to do.'

I looked at her sideways. Asha never had a nice thing to say about Jeh when he was alive. In death, she gushed about him like a schoolgirl fan. 'Dad was actually useless in an emergency.

Remember that time I broke my wrist? He took us to the wrong hospital. You yelled at him on the street.'

Asha gave me a look as angry as a bird's eye chilli. 'Everyone has their flaws. Your dad was one of the smartest people I've ever met. He'd read everything. Everything! When he died, it was like a library burned down.' She pointed a finger. 'Why would you talk about him like that?'

'What the hell, Mom!' I said. 'You spent every minute of Dad's life criticizing him. You made both our lives a nightmare. Now that he's no longer around' – I took the remote from her to switch channels – 'you've turned him into some kind of a saint.' I looked at her. 'What's changed all of a sudden?'

'You're very cruel, Noomi, do you know that?' Asha snatched the remote back. 'Go away and let me watch the news in peace.'

I was angry but stayed quiet so as not to wake up Maya. The news channels couldn't get enough of this 'Frankenstorm'. TV anchors brought on a kickline of experts with charts, graphs, spaghetti models. In the next forty-eight hours, four days before Halloween, they predicted that the hurricane, which was flying north off the east coast, would turn sharp left and slam the New York City area. In the bassinet, Maya wriggled, then threw out her hands, scrunched her face, and revved up to bawl. I scooped her up in my arms, making the whooshing noise that baby books said mimicked the womb.

'You know, you'll spoil her by all this picking up.' Asha turned the TV volume higher.

'Ugh, my breasts are leaking,' I said, trying to fix my nipple into Maya's tiny lips. 'I need to lie down with her,' I plunked down on the sofa and nudged Asha with my hip. 'Ma, move to that chair.'

'Go to the bedroom,' Asha said, flipping to another news channel. 'I want to watch TV.'

'I'm trying to get Maya to settle down.' I snatched the remote from her hand.

'I'm not your bloody peon,' Asha snapped. 'You can't order me around. Go here, go there.'

She got up and stomped off into the kitchen. Pressing Maya to my chest, I muted the TV and willed myself to lie down without getting into a fresh fight. I coaxed Maya to latch on. Breastfeeding had turned out to be the worst part of motherhood. Maya's cries made me feel weak. Or they brought forth bouts of rage, rushing out like blood clots from a broken nose. Where was Veer when I needed him? On a work trip somewhere in Bumberfuck, USA. He'd wheeled his bags out, and then came back through the door to kiss me. 'I'll be back before the show!'

There was a sound of glass breaking. With a hand under Maya's head, I rushed to the kitchen.

'What happened?' I asked. The lights in the ceiling made moons glow on the black-tiled floor. Across the moons was a comet's tail of broken glass: a bottle of expensive lemonade that I'd bought for myself as a treat. I was planning to drink it with ice in a wine glass.

Asha lowered herself to the floor. The inflamed joints of her knees made her wince with pain. She stumbled, toppled over, and was stabbed in the leg by a shard of glass. Blood poured out of the tear in her cotton pants. I put Maya back in the bassinet. She resumed her wailing as I fetched a dustpan from the closet. I began sweeping up the glass.

'Leave it be, Ma,' I said. 'There's bandages and ointment in the bathroom. Go clean up that cut.'

'Can't you get her to stop screaming? It makes me very anxious,' Asha said, holding her knee.

Whenever we'd speak on the phone, Asha always talked about how she couldn't wait to see Maya, how I was a terrible person to keep her only grandchild from her. I stared at her, incredulous.

'Don't make that face,' Asha said.

'What face?' I said.

'That contemptuous face,' Asha said. 'You've looked at me that way since you were a little girl.'

Maya let out another scream. Breast milk dripped from me on to the floor. I wiped the drops off with the towel I'd used to pick up the pieces of glass. I glared at Asha. 'How should I look at you?'

'A little appreciation would be nice.' Asha crossed her arms. 'For coming all this way to help.'

'Help?' I said, tossing the crunchy glass into the trash can. 'Is this what you call helping?' I went to the sink and scrubbed my hands in hot water. Maya's screams were so high-pitched it was a miracle the windows didn't shatter. I began anew the torturous process of getting my red, pucker-faced infant to accept my breast.

'You were more easy-going as a baby,' Asha said, coming up behind me. 'To relax you, I had the maid give you a massage. You should be massaging your baby too.'

'Stop acting like you were mother of the year, okay. Because you were anything but,' I said. Maya latched and finally started sucking hungrily. I slumped my shoulders and let out a sigh. 'And baby oil is dangerous for infants.'

'If you hate me so much,' Asha said quietly, 'why did you ask me to come all this way?'

'I didn't,' I said. 'Veer decided to surprise me by buying you a ticket.'

'Oh,' she said.

I sat down, putting the nursing pillow under my aching arms. 'The next thing I know, you're here.' I stroked the top of Maya's head. The urge to get drunk hijacked my brain. The Rat Park scientists had found out that alcohol mimics the comfort one feels in a parent's arms.

'Did I ever tell you that I chose to have a C-section?' I said, shifting Maya to my other breast.

'You wanted the easy way out.' Asha shrugged sullenly, sipping a cup of cold tea.

I turned my head to stare at her. 'There's nothing easy about having your body cut open. And this,' I added, indicating Maya at my breast, 'isn't easy. I wish you were more supportive.' Tears pricked my eyes. 'I was scared that,' I kissed Maya's head, 'if something went wrong during the birth...'

'Bullshit,' Asha said. 'When things don't go your way,' she slammed her mug down on the table, 'you find someone to blame. Me. Your husband. The whole bloody world.'

'What is wrong with you?' I said. 'Why can't you give me what I need, for once?'

'I don't know what you need, Noomi.' Asha stared at her feet, arms at her sides. 'I have nothing.' She showed me her empty hands. 'You're the one with everything. A husband, a beautiful child. And yet, you can't stop whining. Why won't you stop whining?'

Rage made the edges of my vision go dark. I needed to get out of the apartment, get away, or I'd explode. When Maya fell back asleep, her eyes half closed with the whites showing through like crescent moons, I put her in the bassinet. Without bothering to change out of my pyjamas or swipe on lipstick, I grabbed my coat. 'I'm going out for a walk,' I said over my shoulder.

'But Noomi, the hurricane,' Asha came trailing after.

'Relax,' I said. 'Landfall isn't until late tonight.'

AROUND THE BLOCK WAS a line of people huddled under their umbrellas, checking their phones, waiting to grab what remained on the almost bare shelves at the supermarket. Folding my arms against the rain, I walked past the shoppers towards a liquor store which, shockingly, had no queue. I paid for a vodka fifth and flashed a smile when the storeowner asked me if I was headed to a hurricane party.

'Sort of,' I said.

The East River usually billowed gently, like a silk scarf in the breeze. But the storm surge had made it gallop in crested waves up to the riverbank, spilling on to the boardwalk. The wind hissed through the trees, sounding like boiling water, plucking off what remained of their leaves. People around me held up phones, hair whipping across their faces, to film the surge. I ignored them and walked to the railing, unfazed by the dirty water soaking the cuffs of my pyjama bottoms. A plastic pumpkin, the sort kids use to carry treats, bobbed past me with a friendly, gap-toothed smile. I unscrewed the red cap of the vodka and kissed the bottle's mouth.

'Oho! Big American you'll become,' Zal Papa had said when I told him. 'There'll be no cook, no driver. You'll be back in a month or you'll start drinking. Remember, alcohol can be dangerous to a baby.'

'Not baby,' I said, flatly. 'Foetus.'

Zal Papa made it a point to call me at least twice a week. With the phone wedged between my chin and shoulder, I'd listen as he gave me the latest news about Kamalpur – who said what to whom at what party, who was having an affair, who'd built a new house, while I breastfed Maya or rocked her to sleep. His calls made me ache for home, but I was also relieved to be raising Maya far away.

The calls started off as light and funny, but then pivoted to amused disparagement on Zal Papa's end and slow-boiling rage on mine. Like a bird that builds a nest out of anything it finds on the ground – Zal Papa weaved criticism of me into every conversation:

'The pictures you sent of Maya are sweet. She looks like a good baby. When she's older, I must tell her what a difficult and angry child you were.'

'Your cousin Adil has moved into a flat. I must say he is very good at saving money. You on the other hand are not so good. I've heard you're spending your husband's money faster than he can earn it.'

I stopped taking his calls. And for the first time, there was no one to tell me who I was, how I should behave. Like roommates who become intimate with each other's habits and quirks, I began to get to know what I liked and didn't like. Instead of the words that had been used for me my entire life, I finally had the freedom to use words of my own choosing to describe myself.

But which words should I choose? Lonely, was one. Above the East River, flying in the murky sky, was a seagull whose call brought my eyes to it. The seagull was struggling to catch an updraft to glide on. Violent gusts of wind batted it away like an invisible hand. But the gull kept fighting the storm. For a moment, it looked like it would drown in that lead-coloured sky. Then it found a way to surf the air and sailed away, disappearing from sight like a remnant from a dream. In my next life, if there is such a thing as a next life, I want to come back as a bird. Watching the seagull was like being slapped by god. The vodka burned in my mouth; everything I'd lose by getting drunk flew across my mind like a flock of birds. I closed my eyes, spat the alcohol out and wiped my mouth with my sleeve. Someone yanked me back from the water towards the street, but not before I'd stashed the vodka bottle inside my coat. The police began yelling at people to go home. Walking past a trash can, I threw the bottle into it, and then trudged towards my apartment.

MAYA TRIED TO LIFT her head off Asha's shoulder and focus her eyes on me, her disgrace of a mother. I heard Asha whispering words like 'good', 'strong', 'clever' in her little ear. Maya seemed to be listening intently. I tiptoed past them to the bedroom and shucked off my clothes. I stood under the shower for a few minutes, washing away the rain, and then reappeared with a towel on my head. Maya held up her fists and kicked out her legs, bawling.

'I tried to feed her a bottle while you showered,' Asha said. 'But now that she's seen you, I think she wants the real thing.' She handed Maya to me, and I pulled out my breast meekly, ashamed at what I'd almost done. 'She's stubborn, like her mother.' Asha smiled at me. It was an apologetic smile.

I walked about the room, swaying Maya to the rhythm of the whooshing air outside the window. 'What were you saying when

I walked in?' I asked, turning to look at Asha. 'Good, strong, clever, etc.'

Asha folded her arms around her shoulders. 'You must speak life into children. I used to do that with you too. That's why you've turned out to be so resilient.' She admired me like I was a painting.

For a few minutes, neither of us spoke. I stared out the window, with Maya sleeping in my arms. Then from her pocket, as if she'd been waiting for the right moment, Asha took out a photo. 'Here,' she said. 'Take a look at this, before you blame me for anything else.'

The picture was of me at six years old, sitting with my doll on Asha's lap. She is in a wheelchair. What protrudes from her spindly body is a big, pregnant belly. There are hollows under her eyes. She is holding me like I'm a lifesaver thrown from a boat.

'We wanted to name him Adar,' she said. 'It means wealth, respect. But he came early, and his poor lungs ... Anyway, the worst was that they still put me in a ward with other nursing mothers. The nurses would bring each her baby in the morning. My breasts would start to leak and leak, watching them. I begged Jeh to get me out. I begged him. He said I couldn't until the doctor gave the all-clear. Meanwhile, your grandparents made very sure I knew it was my fault that the baby had died.'

'Is this why you didn't want to be around me?' I said, holding up the picture. 'Because of this baby?'

Another long pause. My mother stood up and crossed the room. She took my hand. 'You're nothing like me,' she said, pressing it to her cold, wet cheek.

When she woke up later that night, I brought Maya into the bedroom. Sitting cross-legged in bed, I changed her diaper. Then I walked about in circles, jiggling her up and down. It was getting chilly. I took Veer's sweatshirt from a pile of clothes and pulled it over us both. There was a commotion in the living room. I heard the front door open and Veer's voice rang out in the silence. 'Hi there ... Mom? Noomi? Maya? Where is everyone?'

'In here,' I yelled.

Veer walked in, smelling of rain, of winter cold. 'I managed to get the last flight out,' he said.

'That was risky,' I said, pulling him in for a kiss. 'It must have been a very bumpy flight.'

'It was,' he said, putting his arm around me, touching Maya's silky face. 'I didn't want you guys to be by yourselves.' He smiled. 'This is our very first hurricane as a family.'

We stood at the window. The storm clouds broke open for a moment, revealing an impassive moon. The rain made the window into a mirror that threw our smiling reflections back at us. Me, Veer and Maya. For the first time, I didn't feel the urge to immediately look away.

'Look, Chanda Mama,' I said pointing, calling the moon by a lullaby name. Thirty storeys down, trees flailed in the wind. The hurricane was on its way. Lightning cracked the sky in half. Yet the moon, like a large ship on a choppy sea, remained steady.

Maya looked at the moon, and the moon looked back at Maya.

I hugged Veer a little closer. He said, 'The show's about to begin.'

ABOUT THE AUTHOR

NAHEED PHIROZE PATEL received her MFA in fiction from Columbia University's School of the Arts. Her writing has appeared in *The Guardian*, *HuffPost*, *The Rumpus*, *Scroll.in*, *New England Review*, *BOMB Magazine*, *EuropeNow Journal*, *PEN America*, and elsewhere. She lives in the greater New York City area and works as a freelance essayist, interviewer and critic.